Confidential
Communications

Confidential Communications

J.R. Reardon

To order additional copies of this book, contact:
Xlibris Corporation
1-888-795-4274
www.Xlibris.com
Orders@Xlibris.com
47059

This book is dedicated to my family and friends—both those who have moved on and who are with me still—who (perhaps unknowingly) guided me in their own ways to pursue my dreams. I consider myself blessed to have had such wonderful people in my life who are just as crazy about life as me. I love you, guys!

To my precious little girl and her father, my husband, David M. Reardon, Esq. David, you are my everything, you share my soul. Thank you for picking me. I love you both.

WHAT IN the world ever possessed me to become a lawyer? I honestly wish I knew. I was raised in the suburbs in a normal, middle-class Irish Catholic family. My parents rarely, if ever, argued about money. I never knew anyone personally who was involved in a lawsuit. Neither my twin brother nor I ever had any problems. Even our dog was loved by everyone she met. Now the dog is long gone, and my family is four hours away. I have made my home in a quaint little Vermont town known as Deering, in a cabin I bought for a song my first year out of law school. It still needs a lot of renovations, but I don't mind. It has character.

When I first purchased the cabin, I was told that an elderly couple had made it their home for over fifty years. The husband built it in 1941. In the olden days, people lived in their homes until they died. Today science has taken over. People are living long enough to die at an age where they no longer know their names or the names of those they cherished for so many years. Not too long ago, I longed to die the natural death my forefathers experienced. Now I want to live forever.

My cabin is the typical log cabin seen on the covers of *Better Homes and Gardens*, albeit a bit less decorative. The front porch so typical of years ago, for instance, displays two gray metal folding chairs, the second of which serves as an ottoman. Inside, a large living room is located to the left, and a large fireplace dominates the far-left wall. A blue-brown-and-red braided rug and a black-bear rug lie in front of the fire screen, I think left by the elderly couple. The bear rug (which I sarcastically named Smokey) was a little creepy at first, but I slowly became accustomed to it. A small couch I bought for about $250 is along the wall to the right of the fireplace. Two chairs are placed near their end tables, with matching lamps along the front wall of the house, one in each of the two windows.

Beyond the living room is a small eat-in kitchen, and to its right is a dining room. My goal is to repaint those first: the paint is peeling from years of summer heat and is, I think, the same lovely sea-foam green color as most operating rooms of the 1970s. Then again, so is the refrigerator, and so is the gas stove. Another goal is to replace those too.

To the right of the living room is a set of stairs that leads to a second floor. A bathroom sits at the top with an old-fashioned porcelain bathtub. I am told that I could get a lot of money for a tub in such prime condition. The wife must have polished the tub's brass fixtures at least twice a week. The master bedroom is to the right—I refer to it as the master bedroom, but I don't think it is that large compared to the bedroom of my parents back home. To the left is another room, which I have made a study. Right now it contains two folding tables and two more folding chairs, but along the remaining two walls are two massive built-in bookcases (perfectly sized for the law books that I refuse to throw away but rarely read). Despite unsolicited parental criticism, the study proves useful to me. I haven't found a desk that I really liked yet, so I have hesitated. What my parents don't seem to appreciate is the state-of-the-art computer with modem, the fax machine, and the photocopier in which I have invested. I enjoy my study because I can still work if I am sick or snowed in during a blizzard. My father thinks that if we are sick or stuck in a blizzard, it is God's way of telling us to take the day off. Now that I think about it, he is probably right.

There are two other smaller rooms on that second floor: one with an extra bed for visitors and the other with a myriad of boxes containing, I think, law books (although all of them are labeled "Kitchen"). I'll get around to those someday. I know, I know: *keep telling yourself that, Rebecca*. There is an attic, but I can count on one hand the number of times I've actually gone up there. The spiders who habitate the area are from a long line of spiders dating back to when the house was first built. Despite my numerous notices to quit, the squatters have held firm. Until I bring in an expert with an honest-to-goodness samurai sword, we have a mutual understanding: they stay in the attic, and I stay out of their way.

Although I've admitted it to few, I actually go to the local cemetery on occasion to visit the elderly couple's grave. As I had originally anticipated, the graveyard is nothing spectacular. I guess living in a house occupied by the same people for so long, with my family so far away, some local family with whom I could attach myself is nice. I never visit the couple because I am morbid or depressed. I visit because I am thankful. Deep down, I am certain that their children have not been back to visit the grave site since the last funeral, and that's just a shame.

I have been told for many years that the best place to start a story is at the beginning. My beginning used to take place in the suburbs of Boston sometime before law school. That being said, Boston's Trenstaw University Law School is where this tale begins.

CHAPTER ONE

N O ONE I knew outside of the legal profession (and actually a few inside) could understand why I accepted Trenstaw's invitation to attend their school. Nothing against their school, of course; it was the idea of going to law school in general. Law school is oftentimes seen as an invitation to emptiness: endless nights of reading countless numbers of cases, missed holidays, missed Sunday dinners, and missed reunions. Only my colleagues truly understood my emotions. To my family and friends, I became a perfect topic to fill a lull in a conversation: "So whatever happened to Becky Lawson?" I wasn't even sure why I accepted the offer. I simply decided to go.

After three years of sweat, pain, and a few unavoidable tears, Trenstaw finally released its catch of three hundred wannabe lawyers—my little five-feet-three-inch, 114-pound Irish Catholic self included—back into the sea. As the ultimate gift given by every law school to hundreds of graduates all over the country, I was given a piece of paper, which basically tells others that I love to read, I read a lot, and I learned something in the process. I happily accepted that we graduates could have purchased a few decent midsized cars with the money we instead spent on tuition. By the time graduation came around, I felt that not being invited back to graduate with the following class was the gift I cherished the most.

Two months later, I was scheduled to prove what I had learned alongside about three thousand others. My family and friends could not understand why graduation was not overly exciting for me. But if they too were preparing to experience twelve more hours of the *ultimate* sweat, pain, and tears, perhaps they too would understand. Perhaps I sound a bit cynical. It was just too difficult having to wait four more months to find out whether or not I should have given back my gift to Trenstaw. For me, graduation would have been much more enjoyable *after* the last twelve hours of sweat, pain, and tears.

Fortunately, the bar examiners welcomed me into the legal arena with open arms (or at least an open hand to accept big bar dues), and I was finally able to move on. My mother was not thrilled to learn that moving on for her daughter meant moving to another state. The fact is I never thought I would leave my mother's house until I married. Suddenly I found myself sitting in a pair of jeans and an oversized flannel shirt, my long light brown hair pulled through the back of a baseball cap, in front of a roaring fireplace—a fireplace located in a log cabin that I proudly called my own.

I found myself surviving the New England snowstorms in a new way and enjoying the famous foliage before everyone else back in Massachusetts. Conveniently, I was no longer involved in a serious relationship. Perhaps that is part of the reason why I moved. Frank, my nonlegal boyfriend of two years, four months, and eighteen days (not that anyone's counting) before law school, quickly became unappreciative of his "female investment" and lasted until about March of my first year, one week after he conveniently forgot my birthday. After that, the male law students I met were too intense, and I wasn't exactly bold enough to freely hand out my unlisted telephone number to anyone I met in a club. That was how Frank met my replacement. I was too busy studying anyway.

I love my little town in Vermont. It is quiet, and the population is only about one thousand. There are few stores in my town, but they suffice. I think it is about an hour's drive to the nearest shopping mall.

Quiet is how I describe my little town in Vermont. Quiet until about eight months after I became a resident.

CHAPTER TWO

I T ALL began the Saturday morning when I walked into Ken's Country Store, a small but popular grocery store located in an old white clapboard building built in the 1800s with a big front porch in the center of town. The store specialized mostly in scrumptious breads, cheeses, jellies and jams, and, most importantly, a vast array of penny candy for the children (or those of us pretending to buy for the children). On a desperate search for Ken's terribly addictive homemade bread, I inadvertently knocked over a display of maple syrup. I originally expected old man Ken to come racing out of the back room with a mop and some old-fashioned miracle to clean up my design, but instead, out walked Charlie McCabe. I am not quite sure exactly how long it took Charlie to clean up the syrup. For me it was not long enough.

"I am so, so sorry," I said, both my hands dramatically covering my mouth. *But then again, this is nice*, I thought. "Hey, don't worry about it," he replied in a sexy Vermont-ish twang. "It's no bother at all." Did Vermont residents even have an accent? I could listen to this guy talk all day.

"My name is Becky. Becky Lawson."

"Charlie McCabe. Pleased to meet you." I immediately reached out to shake his hand, but to my dismay, he quickly pulled back. Was he psyching me out? How rude.

"Whoa, nelly. You're already sweet enough." Charlie wiped his big strong hands on his white apron, which was fashionably draped around his waist. "Let me get cleaned up, and then we'll reintroduce ourselves like mature adults," he said. I laughed, feeling angry with myself for thinking that such a beautiful specimen of a man could have inappropriate personality traits. Normally, I'd be turned off by such a pickup line, but Charlie's delivery was just right for me. Actually, I hoped it was the delivery. I would be greatly disappointed to think that three years of law school destroyed my female defenses; although admittedly, I did picture him out back with a dark red plaid flannel shirt, rolled sleeves, teasing me with strong muscular arms that chopped wood as easily as if it was a piece of cooked pasta. *Oh. Oops. Perhaps I went too far there. Defenses, Rebecca.* Right.

"Tell you what, you finish your shopping, and I'll be over when you're ready to ring it up. I'm working alone this morning. My dad's off this weekend, and I'm minding the store."

"You're Ken's son?" I said.

"Why, yes, unless of course you don't like Ken," he replied. As he smiled, I began to see the hidden resemblances. "So are you new to Deering, Ms. Lawson?" he asked. I hoped my laughter did not come across as too girlish. *Should I change my laugh? Is my voice pitched too high? Am I giggling? Oh man, Rebecca, focus. He just asked you a question.*

"Actually, I am. And please call me Becky. I just moved here not long ago, and I don't know many people in this town. Actually, I feel quite lucky to be on a first-name basis with your dad. Of course, I suppose every stranger traveling through Deering, Vermont, is on a first-name basis with Ken of Ken's Country Store."

"Yes, they generally are. However, not many are on a first-name basis with Charlie. Tell you what, if you like, I'd love to show you around the area sometime." Was he kidding? *Quick: someone pinch me! Right: focus, Rebecca.*

"I'd like that," I replied and followed him to the register.

"Say, why don't you and I go to the Fall Festival? That is, if you're not doing anything. It's supposed to be really good this year." Even Charlie seemed a bit nervous.

"Sure, sounds great," I replied, hoping that I didn't sound too terribly excited. "Well, off I go. See you around?"

"See you around," said Charlie.

Leaving the store, I prayed to every saint in heaven that I wouldn't trip down the old wooden steps. I could hear Charlie rattling around with a box in front of the store, doing the gentleman thing: waiting for me to completely leave. Luckily, I made it down the stairs without incident, but did catch my toe on an oversized rock embedded in the dirt walkway just as I was out of Charlie's sight. With my now-crimson visage, I turned around to see if he was still there. Thankfully he was not. Or if he had been, he ducked in time to save me the embarrassment. Ah, a true country gentleman.

I had never been to the Fall Festival, but I had read about it in the local papers. The festival boasted all sorts of old country arts and crafts, animals, and food. It seemed like a lot of fun, so much that I felt like a little girl anticipating Christmas. That is, until the next day when I bumped into Ali, a clerk at the courthouse.

"What do you mean they have rides there!" I exclaimed, horrified. I hated rides.

"They have rides there," she repeated in a warning tone. My eyes were bulging, nostrils flaring, lip curled, heart pounding in my chest.

"Oh no! What am I going to do?" I exclaimed, dropping my briefcase on the cement floor. "He's going to hate me. Is that why he wants to go there?"

"Probably. Why would a guy his age be the least bit interested in who won the biggest gourd contest?"

Ali was right. I was doomed. For the next few days, I walked around in a nervous yet serious state, playing over each and every ride in my head, again and again. I pictured myself at the top of a Ferris wheel, whipping around on a roller coaster, and swinging high on a pirate ship, convinced that I would die.

The following Thursday, I sat on my couch listening to the radio. Christmas came early. The weather report for the next five days was rain, and a lot of it. I was saved! I could not get to the store to buy a gallon of milk (that I really didn't need) fast enough.

"Hey, so . . . uh, I guess our plans might be a little rained out," Charlie said sadly when I walked through the door. "I guess so," I replied, faking my disappointment. "We could always do something else instead, if you want?" *Please don't suggest another Fall Festival in New Hampshire instead.*

"How about the movies?" said Charlie.

The movies! Perfect! A nice story on a big screen, and all I had to do was sit in a chair bolted to the floor and eat popcorn. "Sounds fantastic! I'd rather do that anyway. Not really in the mood for the festival." Charlie laughed. "Then the movies it is."

We ended up choosing the typical, safe first-date movie: a comedy. As far as I was concerned, it was hysterical, although I never did catch the title or follow the storyline. I was quite content with my company, extremely thankful that I was not sitting in the chair of an amusement park ride.

After the movie, we grabbed a bite to eat and drove by one of the many local lakes. Thousands of stars illuminated the dark sky, and there was a slight chill in the air. "Do you want to go for a walk?" asked Charlie. "Sure, let's." I replied. How romantic can this be? They do this in the movies. They do this on television. Wow.

As we walked, I began to shiver, partially from nerves and partially from the night air. Charlie took off his jacket and draped it across my shoulders. I looked at him and smiled. "Thanks," I said. "It's a little nippy out here." Charlie turned and drew me into his arms. As I all but melted, he placed his hands gently on my shoulders and pulled me in closer. As our lips met for the first time, I spied a star zoom across the Vermont sky. "Did you see that?" said Charlie, seeing it too. "Good sign, I think," I replied, savoring the moment.

We continued to walk through the crisp night air for a while, and eventually, it was time to go home. As we approached my cabin, Charlie clownishly leapt out of the car and greeted me by opening my door with a reverent bow. "So this was fun," he said, smirking. "It was a lot of fun," I replied. *Please keep talking. I don't know what to say here,* I thought. *Plus, yes, I had a great time, and you're handsome, and I pray that you ask me out again, but please know that I am not inviting you in.*

"Well, I guess I'll see you at the store. Maybe we can go out again next weekend? Maybe dinner or something?" He asked me out again. Wow!

"Sounds great to me," I said in the coolest voice I could manage. "Well, I'll see you at the store." Charlie gave me one last kiss good night, and I slowly walked up the driveway and onto the porch. Miranda was gently pacing in the window in obvious approval. This time, I kept my footing.

CHAPTER THREE

A S TIME went on, Charlie and I continued to date, and I began to feel like we were a true "item." Still, we had never discussed it, so I did the thing that girls naturally do. I needed to concoct a little white lie.

"So this guy hit on me today at the courthouse," I said, sitting with Charlie on the front steps of the store. "It was pretty funny."

Charlie suddenly grew territorial. "Who?"

"Actually, I've seen him before. He's some attorney that I've run into in the civil session from time to time. Hey, better than having a pervert hit on you, right?" I laughed and continued munching on a bag of pretzels.

"So what did he say?" asked Charlie, suddenly through with his pretzels, extremely focused.

"Oh, I don't remember—just wanted to go out sometime."

"Well, you told him that you were with me, right?" Charlie's knee began to bounce up and down. Good. Progress.

"I just said that I've been seeing someone. That's all. But what was interesting was the compliment he paid me. He said he'd never seen someone's suit bring out the color of their eyes like mine had today. And he had never seen green eyes like mine before. Anyway, it's all good." Safe enough. And vague enough.

"I mean, we have a really good thing going, don't you think?" questioned Charlie, still worried.

"Of course we do." I picked up another pretzel. "Hmm . . . do I detect some jealousy?"

"I just don't appreciate people messing around with my girlfriend, that's all," Charlie said.

"Oh, so you mean to tell me that you would not want me dating other people?" I replied, a chill of excitement electrifying my spine.

"I'd be very upset," he continued, anxiously resuming his pretzel feast.

"Well, I'd be upset if someone were trying to go out with my boyfriend, so I guess I know how you feel," I replied.

"Come here." Charlie gently but forcefully cradled my face and kissed me. "You don't need to worry about that, though, do you?"

"Good thing," I said, smiling back. It was official. I was his girlfriend, and we were exclusive. Wow. I belonged to someone who loved me for who I was, unconditionally. He would protect me and love me, and we would live happily ever after. Well, if that was fate's master plan.

"Okay, new subject," he said, glancing at his watch. "Where shall we go as for the mayor's Halloween party?" Uh-oh. I had to be creative. "Because I was thinking that we should do a fun couple's theme. These parties are really cool. They rent a hall at one of the local golf courses in the middle of the woods. Pretty spooky. But everyone goes." I had to think fast. I needed a costume, which, of course, did not make me out to be ugly but not send the wrong message. "What about Zorro?" I asked.

"Done," replied Charlie excitedly. Thank goodness that was settled. I could wear a sexy black dress. And of course, I'd wear my long auburn hair in curls, and extra makeup. Perfect.

A few weeks later, Charlie picked me up in full costume. I had to admit, the costumes were great, although I was a tad disturbed at not seeing Charlie's full face. It was more important at that point in time not to be rejected after dressing up in an ugly costume. Perhaps he would take the mask off later at the party.

After a while, Charlie introduced me to a friend of his. "This is Leo," he said as I shook the hand of a heavy metal guitar player.

"Nice to meet you, Leo," I replied, hoping I would recognize him later without the costume and, of course, hoping that he was in fact wearing a costume.

"I've heard a lot about you," said Leo, smiling. "You've been the talk of the town since you arrived." I smiled, surprised but flattered.

"Anyway, I'm running outside with the old ball and chain for a bit. Join us if you like, okay?" With that, Leo rocked away.

Charlie turned to me, noting my concern. "They're going out there to get high. But they are good people. We can go out if you like, and I'll introduce you to Carla."

"I take it that she's the 'old ball and chain'?" I said.

Charlie laughed as he grabbed my hand and headed for the door. "Yes, that's Carla. Nice girl. She'll just be hanging out there. No worries."

We walked outside into the darkness, and I could smell the sweet smell of marijuana smoke already. I, of course, held my breath as much as I could, taking only the tiniest of breaths through my nose.

After the introductions, we walked back to Charlie's car. Charlie leaned with his back to the car and pulled me close to him. "Nice people?" He smiled, looking into my eyes.

"Yes, they do seem nice. You've known Leo a long time?"

"Oh, we go back years. He gets himself into trouble every once in a while, but he's one of my best friends." Charlie drew me in closer, and we began to kiss.

This kiss, however, was different. I embarrassingly jumped. Instead of Charlie's familiar soft gentleman's kiss, I felt his snakelike tongue being jammed into my mouth. Gross. An invasion. Now what was I supposed to do with that thin slippery thing slamming across my teeth?

I decided to just let things be for a second and let him do the work. Despite my age, suddenly I had no idea what I was doing. No one had ever done that to me before in quite that way. Or perhaps they had, but I was so taken aback by Charlie that I felt like a schoolgirl experiencing her first make-out session.

I'd better let this go, I thought. What would Charlie think if I didn't let him kiss me? *Oh boy. Too much thinking again, Rebecca. Now how the heck are you going to deal with this? Is his spit in there too? Okay, now there is just way too much spit in my mouth. Oh God, this is the big gulp. I feel sick. Things are too intense.* "Everything all right?" he asked. "Oh yes, fine. I just thought I heard something behind us in the woods. Startled me for a second, but I think we're fine." Okay, so I lied. But I had to say something. At least we were just talking at this point. I really needed a break.

Charlie, on the other hand, was not ready for a break. And just as I was wishing that he would put the mask back on, I felt something on my right thigh. Still stunned with the kissing incident, I had no idea what it was, so I pulled my leg back.

It was then that I realized. It was *it*. Oh good God. At least it remained in his pants. But still, we'll have none of it. There is no it until I'm married. Or, I suppose if I find myself in a situation like in one of those romantic movies, completely caught up in the moment and absolutely sure that I'm with the right guy. Could Charlie be the right guy? Would I accept a diamond if he got down on bended knee right now? Until now, he has seemed like my idea of the proverbial Mr. Right. Either way, I am not caught up in the moment, have no idea what I am doing, and tonight is not the night. Get it out of my way! Put it back! Please, put it away! I pulled back again, desperate to break the chain of events. "Did you hear that?" I asked. Perhaps I could scare it away. I had heard that fright can do that to some guys.

"Hear what?" Charlie was obviously wanting to continue the moment.

"Now I know I heard something back there, and I don't really feel like getting attacked by a raccoon or something. I had an uncle who was attacked by a raccoon once pulling his garage door down. Damn thing attached itself to his head, and my aunt ran inside the house, leaving him stranded out there. Why don't we go back inside?"

"Okay," Charlie said sadly, following me back to the party like a lost puppy.

That night after I went to bed, I kept replaying the events in my head over and over again. Was this what serious dating is like? *He doesn't expect anything, does he? What if he tries something?* I knew I would reject him, but at the same time, I'd be heartbroken if he broke up with me. And if he did break up with me, would he tell everyone in the town that I was just some prissy girl? Probably. We were adults after all. Great. I decided as the sun came up that I was just going to be me. And if Charlie didn't like me for me, there was someone else out there.

I remember when I was a little girl, I asked my mom, while she was doing the dishes, whether or not I'd be married when I grew up. "Of course, you'll be married," she replied.

"But to who? What will he be like?"

"I don't know, honey . . . and the word is *whom*," she replied with a smile. "A handsome businessman. He'll come in the back door with his suit and his briefcase. Just like Daddy." And that's what I always pictured: faceless man dressed up in a suit with his briefcase. Could Charlie be the faceless man? Only time would tell.

As the weeks went on, Charlie and I took walks at the lake, went ice skating on local ponds, and attended a few town social events. He must have sensed my pressure at the Halloween party, as *it* thankfully never reared its head again. Needless to say, I was relieved. Kissing took some getting used to, but now that I was more comfortable with Charlie "the Charmer," it became more enjoyable.

Every weekend for the next ten months, we took rides, and I quickly learned the area. Charlie introduced me to just about everyone in town. Those I didn't know I met hanging around the country store. I suppose being a licensed attorney and all, I was building my future clientele. Even the richest people in the area have to buy necessities sometime. I began drafting wills for a bunch of elderly townsfolk and a few purchase and sale agreements for vacationers purchasing cottages. People drive slow in Deering. I think the last motor-vehicle accident was about seven years ago, between two out-of-staters. At any rate, I am one of three attorneys in the area, and my neighbors give me enough business to put food on my little table. Trenstaw's gift was certainly working out well.

Ken and I became famous friends too. I would eat dinner over his house with Charlie quite often. Apparently, Mrs. McCabe had passed away about ten years prior, but the grief never subsided. Charlie never mentioned his mother much, I think because they did not get along very well.

Apparently, Charlie moved out of Deering when he was eighteen, without any notice and without any indication of where he was going. In fact, he did not even show up for his mother's funeral. When he met me, he had resurfaced, as quickly as he had left. At least Ken seemed somewhat happy again.

Only on one occasion did I ask Charlie what he did for all those years away from home. He immediately became tense and attempted to change the subject. Of course, I let him. For the time being anyway.

One Sunday, Ken called me at home. He sounded as though he had been crying. I asked him if something was wrong, and he requested I stop by the store. I quickly grabbed my keys and my purse and met him right away. He was sitting alone on the steps.

"Ken, are you all right?" I asked.

"He left," said Ken.

"*Who* left?"

"Charlie." Ken began sobbing. "He left as quickly as he did when he turned eighteen."

My heart sank. "What!" I exclaimed.

"He's gone, Rebecca. His room is empty. The car is gone. No note. Just like before."

"Listen, Ken," I said as I handed him a tissue, fighting back my own tears of betrayal. "What happened when Charlie was eighteen? He won't discuss it with me."

Ken sighed. "I guess I should start by saying that Charlie is my adopted son."

"Really?" I said. "I actually thought he resembled you."

Ken chuckled and looked at his feet. "My wife was raped shortly before we were to be married. She was out with her sister looking for material for her wedding dress. Can you believe that one? All the girls in her wedding party were going to sew the gown together. My wife thought it would be so special to hand down to one of our little girls one day, or a granddaughter."

My eyes began to fill with tears, and Ken continued. "Anyway, on the way back to the car, my wife was grabbed from behind, and her sister was grabbed too. They were both dragged into the woods and raped."

"My god," I whispered.

"We, of course, called the locals, but they didn't do anything. There was no evidence, and back in the day, DNA testing wasn't as reliable or used as often as now."

"I am so sorry, Ken," I said, not knowing what to say.

"Anyway, we didn't tell a soul around here. My wife swore me to secrecy. But a short time later, after we were married, we found out she was expecting. Everyone thinks Charlie is my natural son, but if you do the math, by a few short weeks . . ."

"Oh no."

"Yes. Some of his friends assumed my wife didn't want to wait 'til our wedding and teased Charlie as Charlie got older. Charlie didn't know what to say. He was convinced his friends were right. My wife said nothing for the longest time and told him he was a preemie."

"Well, he had some nice friends, huh?" I said.

Ken took a deep breath. "Charlie hung out with the wrong crowd when he was a teenager. Can you believe it? A wrong crowd in Vermont? It was a bunch of kids who had moved from out of state. I can't even remember where. Charlie had never left Vermont. We never really went on vacation, with the store and all. Anyway, he was fascinated by the stories he heard from these kids and left when he turned eighteen. My wife saw it coming all along. She used to beg him to hang around with the local kids. Eventually she told him the truth about what happened, and when he realized I wasn't his real father, he was furious. It tore our family apart. Especially the relationship between him and his mom. He left without saying a word one day, and was never heard from since. He never even came back when she died. My poor wife was never able to have a child again after what that bastard did to her. I raised Charlie as though he was my own. We were perfect. We went to church every Sunday—the happiest of families. Now I have no family."

"So this must have been quite the surprise when he came back just before he met me, huh?" I said, handing Ken another tissue.

"When he came back after all those years, he never told me where he lived, let alone how he lived. He said he traveled a lot and lived on the road. But really, how can you eat good meals when you don't have a good, steady job? Apparently, he has done all right. He's a good weight. He's in good shape. That's not bad, you know?"

"I know," I said, succumbing to the need for a tissue myself. "He'll come back. Don't worry. And if he is back on the road again, I'm sure he'll call one of us to let us know he's okay. He wasn't mad at us now, was he?"

"I suppose not."

"And he wasn't hanging around with any out-of-staters who had seen more than the state of Vermont now, was he?"

"Yes, he was." Ken smirked.

I could feel my face turning a deep shade of burgundy. "I see you're feeling better. And I see where Charlie gets his sense of humor. But you will notice my official residence is Deering, Vermont."

"I know. Thanks, Becky."

"You're quite welcome," I said. At least things had begun to make some sense.

Five weeks went by, and no sign of Charlie. However, no bodies were recovered according to the news, and I told Ken that was a good sign. Ken was still very upset at Charlie's sudden disappearance but quickly returned to the daily routine he carried on for so long. I was quite busy with my clients, and although I thought about Charlie daily, I was able to manage. Law school does that to a person. We learn to adapt. My problem was not only was I growing tired of adapting, but I didn't want to deal with the repercussions with Ken. I could eventually write off Charlie and go on with my life, deciding that I had been dumped and used. At least I hadn't slept with him. Although perhaps I should have. Ken was like a second father to me, and I wasn't sure I wanted to see his reaction even if I did find another Mr. Right. Ah, the joys of being a girl with Catholic guilt. For now I decided to concentrate on the joys of being an attorney.

CHAPTER FOUR

ALLAN RICHARDS came into my life on a Thursday morning at about eight thirty. The cold weather had returned, and I had stopped at a local coffee shop on the way to the courthouse. All was quiet, until Allan came barging into the store, demanding to see the owner. Mr. Becker came out of the kitchen and asked if something was wrong.

"Yes. Something is wrong. I mean, no. Not here. You live here long?" asked Mr. Richards.

"Of course, my whole life. What is the problem?"

"Do you know of a good attorney in this area?" My ears perked up like a golden retriever.

"She happens to be drinking a cup of coffee, right over there," said Mr. Becker with a smile. I had just probated his sister's estate the prior week. She had left her entire estate to him. Of course I was a good attorney.

Mr. Richards rushed over to me. "Hi. I'm Allan Richards. Can I speak with you for a moment?"

I put down my coffee cup. "Rebecca Lawson. What can I do for you?"

"I need a lawyer," he said.

"That's the rumor." Mr. Becker laughed. "Look, I have to be in court in a half an hour, and I would rather speak with you in private. What's your schedule look like today?"

"I'll make time." Mr. Richards handed me a business card. "I'll be in my office all day. It is located about four blocks from the courthouse. Can you come over when you're through?"

"I'll be there as soon as I can. Let me ask you this: what type of case is this?"

"Corporate. No, criminal. No, corporate. Definitely corporate." Mr. Richards shot a dirty look at Mr. Becker, who could be no more obvious in his eavesdropping.

"I have a hearing at 9:00 AM. Hopefully, I'll be through around ten o'clock or ten thirty, at the latest. Would you like me to call when I'm on the way?"

"No. Just come over as soon as you can. I'll be waiting." Mr. Richards left just as quickly as he had arrived. I finished my cup of coffee, waved good-bye to Mr. Becker, and went to court.

Normally, I loved going to court. I knew everyone there, and although some days I wouldn't get what I was looking for, I truly loved my work. This day, however, was different. The events of the morning made it difficult for me to concentrate on presenting my motion. Even Judge Haley noticed. "Counselor, may I see you for a moment at the bench?"

"Certainly, Your Honor," I replied. I approached the bench immediately.

"Are you all right, Becky? You seem a bit distant today. That is not like you."

"Oh, I'm fine, Your Honor. I apologize. I have a meeting with a potential client when I leave the courthouse this morning. I met him in Mr. Becker's coffee shop a little over an hour ago, and I am just curious as to why he is seeking legal advice. He seemed very intense."

"Well, I suppose congratulations may be in order then. The more clients the merrier. You seem to be doing quite well for yourself. You have worked very hard and have certainly come a long way," said Judge Haley.

"Thank you, Your Honor. This case may be involving corporate and/or criminal law, and that is a new twist for me, and I love to think. Right now I am just used to doing the usual for this little town." Judge Haley laughed.

"I am sure you'll do just fine. Now let's finish up this hearing so that you may go meet your new client."

I left the courthouse as quickly as I could for someone in heels. Judge Haley was right. I had come a long way. I lost nothing by moving up to Deering. I knew no one in the legal profession back home, except for professors and colleagues with whom I didn't care to become friendly. Not that many were eager to help anyway. The closer the date of graduation, the less people could be viewed as contacts. Most were still practicing attorneys, and many specialized in fields of their own interests and also, oftentimes, unfortunately, in themselves.

A reoccurring problem among members in the profession is the lack of any willingness to share information or a case. Money, unfortunately, becomes the driving force among many attorneys. And for the most part, most attorneys listening to another's windfalls are more envious than congratulatory.

Fortunately, I had Judge Haley and his clerks to encourage me. I learned in school that the Rules of Professional Conduct encourage the sharing of information and helping others who are new to the profession. Judge Haley and the clerks in Vermont were always living by this rule. They were all truly honest people, and quite helpful if I had a question. Not that I asked that many questions, because I was great at the research. I spent hours photocopying files of closed cases in the archives of the courthouse. It was well worth my time since I began my new life with literally no clientele. I vowed to always follow Judge Haley's good example as I became more experienced myself.

The office of Allan Richards was quite large for Deering. It was located in a fairly new building, rising six stories high. I knew the building was new when I was able to take a comfortably sized working elevator to the sixth floor. The receptionist seated high behind a crescent-shaped desk greeted me as I opened the giant french doors to an impressive lobby. Everything was brass, glass, and oriental rugs. I was thankful I was dressed for the occasion.

"Oh, Attorney Lawson. I am glad you could make it. Come in. Come in." Mr. Richards came rushing down a long hallway.

"Hello, Mr. Richards. I came as quickly as I could," I replied.

"Call me Allan. Let's talk in the conference room." Allan, who had already begun walking, led me back down the hallway. I counted eight offices on the way to the conference room, all filled with persons acting busily or busily *acting* as in most businesses. Appearance is key in the working world. I learned that in Boston.

The conference room was huge. It had an oak table, which appeared to be about fifteen feet long. Leather chairs encompassed the table. Four telephones were strategically placed around the room, all, of course, equipped with multiple lines for conference calls. Allan closed the door, muffling the cacophonous sounds of people, phones, computers, keyboards, printers, and fax machines.

"I didn't mean to scare you this morning. It's just been a little hectic around here."

"Listen, Mr. Richards—I mean, Allan—most attorneys don't meet clients with a positive karma. In today's age, people don't introduce themselves to attorneys unless they have to." Allan rolled his eyes in agreement.

"The reason I need a lawyer is because my business is in deep trouble. One of our employees is involved in something highly illegal. I just know it. Now I cannot emphasize enough that *I am not involved.* I am not even sure what illegalities this guy is up to. But I know enough that since it is my business, and if he is using my business to conduct affairs not our own, I have a big problem."

"Allan, is he here now?" I whispered.

"No. He left for vacation for a week," he replied. "I assure you, we're safe here."

"Look, Allan, I don't want to alarm you, but I think we should speak somewhere else." Allan looked concerned. "You don't know who else may be involved."

"Who would be involved?" said Allan, obviously not eager to venture into foreign territory. *Odd,* I thought, given his demeanor in Mr. Becker's coffee shop just a short time ago.

"Listen to me." I handed him a card. "This is where my office is located. It is small and nothing as elaborate as this, but I know we can talk there. Can you go there now?"

Allan picked up his briefcase. "Let's go," he said.

CHAPTER FIVE

T WENTY MINUTES later, Allan and I sat in my little office, located in an old three-story sand-colored building above a hardware store on Main Street. Sipping on an extra large cup of coffee from the bakery next door, Allan discussed in great detail his background, his business, and his clientele. He told me that he grew up in Schenectady, New York, in a middle-class neighborhood. His parents owned a pub in the center of town and worked there until they passed away. Like him, Allan's two brothers were both involved with finance: Jim Richards was an accountant in New York City, and Ted Richards was a vice president of Aquicard, the biggest international credit card company in the world. Ted's office was located in Denver, Colorado. Allan, following in his brothers' footsteps, received his graduate degree in business at Columbia University in New York and landed his first job as a financial advisor. Desperately wanting to make money on his own fast, he established his own financial-advising business, Financial Investments. Once the business started doing well, Jim put together a presentation for Ted to pitch to Aquicard. The pitch was convincing, and Aquicard invested with Financial Investments immediately. Soon others followed, trusting Aquicard's every move.

Eventually Allan began offering investment opportunities in Financial Investments for his clients as well. Fortunately for him, his company quickly branched out, and only recently did Allan decide to open offices in Vermont. Apparently, he had a passion for skiing. In fact, the home he had built not far from Deering was a giant log cabin: A-frame style, with two decks at the top of a small mountain, every amenity imaginable included. On one side, just below the decks, was the top of a ski lift, which spilled his friends and family onto three trails of their choice: black diamond/expert trail, an intermediate trail, and a novice trail.

"Now who's this guy in your office that has you so concerned?" I asked.

"His name is Brent. Brent Thompson. He has been working with me for, oh, about four years. Never met his family. Never met any of his friends. Oh wait, one friend: Allison Hatchfield. I met her a few times. He dated her for a while. I think he still does on occasion. I'm not sure."

"Okay," I said, feverishly jotting down notes. "What's his work schedule?"

"His job is full-time, and he's a workaholic. He works early in the morning until late at night. Generally, he's the last one to leave. On some occasions, he leaves with the last employee, has dinner, but the light has been seen back on in his office until the wee hours of the morning. Each time I've approached him to discuss his clients, Brent has had some excuse to dodge the conversation by meeting with a client. I've never really found anything of great significance in his office files, although he routinely brings two large briefcases to and from the office. His productivity level has always been consistently high for the office, and he was promoted at one point to junior office manager for his unit in addition to his duties as financial advisor. I can't simply fire him because I think he's doing something illegal. I've got no proof, and I'm not dumb enough to open up myself and my company to a lawsuit. I just have a bad feeling, and I don't know what legally I can do."

"Have you ever been audited?" I asked.

"Sure, we conduct internal audits quite often. My brother takes care of it. I actually enjoy being audited, believe it or not. My company is becoming too large, and I would rather that the problems are caught before they become monsters. Besides"—he chuckled—"it's my only way of monitoring Brent." Allan suddenly stood up. "I suppose there is nothing I can do, huh?"

"Look, why don't you give me all the information you have on Brent. His personnel file, his client files, et cetera. Photocopies will be fine for now. Do it, though, when you are alone in the office so nothing is ever missing. I'd also like some general information on your other employees from the Deering office. Later, if necessary, we'll check out the employees in New York. As for the financial reports, get me copies of those too, as well as the audit reports for the past five years. We'll go from there."

"Thanks, Attorney Lawson. I'll get them to you right away."

"Becky. Call me Becky. And don't talk to anyone about this without checking with me first. Do you have another corporate attorney with whom I should be speaking?"

"No. We don't. Well, I suppose you are now, if you want."

I was both flattered and excited at the same time. "I'd be more than happy to represent your company. Now if anyone asks about me, including Brent, tell them that I can be reached at any time should your business require. That way, they won't be suspicious if they see me with business files or speaking with you." After a standard-fee agreement was signed, Allan left the office, and I was a real corporate attorney.

CHAPTER SIX

T HAT EVENING, I made a spaghetti dinner, drank a couple of glasses of Pinot Grigio, and curled up on the couch with one of my old business books in front of the fireplace. Although winter was still a few weeks away, it was snowing outside. Miranda, my brown-beige-and-black cat, was at my feet, innocently staring up at me with her big green eyes. The phone had not rung all evening. We were both quite content.

Despite the events of the day, I still could not erase Charlie from my mind. The sorrow in Ken's eyes, as we sat on the steps not long before, had deeply affected me. I supposed I also felt a bit guilty as Ken's emotions resembled the sorrow in my mother's eyes the day that I left for Vermont.

"You sure you have everything now, dear?" she said, watching me stuff the last of my bags into the trunk of my car.

"Yes, Mom."

"And your bar review materials for the Vermont exam?"

"Yes, Mom."

"And you have your map, and enough money?"

I grimaced, turning to face her. "Yes, Mom."

"Now about what time will you arrive? I hope you'll at least call when you get there." My mother's eyes began to water.

"Of course I'll call. I'll probably be there by four. I have my cell phone if you are looking for me." Desperate to put an end to the uncontrollable (and far too public for an Irish Catholic family) display of emotion, I hugged my brother, father, and mother good-bye and started my car. As I drove away, my eyes watered too.

Missing my family, I felt compelled to pick up the phone and call Massachusetts. But at 11:15 PM, I was hesitant. The last thing I wanted to do was to worry my mother that her successful lawyer daughter was unhappy and alone in the backwoods of Vermont four hours away. Instead, I held our family picture for about five minutes and kissed her face good night. "Good night, Mom." Miranda meowed.

The next morning, I slept late. My calendar was clear for the next three days, so I took my time before heading for the office. I had no secretary; I didn't need one yet. I had an answering machine for the time being, and that was enough.

As I was fishing for my key, I heard someone leaving a message on my office answering machine. It was Allan. "Hi . . . uh, Attorney L . . . Becky? It is me. Allan Richards. From yesterday? I was wondering if I could set up an appointment with you sometime soon. Please give me a call when you get a chance. I'll be at the office. Thanks."

Once inside, I read my mail from the previous day. No settlement checks: in other words, no good mail. I listened to the rest of the messages on the machine, called those requesting a callback, and began fishing around for Allan's office number. Finding his business card, I began to dial. Allan answered the phone. "Good morning, Financial Investments."

"Yes, may I speak with Allan Richards, please."

"May I ask who's calling?" said Allan, obviously screening the call, although I wondered why he hadn't picked up my name, which would have been prominently displayed on the caller ID. "Sure. It's Attorney Lawson."

"Oh, hi, Becky! It's Allan. How are you?" His voice was loud and much too happy for my taste. It never ceased to amaze me when people assumed they could mask their emotions by the tone of their voice: a little pet peeve of mine.

"I'm fine, Allan. I just received your message. Would you like to come down to the office?"

"Yes, I'd love to. How's eleven-thirty sound?"

"Eleven-thirty is just fine. I'll see you then." I hung up the telephone and began editing a will for Mrs. Fitchmier. Her estate was definitely not worth the time I had put into the drafting of her will, but *she* had successfully managed to make a project out of it: seven times, as a matter of fact, in eight short weeks.

I looked around my office at the letter-sized manila folders, took a deep, cleansing breath, and began to dream. How I wished each civil case would expand to the point of requiring the brown expandable envelopes. They usually don't. A few do, but rarely do they become the much-desired "big case." The big case is an easy, no-heavy-lifting, open-and-shut case. Perhaps, for instance, the case would be a motor-vehicle accident, which occurred on a bright, sunny day. My client, operating his motor vehicle, would be stopped at a traffic light for several seconds when struck in the rear by a bus driven by an agent of a large financially solvent corporation with maximum insurance. Naturally, this poor, innocent soul would have been a blossoming young athlete with a multitude of offers for professional contracts on the table; now he finds himself a paraplegic. Such cases normally do not go all the way to trial; they are normally settled out of court. But the fee to keep the case out of court would be high, and the big file contained in the expandable envelopes would prove quite profitable in the end. If the case did go to trial, it would be a winner, and my name would be plastered over every local, and possibly national, newspaper. It would be my time to shine—savoring the moment to be relived as a war story for years to come, war stories told to jealous members of the profession, no one truly caring to hear the story but myself, and no one believing that I did truly feel sorry for the victim who otherwise may not have gotten the benefits he'll have for the rest of his life without my help. Mrs. Fitchmier's will was in a brown expandable envelope, but it certainly wasn't the big case.

Suddenly there was a knock on the door. It was Allan. He was early. He carried with him a stack of papers, which he quickly dropped on my conference table, which was actually an old dining room table of Ken's. Ken had kept the table in the cellar for years, unable to bear the thought of throwing it away when he and his wife had purchased a new set twenty years ago. Although the table was purchased when I was in grammar school, it was built in Vermont by a local carpenter, and was sturdier than any table one would purchase in a shopping mall today. True carpenters take great pride in their work. Their work is a form of art that they hope will be handed down from generation to generation. National chains take great pride in the dollar sign. They manufacture items that will last for a limited period of time; they want to see their customers spend money in their stores more than once in a lifetime. Their hearts are not in the craftsmanship of true carpenters. I love Vermont.

"Here's all I could find on Brent Thompson. I even have a picture of him with Allison Hatchfield at one of our business functions." I studied the picture carefully. He looked normal to me. Tall, lean, and toned, with clean-cut brown hair and dressed quite nicely for the occasion. I suppose deep down I expected them to look like Bonnie and Clyde. *Wake up, Becky. Live in the now.*

"You have done well, my son," I said. Allan chuckled. "Are you a big *Star Wars* fan?" he said, looking around at the law books I kept in three old cherrywood bookshelves kitty-cornered on one side of the room. *Those bookshelves would last too*, I thought. They were made in Vermont as well by the same local carpenter who crafted the table.

"Oh no," I replied. "I just thought the line would fit. Aside from obtaining this information faster than I ever anticipated, has anything else come up?"

"Not really. Brent is planning on taking a vacation, though. I am not sure where. He didn't say. I did overhear him on the phone discussing flight times with Allison. I suspect they are traveling together. The more I think about it, he did mention another two people—a male and a female, I think—going on vacation too."

"How much vacation time are your employees allowed per year?" I asked.

"Four weeks. We don't really have a busy season, but we normally set the maximum time out of the office at two weeks. A desk left empty for one month is extreme in any business setting."

"I understand. Well, he may be just taking a vacation. Do you know the airlines he may have used?" As I watched Allan continue to glance nosily about my office, I made a mental note to reorganize it and give it a proper cleaning. After being in the lobby of Allan's building, the office of his corporate attorney definitely needed to look the part as well. "Not a clue," Allan replied.

"Well," I replied, "not a problem. Tell you what, I need to look over these papers. Why don't you go back to the office, and I'll give you a call in a couple of days." *Yeah,*

Rebecca, after you hire an emergency redecorator. "In the meantime, act natural, but keep your ears open. And keep me informed, okay?" Allan sighed. "Okay. I'll keep in touch." Allan grabbed his keys and was out of the office as quickly as he had arrived.

For the next two and one-half hours, I read over the paperwork, making notations as needed on legal pads and yellow stickies. Brent appeared to have a clean background, good business education, well-developed résumé, and no gaps in his history to suggest a criminal record. The fact of the matter was I could find nothing wrong. He happened to put in a lot of overtime and didn't socialize more than the minimum with the employees of Financial Investments. Sure, he didn't announce where he could be reached on vacation. But isn't that what vacations are all about? Nothing in the Financial Investments employee handbook stated that one had to disclose all the particulars about his vacationing. I would have to dig deeper.

Taking a few of the documents with me, I left the office and ventured to the old courthouse. My friend Tyler Walker served as the chief probation officer. Tyler had a lot of time on his hands, since Deering wasn't exactly the crime capital of the United States. Tyler could always be convinced to dig up criminal records for defense attorneys in need. I was "in need" and pleased to find him in his office when I arrived. "Hi, Tyler. How are you doing today?"

"Becky! I'm great, how are you? I didn't see you this morning."

"Oh, I didn't have anything on for today, so I went to the office. Listen, I need a favor from you."

"Oh, you do now, huh?" Tyler rubbed his hands. "Whatcha got?"

"I need you to do a check, local and national, on a fellow for me. But I need you to keep this quiet as he has not been charged with anything as of yet, and he lives around here. Can you promise me that much?"

"No problem, darling. Got a name, address, and social?"

"Sure do. His name is Brent Thompson. He lives at 12 Crickety Creek Drive, Deering, Vermont. Here is his social and DOB," I said, handing him a slip of paper.

"I'm on it, darling. Anything else I can do for you?"

"Well, . . . since you're asking, I'd like you to check out his girlfriend, if you can. I only have a name of Allison Hatchfield. She is around the same age and lives somewhere in Vermont. I am not sure where."

"I'll see what I can do."

"Thanks, Tyler. You know where to find me." Tyler waved good-bye, eager to solve his new mystery. Tyler had been working in the courthouse for many, many years and took great pride in the fact that he knew just about everything about everyone. He was a short, stocky man in his forties, married with six children. He had black hair and wore glasses and a white button-down oxford shirt every day. As I left the courthouse, I thought about getting him a new shirt for his birthday. Blue might flatter him. I supposed I would need to have someone else do a background check to find out when his birthday was and what size he actually wore.

CHAPTER SEVEN

B ACK IN the office, six messages and three hang-ups greeted me on the machine. Strange, I thought, but it was possible that the hang-ups were wrong numbers. One of the many ethical rules an attorney is obligated to follow is to always return a client's phone call no matter who the client is. I didn't have time to hypothesize hang-ups. After listening to the actual messages, I was grateful that the rules required only one return call. Mrs. Fitchmier had called all six times.

"Hello, Mrs. Fitchmier," I said.

"Oh, Becky, I am so glad you called. I have a question about my will." Glancing at my scales of justice on top of one of my now-noticeably-dusty cherrywood bookcases, I began to rub my forehead. Couldn't I have just finished this draft? Mrs. Fitchmier continued. "Do you remember the watch that I was going to leave to my niece Laura? Well, I can't find the watch, and she didn't send me a get-well card when I had sinusitis last week. I have decided not to give her that watch anymore. I hope that's not too much of a bother for you." Mrs. Fitchmier's voice reminded me of Mrs. Potts in Disney's *Beauty and the Beast*.

"No bother at all, Mrs. Fitchmier. I can delete it quicker than you can make a cup of tea." Mrs. Fitchmier laughed, and I printed draft number 8 of the Last Will and Testament of Alice Fitchmier. Snow had begun to fall outside, so I filled my briefcase with Allan's files and went home. *Hmm, lots of accordion files*, I thought.

By the time I arrived at the cabin, three inches of fluffy white snow covered the ground. Strangely, I noted a fresh set of footprints coming from the left side of the cabin, out to the walkway, then heading toward the street. Someone had been walking around my home, and it wasn't the electric or cable companies. They had been in the neighborhood earlier in the week. Fortunately, the prints were pointed in the direction of the street. I had watched enough mystery movies to assume that the person had left. At least I hoped that the person had left.

I cautiously opened the door and secured it behind me, the sound of the deadbolt lock chilling my spine. My antiquated answering machine beckoned in the background with repeated computerized beeps, indicating that I had at least one message. The machine would have to wait while I searched the bottom floor of the cabin, ensuring no one but myself was within. When I was comfortable that the bottom floor was clear, I ventured upstairs, but not without a kitchen knife.

My study was empty. The spare room also appeared safe. The last room to check was my bedroom.

At first glance, all appeared clear. Phew. Walking over to the window, I peered outside toward the footprints, which were vanishing as the snow fell. There didn't appear to be any tracks in the yard or in the surrounding woods as far as I could see. It was comforting to see the snow brighten up the area, even though night was approaching. I decided to go downstairs and start a fire.

Turning around, I noticed that the lace on my left shoe had become undone. Spying my moccasins, which were sticking out from under my bed, I decided that I would be more comfortable in a pair of sweatpants and an old flannel shirt. Sitting on my bed, I reached down for my moccasins when something sharp suddenly pierced my right hand. "Ouch!" I cried out, leaping off the bed and into the hallway.

Peering back in, I looked down to see the playful eyes of Miranda peering back at me. Now cradling my bleeding hand in pain, I screamed at the cat: "That was *no*, Miranda!"

Miranda darted from the room and ran downstairs. Thankfully, I was not holding the kitchen knife at that time, else I would be taking a trip to the veterinarian with my pawless cat. Cats were supposed to be so smart. How could they have the nerve to be so stupid? Some say that one does not have a cat for a pet; they have a cat for a roommate. I had a cat for a *pet*, and if she pulled that stunt again, I would ensure that she exercised her right to remain silent.

After taking a minute to collect myself, I ventured downstairs to light my fire. On the way, I pressed the button on the answering machine and prepared the logs. The first call was my mother, who had heard that it was snowing in Vermont, and she wanted to make sure that I was prepared for it. Not that there was anything she could do, but the thought counted. Call number 2 again was my mother, who had forgotten she had already called before: "I enjoyed listening to the sound of your voice anyway, honey. Talk to you later."

Call number 3 was Ken, wanting to see if I needed anything from the store because the storm had a high chance of dumping up to twelve new inches of snow on Deering. Since every storm I had experienced so far in Vermont posed the same threats, I chalked the call up to loneliness. Too tired to chat, I made a mental note to call Ken later.

The final two calls were hang-ups. Unusual, given the hang-ups at the office earlier, but I was too tired to care. I was more focused on the fact that there were no clients that I had to call that evening. I had plenty of time to relax and go over Allan's file once more while Miranda curled up at my feet in front of the fire. I stretched out on the couch with a cup of hot chocolate and began to read when the phone rang again. *Ugh*, I thought. Just when I got comfortable.

"Hello?" Click. Dial tone. I shivered, wishing that I had some form of caller ID. The phone rang again.

"Hello." This time my voice was stern and authoritative.

"Becky?" A man was on the other end.

"Who is this?" I asked firmly.

"It's me, Allan. I'm sorry, did I catch you at the wrong time?"

I breathed a little easier. "Oh no, Allan. What's new?"

"Well, I just wanted to check in. I called your office, and you weren't there. Given the storm, and the fact that you live alone, I figured that you went home. You do live alone, don't you? I don't want to be bothering anyone else sleeping, or if you have children—"

"No, Allan. It's just me. Did something happen at the office?" *Okay, Allan, don't dive too far into my personal life, okay? Not a good time.*

"Brent left today. He left for five days. Allison went with him. That's all I know."

Not much information to work with. "Thank you, Allan. I am glad you called. No more information other than that? He doesn't use any corporate cards when he leaves, does he? Perhaps we could find out the airline information that way?"

"Oh no. We're clean when it comes to the corporate expenses. I already checked. I know he went somewhere south, and he is out of the country on some island or something. Look, I'll let you go. I really shouldn't be bothering you at home."

"It is quite all right, Allan. Keep me posted, okay?"

"Good night, Becky." I hung up the receiver and went back to the couch, hoping that Allan wouldn't make it a practice to call my house all the time. The phone remained quiet the rest of the evening.

When I awoke the next morning, the roads had been plowed. I quickly shoveled the walkway to the driveway and ventured out to the office, arriving just after noon. No mail had arrived.

Fishing for my keys, I noticed the pungent smell of a man's cologne. My office was the only one upstairs, and I had no appointments scheduled for that day. Curious, I ventured downstairs to the hardware store to see if Mr. Hatley had come looking for me. "Mr. Hatley?" I called out.

Mr. Hatley was standing on a wobbly ladder, adjusting an old radio that rested on the top of a shelf. He was a tall skinny gentleman in his early sixties. His hair had thinned significantly, but it was still as black as ink. "Becky, what a nice surprise," he said, peering down at me over the brim of his small square spectacles. "What can I do for you, honey?"

"Oh, I was wondering if you had come upstairs looking for me." I quickly noticed the absence of any cologne on dear Mr. Hatley. In fact, I instead suspected that he had been working quite hard, perhaps stocking the shelves for the past two days. Note to self: *buy Mr. Hatley cologne for his birthday.*

"No, Becky. In fact, it has been rather quiet. I haven't seen anyone this morning. The phone did ring about a half hour ago down here. Was the wife. I just hung up, as a matter of fact. I think she's still talking. You know, we've been married for forty-five years. And wouldn't you know it, when I come home at night, she doesn't talk to me. But all day long, she calls and wants to talk about nothing. Like that funny show. *Sign . . . Sign . . . Feeld*? What's that funny show?"

"*Seinfeld*, Mr. Hatley."

"Yes, that's it. Anyway . . ."

Unfortunately, I didn't have time to chat, and Mr. Hatley could go on and on all day. "Actually, Mr. Hatley, I have to fly. I have a lot of work to catch up on. Say hello to Mary for me, okay?"

"Okay, Becky. Have a good day." I went back upstairs.

My office was in the same condition as I had left it. Maybe I was being paranoid. Tyler was the only person on the answering machine, stating that he needed to meet me at the courthouse as he had the information I requested. I grabbed my Burberry overcoat and gloves from the closet, picked up my briefcase, and scurried out the door.

Approaching the courthouse, I saw Tyler on the front steps. He had a cup of coffee in his hand. "Becky! I am so glad I caught up with you. I haven't had any coffee yet today, and I just couldn't wait."

"I hear ya," I replied. "How are you, Tyler? I got your message on my machine and came as soon as I could." We continued up the steps together, past the guards at the door and up some more marble steps to the second floor. We took at left at Courtroom 322, which was in session. We then took a right down a corridor and continued past a series of offices until we reached a door with a sign that read, "Tyler Walker, Chief Probation Officer." Even though I had been frequenting the courthouse for some time, I loved the history it had, which was quite evident in the detail of the rooms themselves. The courthouse had undergone little renovation since its construction over one hundred years prior.

Tyler opened the door, and we were greeted by Tyler's secretary, Kathy Singleton. Kathy was in her midthirties, her auburn hair pulled up in a bun. She wore a different pair of glasses every day, depending on the day of the week, which matched her floral-print dress, again assigned to a certain day of the week. Kathy's desk was spotless: organization was key, according to her.

Tyler's desk had a bit of a different pattern to it. He claimed it was organized, and Kathy was forbidden to touch it. I was with Tyler after Kathy once attempted to organize his desk before going on an unreachable vacation. Poor Tyler: he was lost for two days until he could find his way around. By the time Kathy returned, the desk was back to normal.

The desk's current appearance was no different, but Tyler quickly pulled a bunch of papers fastened together by a paperclip. "Here's all I could find, Becky. Got exactly what you were looking for, I think."

I hurriedly skimmed the papers. Allison was clean, but at least I now had her address. Apparently, she lived a couple of blocks away from Brent. Brent, on the other hand, surprised me. He was clean as well.

"Thanks, buddy. I've got to get back to the office. I'll be back for the first call of the list in the morning. I have a couple of things to take care of. See you later."

"Sure, Becky. Is everything okay?" said Tyler.

"Yes, everything is just fine. This is more than helpful. I owe you one." I hurried past Kathy and shut the door. I ran back down the hall, past Courtroom 322, down the marble stairs, and out the door. I couldn't get back to the office fast enough. On the way out the door, Judge Haley stopped me.

"Becky, I overheard a clerk on the phone earlier today. Someone was looking for you."

"Hi, Judge. Someone was looking for me? Do you know who it was?"

"No. There was no message. They just called up and wanted to know if you were around the courthouse. Gee, I wish I had known you were. Well, I suppose they will find you if they really want to. How is everything going?"

"Oh, just fine. Very busy nowadays. You know, I have been getting quite a few hang-up phone calls lately, at the office and at home. I have no idea who would be trying to get in touch with me."

"That's strange. Well, I'll alert the clerks to the situation. If anyone else calls, I'll have them get a name first, okay?"

"That would be great, Judge, if it is no trouble."

"Oh, no trouble at all. Listen, I see that you are in a rush, so I won't talk your ear off. Promise me you'll be careful though, okay? If you don't feel safe going up to your office for a while, have someone go with you. You shouldn't be traveling anywhere alone, in case these hang-ups are from a member of our fine system's criminal clientele."

"I'll be fine, Judge. Thanks," I replied, scurrying back down the courthouse steps and out to the rocky dirt parking lot where I had parked my car.

CHAPTER EIGHT

T HE STAIRWAY to my office seemed much longer than usual, and remarkably narrower. Sure, it consisted of twenty-two stairs straight up (except for the last three, which bent around the corner to my office door), but I was in good shape and used to the climb. I supposed my lack of oxygen didn't help—running from the courthouse to my car and from my car to the building, only to travel up those twenty-two stairs. Subconsciously, I was anticipating the scent of men's cologne upon my arrival. Nothing. I was safe. Just the smell of sawdust from the hardware store below. Well, unless whoever the person was smartened up and ditched the cologne. Honestly, if I was being stalked by some strange mass murderer, I wished that he would choose a different cologne. That particular scent was extremely offensive to my delicate sinuses.

I was relieved to find the answering machine free of messages. Not that I expected any. It was just one of those days. Snowstorms in Deering always quieted the town. Everyone took life a bit slower. That had to have been the reason why the townspeople seemed to live so long. I began to wonder if I too would live so long. My roots were, after all, still based in fast-paced Boston.

Spreading the Financial Investments paperwork around the table, frustration began to rear its ugly head. Why was I not finding anything? I supposed that since I landed the Financial Investments account, I should learn the company inside and out. Tedious, but necessary and, with any luck, worthwhile. Still, I couldn't help but ponder Allan's great fear of Brent. Brent was productive, showed up for work on time—early, in fact—and often stayed late. He may have seemed secretive, but his record appeared clean. The company files appeared clean at the outset as well. Perhaps Allan just wanted to keep his record flawless in an overly litigious world.

Allan's clientele was, as I suspected, vast according to the paperwork he supplied. They ranged from parents investing for children, grandparents investing for grandchildren, and business-degree candidates hoping to get a jump start on retirement. Nothing out of the ordinary. Amounts varied as did the clientele. And the companies in which Allan invested were all over the world, ranging in anything from meat and other food to gas to credit cards to real estate. Everything appeared solid.

My stomach alerted me that dinnertime was approaching, and it was already dark outside. People were leaving work early, and given the fact that my route home was not well lit, I decided I should follow along with the traffic. I left the Financial Investments file, grabbed a few personal injury files demanding my attention, and headed for home.

As I turned into my driveway, I scanned the lawn for footprints in the new fallen snow. Thankfully, the snow was untouched, with the exception of a few squirrel prints. Ken's familiar voice was on the answering machine, and I dialed his number after a quick, uneventful check around the house.

"Hello?"

"Hi, Ken, how did you survive the snow?"

"Oh, I survived. I just called to say hi and to see if you had spoken with Charlie."

"I'm sorry, Ken. Actually, I was hoping that *you'd* spoken with him."

"No. He hasn't called." It broke my heart to hear Ken's voice so forlorn.

"Ken, listen. Why don't you come over tonight, and I'll make you some dinner?"

"I'd love to, Becky. But I don't want to put you out or anything."

"Ken," I said sternly, "please come. I could use the company."

Ken's voice grew more excited. "Okay then. Can I bring anything?"

"No. I was just going to whip up some spaghetti. I have homemade sauce defrosting."

"That sounds good. Tell you what, I'll bring the bread and some dessert. Apple pie okay?" Two of my favorite things.

"That would be perfect. See you in a bit." I hung up the phone and began to set the table. Miranda was pitifully walking around the kitchen, seeming apologetic for the prior incident under the bed. I picked her up and began to stroke her furry little head. "It's okay, little one. Just don't do it again, okay?" Miranda purred in contentment.

Soon Ken was at the front door, bread and apple pie in hand. Dinner was perfect. Ken told stories about his childhood, his wife, and about Charlie. We talked about the town and how it had changed over the years and how he hoped it would not change much more. I told him about my childhood and my family back home. He could not understand how anyone could spend so much time living around such a busy city as Boston. I told him that I did miss it, if only a little. I was also quite shocked to hear that Ken's precious town had really changed at all.

Ken left after a few hours, and I began to review my personal injury files. Personal injuries were almost always slow-moving cases. Generally, the clients had to finish treating before I submitted a demand package to an insurance company. Then it was up to the insurance company to set the tone of negotiations by the way they evaluated each case. Sometimes they were favorable, and sometimes they made mistakes. The only time I took real offense was if my client was injured more than the victims in most other personal injury cases. If the client played according to the rules, mitigating his damages, and the insurance company deliberately quoted low,

I took it to heart. I always treated each client the same, of course, but I truly needed to vent my emotions via a long, arduous workout when an insurance company tried to take advantage on the cheap, particularly if they suspected the client was hard up for money. That is not the way the system is supposed to work. That is not why I became a lawyer. It was just one of the many reasons why the general public no longer trusted the system.

I supposed the only way I felt that I could make a difference in the games people played would be if I were to become a judge. Judge Haley always told me that he felt he made a difference through his position every day. Should an insurance company even attempt to take advantage of a client in such an instance, he would order the appropriate penalty; and with the strike of his gavel, justice had been served. He did tell me one day that I was making a difference, just as he was, by pointing out the mistakes of such slippery defendants. Otherwise, he would be powerless in most cases to make any move. I supposed that there was some truth to that statement.

I wasn't quite ready for bed until after the clock struck twelve. By then, everything appeared to be in order: my files were up-to-date, the house was clean, and the dishes were done and put away. I pulled out a suit for the next morning, found a pair of nylons, and went to bed. I didn't have to worry about shoes. Basic black worked with most of my suits and would work just fine in the morning.

Neither Judge Haley nor Tyler was anywhere to be found at the courthouse the next morning, so after I finished my business, I went back to the office. Putting down my briefcase and keys, I realized that there was a message on the answering machine. Pressing the button, a computerized voice resonated throughout the room:

"DO *not* represent Financial Investments or any of their employees. Withdraw from any representation on behalf of that company *immediately*."

I just stood there in the center of my office, my coat still halfway on, frozen. I could barely breathe. The sound of a horn outside woke me from my trance, and I replayed the message. Quickly I took the tape from the machine and put it in my desk drawer, replacing the machine with a new tape.

My eyes then focused on the center of the table. My first corporate account. Since I met Allan, I had tracks in the snow around my house, hang-ups, and now a computerized warning on my machine. Suddenly, the phone rang again. "Hello?" I said.

"Hi, Becky. It's me, Allan."

"Hi, Allan." I sat down, obviously not thrilled with the call.

"Is something wrong? You don't sound like yourself."

"Oh no. I just walked in the door. How are you doing?"

"I'm okay. Nothing new to report. Business is going fine, as usual. Nothing abnormal since our boy has been on vacation. Did you find out anything?"

I walked over to the windows and peered outside. "Well, my initial check both state and federal appears clean as to both Brent and Allison. I don't see anything as of right now in the paperwork you gave me either."

"I have to get rid of him, Becky. I just don't trust him. But I can't get rid of him without cause. I just don't know what to do. I mean, he is a good worker. You can see that. But the late nights, and the secrets . . . I just don't feel I can trust him, and he would never talk to me about it. He just leaves me with a bad taste in my mouth."

"Perhaps you can set a new rule forbidding any work past eight o'clock?" I suggested, now pacing around the office and straightening up the Financial Investments files on the table.

"Yes, that's a good idea. Then I can keep an eye on him," said Allan. "I certainly don't need to work late nights at my age." *What exactly do you do?* I thought. "And everyone else too, right?" I said, reminding him of his other employees. "Of course," Allan replied. "Listen, why don't you bill me for the time you have put in thus far, and if anything new comes up, I'll give you a call." Ugh. For the first time, I didn't want to bill a client. "I really haven't done anything yet, Allan."

"Sure you have. Call it research and review, right? I'll expect it, uh, what do you lawyers say . . . *forthwith*?" Desperately wanting to end the conversation, I caved. "Sure, Allan. I'll put one in the mail this afternoon. Good-bye." I hoped that my bill would be the last of Financial Investments. How did I know that my phone was not bugged? What if someone was watching me through some high-powered binoculars outside the window? What if someone was waiting for me outside the office door? Would I have even heard anyone coming up the steps? Maybe I shouldn't have even spoken with Allan. Maybe he was right, and Brent was tracking me down like a baby deer. Should I even be putting anything in writing? *Breathe, Rebecca.*

I collected my thoughts and decided that I had the right to bill for the initial investigation and my opinion as to the situation. I hadn't done anything wrong. I quickly typed a detailed letter to Allan and enclosed a bill. I did not have to accept or keep anyone as my client. I certainly could withdraw from any case with just cause. I was still in control.

I finished up a few other matters that I had put on hold and packed up for home. Taking a different route this time, I stopped at Ken's Country Store for a gallon of milk and some more of his terribly addicting bread that I knew would make me feel better. I had no mail at the house, although the answering machine was calling to me when I entered. Reluctantly, I pressed the button.

"DO *not* represent Financial Investments or any of their employees. Withdraw from any representation on behalf of that company *immediately*."

Once again, I thoroughly searched the cabin. No one was inside. Miranda followed me around each room, sensing something was wrong. "That's it!" I said as I packed a bag and threw it on the couch. Nothing was pressing for a few weeks. My next court appearance wasn't until the end of the month. I could go home for a while—take a vacation and see my family.

Suddenly there was a knock on the door. I ran to my bedroom window and peered down below through the curtain, only to find a set of eyes peering back at me. It was Ken. "Becky, can I come in? It's awful cold out here."

"Ken, what a nice surprise. What are you doing here?" I asked, glancing out to the street behind him. "You left your change in the store. Fifteen dollars." He handed me the money and glanced around the room. "Are you going somewhere?" I knew Ken sensed my anxiety. "I thought I might take a trip to see my folks. I haven't seen them in a while."

"And you are taking your cat, I see? I suppose I am no longer the designated cat feeder?" Miranda playfully brushed up against Ken's ankle. "Oh no, Ken. You are a wonderful cat feeder," I replied, unable to get the computerized voice out of my mind. My breathing grew heavy again.

"Becky, are you all right? What is wrong with you? You look flushed."

"It's nothing. Actually, I am getting these strange phone calls at the office and home, and I am a little nervous." Ken insisted I play the message for him. Halfway through, he demanded I spend the night at his house, cat included. "After all, Becky, Charlie is not here. You can use his room. It will be safer. Tomorrow, we'll go see the sheriff and report the incident, but you two will stay with me for a while. What's a couple of lonely people to do right? Besides, you're like a daughter to me. Anyone threatens you, and they have to deal with my itchy trigger finger!"

"Thanks, Ken," I said, laughing, picturing Ken's osteoarthritic trigger finger. I gathered my things, put them in my car, and followed Ken down the street. Once we arrived at Ken's house, we decided to call the sheriff, who immediately stopped by to listen to the message and take my report. He assured us that he would personally stop by and check my house before returning to the station. After he left with the tape, I said good night to Ken and prepared for bed.

Unfortunately, the adrenaline was too overwhelming, and I didn't sleep much that night despite the nice cup of warm milk Ken made me drink. Even if I could somehow block Financial Investments from my mind, all I could think about was Charlie. After all, I *was* spending the night in his room. Glancing around, I admired the dusty Pop Warner football trophies and little league plaques. A soccer ball rested in the corner of the room on top of some old hooded sweatshirts. A few partially filled bottles of familiar cologne stood on top of a scratched chest of drawers. An old picture of him, his mother, and his father at some outing stood behind the cologne. Charlie must have been no more than ten or eleven year sold in that picture. They seemed so happy then. A picture of innocence on so many levels. Little did that happy little family know the avenues life would take them down. As I lay in Charlie's bed, all I could think about was which avenue he was on, and whether he would ever find his way back down mine.

CHAPTER NINE

I AWOKE the next morning to the delicious smell of bacon wafting through the house. Ken had been awake for some time and prepared quite the scrumptious feast. By the time I made it downstairs, I was greeted with a smorgasbord of pancakes, eggs, sausages, bacon, and toast. Despite the fact that I could not help but remember the terrifying message on my answering machine just hours before, I was able to enjoy breakfast. Still, Ken sensed my anxiety. "I wish I could make you more comfortable in my home," he said as he cleared the dishes.

"Oh, Ken," I replied, "it's fantastic here. It's just that being in a strange place, not by choice, reminds me that there is someone out there who desperately wants to either help me or hurt me. And given the tone of the voice on my machine, I'm thinking helping really isn't the intention. Either way, I . . . I'll be fine in a couple of days."

On the way to work, I picked up the local papers and was horrified to see Financial Investments staring at me on the front pages of each. The same picture headed all the articles: Allan leaning against the front of his impressive building, dressed in a blue Armani suit, with the Vermont morning sun reflecting off the building's mirrored windows. Apparently, the excitement wagon hadn't visited Deering in quite some time, so the newspaper editors decided to run business success stories. Since Allan was doing so well, they decided to hit him first.

The first paper did not seem threatening. The second paper, however, hit me like a brick. At the bottom of the page, the reporter asked Allan if Financial Investments had an attorney. "Why yes," Allan replied, "Rebecca Lawson."

Panic instantly set in: I began to breathe heavily, and my mind began to race. What if the person who left that message read the article? Well, I did not get the message until after the paper's deadlines were closed for the day. Still, should I just cut my losses and pull out of the case? If I did, at what cost? Definitely unfavorable advertising for me: "Local Lawyer Rebecca Lawson Backs Out on Major Vermont Corporation." That would certainly boost my corporate clientele. What would Allan do if I backed out? What if he was somehow linked to that message? But then again, what if he was not? I began to wish I knew Brent's whereabouts probably more than Allan's.

There was nothing I could do but go to work. I had other clients who needed my attention. Still, my mind continued to wander. During my first year out of law school, the most anxiety I had was making my way through the intricacies of the probate and family court. I could still see myself walking through the courthouse halls dressed in my brand-new but poorly fitted suits. The biggest challenge that I faced then was that the rules of evidence, which I had feverishly studied, did not apply when dealing with family disputes.

The cases themselves, particularly motions for termination of visitation rights of parents, were especially draining. The standard was the "best interests of the child," but courts were generally reluctant to terminate parental rights no matter how mixed-up the parents may have appeared. After the smoke cleared, all that was left was a heated argument between a mother and a father or a parent and a grandparent over visiting a minor child (the true victim), who would be more confused than ever. Social services, therapists, doctors, lawyers, judges, victim and child advocates naturally were eager to help, but the child always ended up reiterating a tragic story endless numbers of times to these strangers claiming that they were trustworthy because they said so.

I just felt that children should not have to spend their time considering which parent they were supposed to side with, rather than which toys to add to their Christmas list. Those cases just never seemed to resolve, and I dreaded every last one, mostly because I wanted to save every child myself. I just hoped that by the time the children became adults themselves, they wouldn't reenter the vicious cycle from whence they came, the next time as parents.

That being said, I began to steer away from accepting the juvenile cases, instead representing the occasional adult in the criminal session. What I did learn in the juvenile session I took to the adults. After all, the better I understood the client's perspective, the better I argued his case.

I began to wonder if Brent had friends or family who were ever involved in the criminal system when he was a child: if he was linked with something illegal, perhaps that would be the place he received his influence. The juvenile system was just as draining for me. Originally, I was under the impression that the juvenile appearances were nothing more than representing smart-aleck children who were just like any other child—just slightly angrier, slightly more daring, and unfortunate enough to get caught. Naturally, I was surprised to find that the problem was much worse than that. The young people caught up in the juvenile system were not just charged with beating up each other, throwing rocks at windows, or stealing a couple of packs of chewing gum. They were minors who were charged with assaults and batteries with dangerous weapons, armed robberies while masked, drug offenses, and other various types of gang violence.

All too often, I witnessed the discouraging scene of a child, no more than ten years old, being accompanied down the courtroom halls in shackles (hand and foot) by a bailiff who was three times his size. He certainly did not understand how the world worked. Instead, he found himself caught up in a bad situation stemming from bad influences and poor decision making.

Sadly, many first offenders performed their stunts to get a laugh out of their peers (perhaps Brent), to look cool, or to get attention. Oftentimes they meant no real harm. Sometimes the acts could be seen as cries for help from adults in their lives who had forgotten that they were parents. Oftentimes the first time around, the judges would go easy on them. However, they usually either found themselves either enjoying the limelight or mistakenly thinking that the system was so weak that they would never get caught again. Temptation for some was, however, too powerful, and many found themselves back in the same courtroom—in front of the same judge, next to the same criminal-defense attorney. I hated being too strict with some of the younger defendants, but if they were not scared, they would usually return on a subsequent offense.

As civil had always been my true love, the criminal cases I had been handling had significantly dwindled. I supposed, though, I had picked up some potential white-collar crime after meeting Allan, but I must admit that it was intriguing. Perhaps my mother was right. I should have gone to medical school.

As I approached the parking lot at my office, I began to think that perhaps I shouldn't have gone to graduate school at all. What I should have done was gotten married, moved into a little white house with a little white picket fence, and worked as a cashier in a local grocery store like Ken's. Sure, I probably would have made only just enough money to get by, but I probably would have increased my personal longevity by eliminating stress from my life. Turning off the engine, I wondered if life was really worth worrying every single day that I could be sued for malpractice, as I learned the ins and outs of each unique court system. I wished that I was taught practicalities as well as theory in law school. At least I had Judge Haley to guide me. He told me when we first met that I reminded him of himself when he first became a lawyer, only he had no real mentor.

Carrying my heavy briefcase up the stairs, I came to the conclusion that my anxiety stemmed from feeling less than total control. I would prepare and prepare cases and situations until I was sure that I could prepare no more. I valued my reputation. I did not want to find myself embarrassed in any situation. As a result, I was embarrassed rarely. I supposed that my attempt of "controlling control" resulted in less happiness, since I was not always happy. Miranda calmed me down. Every day, no matter what happened, she would act as though I was flawless. She was probably the one keeping me alive; otherwise, I would have had a lifetime prescription for nitroglycerin and a bleeding ulcer. If I ever decided to leave the law, I would be an Animal Rescue League person. I could find great peace living with a bunch of animals in my little log cabin. Maybe even some wonderful man would pick me to be his bride, and we would have little children running around. That would be a nice life.

Reaching the top of the stairs, I told myself that I knew in my heart that I could never leave the law. It wouldn't matter if I chose to be an Animal Rescue League volunteer or a cashier or a housewife. I love the law too much. Besides, the law has forever affected my life: I learned in law school that I could be sued for anything, and having more legal experience worsened the deal. Even assuming that I was unfamiliar with the smallest, minutest area of law, people would assume that I was an expert and had billions of dollars to deposit into their frivolous bank accounts. My nature will never allow me to relax.

Inside my office, my answering machine was flashing the number *10*. Ten messages. Did I really want to answer them? I peered out the window into the street. Broad daylight. Who would be stupid enough to pull something in broad daylight? I supposed that if I were to be shot, it would happen after dark when everyone had gone home. Ignoring the machine was no longer an option without violating ethical rules, especially when the messages could affect the outcome for any of my pending cases.

I sat down and pressed Play Messages.

"Hi, honey! It's Mom. I just wanted to say hello and make sure that you wished your grandmother a happy birthday today. I called you last night, and you didn't call me back. Call me when you can so that I know you are all right."

Beep. One down, nine to go.

"Uh, hello. My name is Walter Ericson. I was looking for Attorney Lawson. I might have a case for her. Please call me at 555-7970."

Beep.

"Yes, hello, Attorney Lawson. I'm sure you read Grisham's *The Rainmaker*. Do you want to make it rain? Call me at 555-6435. My name is Varoules. Mikey Varoules."

Beep.

I began to relax. Two potential cases—not bad. I expected such given the newspaper articles. We'll see. Maybe Allan wasn't such a bad guy after all.

Messages 4 through 6 were hang-ups. Nothing to be worried about. I changed chairs. Then the voice:

"Good morning, Becky. Just a reminder—withdraw immediately."

Beep.

Furious, I threw the message pad against the wall as the machine continued playing. "Hi, Becky! It's me, Allan. Can you give me a call when you can? I have a couple of questions for you. Talk to you soon."

The final two calls were Bianca's—from the clerk's office—and Judge Haley's, gloating over the newspaper articles. I grabbed my coat and started for the courthouse. Judge Haley was going down the courthouse steps when I arrived. "Becky! Hello!" said Judge Haley.

"Hi, Judge. How are you doing?"

"I'm doing just fine. Did you get my message?"

"Yes, as a matter of fact, I did. Guess I am famous now, huh?"

"For a little while anyway. Enjoy it while you can. Just remember your ethics—don't let it go to your head."

"Don't worry, Judge. You know me. I think I am the only attorney in the courthouse who dares to ask for a second call if I have to refill the parking meter." Judge Haley laughed. "You are right, my dear. You're lucky I like you. You certainly would never get away with that in Boston. Say, what brings you here today?" Deep down, I knew my business at the courthouse was through for the day. What I really wanted was a pep talk from the esteemed judge. It was amazing how he always cured my seemingly endless waves of anxiety with a mere five minutes of small talk. "Well, I just wanted to make sure nothing new had been filed on a particular case."

"Now that's the sign of a good attorney. Have a good day, my dear," said the judge. "Thanks, you too." Judge Haley disappeared around the corner, two bailiffs at his side. On my way to the first payphone to call Allan, secretly I wished that I was a judge instead—I needed the protection.

CHAPTER TEN

"FINANCIAL INVESTMENTS, may I help you?" chirped the secretary. "Yes, would Allan Richards be there?" I replied.

"May I ask who's calling?"

"Sure, Rebecca Lawson." I decided I needed to be more businesslike. "Uh, Attorney Rebecca Lawson."

"Just a minute."

I waited for about five minutes, then the familiar voice came on the other line. "Rebecca. How are you?"

"I'm just fine, Allan. How are you doing?" I asked.

"Great. Did you read the newspaper articles today? Great for business, both mine and yours, huh?"

"Yes, Allan. You really shouldn't have done that."

"Oh, no problem, Becky. I didn't think you would mind. Listen, why don't we have dinner? I have some things to go over with you. How's seven at Café Mirabelle sound?"

"Sounds great. I'll meet you there." I hung up the phone.

Six o'clock came quite quickly, and I began to get anxious. Perhaps dinner was not the best idea. Still, Judge Haley's pep talk gave me some confidence. If someone was out to get me, they would. If my death was predetermined, and I was shortly to find out the creativity of my maker, there was nothing I could do about it.

Making my way over to the Venetian-style restaurant, I found Allan outside, smoking a cigar. "Hello, Rebecca," he said, snuffing the cigar. "No smoking inside. I hate that."

"Doesn't bother me," I replied. "I never touched the stuff. I suppose my unsuccessful attempts to light matches as a little girl had something to do with it." Allan laughed and ushered me inside.

As I ate my chicken marsala and he his veal cutlets, I began to rethink the dinner idea. Although this was a business dinner, and we did discuss business, his attempt to impress me with his extensive knowledge of fine wine made me extremely uncomfortable. Tuning out the soft Italian music being pumped into the dining area, all I could think about was my tax classes in law school and how our meal was being written off by the company. We did not need to have such an expensive meal. And for that matter, we certainly did not need such a small table. Or a candle.

My thoughts then turned to the starving people in the streets of Boston, people whom I used to walk past every day on the way to the train. They would have loved to have dinner with us and certainly would be able to converse in business for an hour and a half. Too bad we couldn't have invited them. It was a bit disheartening.

"I wanted to talk to you about Brent, Becky." I blushed with fear.

"How is Mr. Thompson?" I inquired. "And Allison?"

"They are both doing well. They have both returned from vacation, and Brent, of course, is back to work."

"Anything new going on?"

Allan sighed. "No. Brent is keeping strange hours as usual, but he is still one of the most productive employees I've got. Have you gone over our files?"

I nodded. "I hate to tell you this, Allan, but I just haven't been able to find anything wrong. I'm really not sure what to tell you at this point."

Allan banged his fist on the table with great force, and the entire restaurant jumped. Allan smirked sheepishly around him at seemingly countless glaring eyes. "I am sorry. Sorry." He then leaned in closer to me and whispered, and I naturally leaned back. "I am just frustrated and nervous. I thought for *sure* that you would be able to find something."

"Mr. Richards," I replied sternly, "I am your attorney, not a detective. True, if I wanted to be a detective, I would probably do one hell of a job, but I don't have the time to follow people around and dig up dirt on them. It's dangerous, and I'm not qualified to do that. I've done everything in my power to check Brent out, and he seems fine. I don't know what else you wish me to do. Now if you find what you think is just cause to fire him, and you want to discuss it with me, no problem. I would be more than happy to do so. Right now, my hands are tied." I faked a sip of my Chardonnay. The glass was still full as I had no intention of drinking with a client. Besides, with all that was going on, I needed to be sharp.

"I understand," said Allan. "We'll leave it at that then. If I come up with anything new, I'll let you know. In the meantime, if other things occur within the company that require legal assistance, we'll still call you. Is that okay with you? I would not want to lose such a brilliant attorney."

"Thank you, Allan," I replied, wondering why he thought I was so brilliant. "I should be going."

"I'll walk you to your car."

"That won't be necessary. I'll talk to you soon. Thank you for the dinner." I walked out of the dining area and stopped in the ladies' room, leaving Allan at the table. It seemed that I was alone, so I took the liberty of splashing cold water on my face and breathed a heavy sigh of relief. *This should stall Allan for a while*, I thought. To my surprise, a woman with long dark hair came out of a stall and began washing her hands. *Funny*, I thought. I glanced under the stalls for feet. There were only three stalls. I guess in my distracted state, I must have missed one. As the woman was playing with her makeup, she turned to face me. "Was that your husband?" she asked.

"Oh no. He's just a business acquaintance," I said, glancing at her expensive-looking compact. "Are you from around here?"

"No. I'm from out of town. Just passing through. Everything okay out there?"

"Yes. Everything's fine." The woman quickly left the ladies' room and disappeared into the night. Strange, I thought. Although Allan's table incident did cause quite the disturbance. Assuming Allan had gone, I walked out the door and walked to my car. For the first time in my life, I looked under the car. Not that I knew what I was looking for. I wasn't really looking for a person. I guess I was looking for a bomb. Not that a bomb would be large enough for me to notice. Not that I would even know one if I saw it. Hey, at least I looked.

Climbing into the car, I inserted the keys into the ignition and discreetly said a quick prayer that my caution had not been in vain. Quickly I turned the key, and the car started immediately. Thankful yet exhausted, I made my way back to Ken's.

Ken was peering through the window when I arrived. All I could think of was my mother peering at me through what we lovingly referred to as her peekaboo window when I was in high school. As I climbed out of the car, he ran to the door to greet me. Miranda brushed against my right leg. "How was dinner?" asked Ken.

"It was okay," I replied. The aroma of warm apple pie and coffee was drifting from the kitchen. "Boy, *that* sure smells good," I said. Ken happily poured me a cup of coffee and sliced me a piece of pie. The store had been usually busy that day, in addition to a recall, which required Ken to pull all the cans and bottles of tomato juice from the shelves. Ken was more than ready for bed. I, on the other hand, was wide awake.

"Have a good night, Becky," said Ken. "And by the way, just so you know, please stay as long as you like. You're always welcome here."

"Thanks, Ken. I will be going home soon, though. I really hate to impose on you like this. You have been more than kind."

"Hey, not bad for an old geezer like me, huh?" Ken started up the stairs. "Actually, I do get lonely in this quiet house. It's been nice having you around. It makes me feel like I have someone to care for." He leaned on the banister. "You know, I have only known you a short while, Becky. But I want you to remember, I consider you family." I smiled. "Thank you, Becky Lawson."

"No. Thank *you*," I replied. Miranda purred. I then did something I hadn't done in a long time. I went to my room and pulled out my old charcoal chalks and a piece of construction paper. For three hours, I drew a picture of an old Vermont covered bridge. Although I had a long day and stayed up quite late, I hadn't felt that relaxed in a long time. And with my old pal Miranda at my feet purring contently, I was soothed.

CHAPTER ELEVEN

I T WAS nice to be comfortable in my own home again. I had been home for about three weeks, as the local police would say, *without incident*. Reluctantly, I had put off working on a couple of slow-moving cases and was finally able to bring them up-to-date. Although I was not that far behind in updating my files, I couldn't let myself do such a thing if I could help it. I silently criticized other attorneys who would not even think about putting a case on for status in their diaries even once a month, waiting instead for the client to call before updating the file. That practice, I felt, was unethical. Given the incidents in my personal life, I had fallen slightly behind, and the Irish guilt had invaded my conscience.

Varoules's rainmaker case did not work out, but Mr. Ericson had an employment law case that posed some interesting issues. I was not really interested in employment law, but several people of my clients were involved in employment disputes, so it was inevitable that I would have to learn. Of course, with Financial Investments, I would definitely need to be current with that field of law.

Winter was almost over at this point, although the calendars clearly said we were well into spring. The snow had pretty much melted away, and the birds cheerfully serenaded me each morning. Easter was just around the corner, and my family was planning on coming to visit for a few days. Since he had become family to me, I invited Ken to join us for our Easter Sunday meal.

Although I was curious about what was going on in Allan's world, I was grateful that I had not heard from him since dinner at Café Mirabelle. In fact, I had picked up some more criminal-defense work and never saw anyone connected to him or anyone from Financial Investments. During each court appearance, I quietly breathed a sigh of relief that I was away from Financial Investments and dealing with "ordinary, decent criminals." At least with them, I knew exactly where I stood.

I did see Allan in the coffee shop on a few occasions, however, but I kept my distance. He and his business also continued to frequent the local papers. Even though I no longer had open projects with the company, I was pleased that no one had been arrested for any illegal activity. The last thing I wanted was to have someone from Financial Investments try to drag me down with them if they were charged. Truthfully, Allan's business was making a real difference in the community. The more Financial Investments grew in Deering, the more jobs were offered to the locals. There was even talk about a summer program with the local high school students to pique their interests in business.

It seemed that the world was at last settling down, and I decided that yes, it was nice to be home. That is, until the phone rang. Fantastic. As much as I wanted to answer it, I was just too tired to talk. Sometimes I felt that after dealing with people's problems all day, I too needed a break. That being said, I let the answering machine do the honors:

"Wise move, Becky. Keep your head. Leave Financial Investments as it is. Do not get involved with anyone there. Particularly Allan Richards."

Click.

Immediately my thoughts turned to Brent and any underworld connections he might have had. Surely Brent was involved in the criminal world, even though he had yet to be caught. Perhaps he feared me getting closer or, worse yet, close enough to have an idea of what he was up to. Great. But closer to what? I decided to clear my head and go for a walk.

What I loved about my little log cabin was the pathway that led to a tiny spring-fed pond not too far behind it in the woods. Since the closest neighbors were almost three acres away, I never had to worry about nosey neighbors watching my comings and goings, let alone any activity on my property, especially when I went to my secret pond.

I walked along a small stream, which gurgled beside the pathway as water playfully splashed over rocks and small trees that the beavers had felled. Approaching my secret pond to which I had not even introduced Charlie, I smiled at a familiar big rock: my thinking rock. I had spent hours sitting on my thinking rock, staring at the lily pads on the water, trying to clear my head and enjoy the sights, sounds, and smells of nature: calming simplicity. I supposed that if I really looked, I could see the little spider bugs skirt across the water. As much as I despised spiders, most days the spider bugs didn't frighten me. I was actually intrigued as the little hungry fish jumped to catch the occasional quick bite to eat.

I sat on the rock for some time and, craving something warm to drink, began to walk the path home. I was feeling refreshed and very determined. No longer was I going to fear the voice on the answering machine. It was time for me to face my fears. I knew that this was not destined to be the last bizarre incident in my legal career. Arriving home, I made a cup of tea, sat down at the kitchen table, and made my list for Easter.

CHAPTER TWELVE

A COUPLE of days later, I went to work, only to find a letter shoved under my door. Strangely, the return address said, "A friend." It wasn't ticking. Good sign. I put my briefcase and purse down on the floor and slowly began to open it. It read,

> Meet me at your little *thinking rock* tomorrow at 8:00 PM.

I nearly fainted. I had told no one about my thinking rock. Who would know that I referred to a rock as a thinking rock? Someone had been watching me, and surely the message was related to Allan and Financial Investments. I grabbed what files I needed for the week, called the phone company to send all calls to the house, and ran to the safest place I could think of at that time of day: the courthouse. It would be my office for the day. Perhaps even the week.

Unfortunately, the day flew by quickly, and the courthouse was soon closing. I had no choice but to go home. My parents were arriving in two weeks, and I had become an emotional wreck. Maybe since Ken had a gun in his house, I could borrow it without telling him. *No, Becky. That's illegal. What about telling Ken?* Again, no. I couldn't tell Ken. He was too old to defend me. If I was killed by 8:15 PM the next day, at least my family would have taken time off from work and wouldn't miss much after my funeral.

On the way home, I made peace with my decision not to borrow the gun. With my luck, I would shoot my cat, myself, or something else enough for me to lose my freedom or my bar ticket. Needless to say, sleep was not an option. Drawing with charcoal wasn't working out either. Instead of pursuing another covered bridge, I drew a haystack. No, I wasn't copying the Impressionists. It made me think of my legal career. Most of what I needed was like finding a needle in one of those foolish things. And wasn't a charcoal haystack pleasing to the naked eye. I crumpled up the paper and threw it away.

The next day, I decided to spend the day with Miranda in my cabin: a jeans-sweatshirt-and-slippers day. Just in case, however, I called Ken and arranged for him to take her for the night and feed her the following day.

"Hi, Ken," I said.

"Hi, honey! How are you doing today?" said Ken.

"Oh, I'm okay. Listen, Ken. Can you do me a favor?"

"Anything for you, sweetheart."

"Can you take care of Miranda tonight and tomorrow? I have a meeting with a client, and I have no idea what time I will be back, so I'll just come back to the house here tonight. I just can't bear to leave Miranda for long, especially after I've been working so much. I don't want her to feel abandoned, you know? Besides, she adores you."

"Well, the feeling is mutual, and I'd be honored. I'll pick her up in a little bit. Things okay there at the house?"

My eyes filled up, thinking that it could be the last time I talked to Ken. "Yes, Ken. Thank you. I really appreciate it. I look forward to seeing you when I'm done. Maybe you can make me some of that world-famous apple pie of yours." I picked up Miranda and held her tight. "I'll always love you, pumpkin. You be good now, you hear?" Miranda purred. Ken picked her up within the hour.

At 7:00 PM, I began to grow extremely anxious and cleaned the house to the point where it was sterile. At the same time, I cautiously began to listen for oncoming traffic or footsteps. Nothing. The only saving grace was that it was still fairly light outside. Soon it was 7:55 PM; I put on my sneakers and reluctantly walked out the door.

The brook didn't act like its usual friendly self that evening. It seemed unusually loud. My steps were loud too, but I was walking quickly. Still, everything around me was loud. I was trembling but had to be strong for doing something that I knew deep down was so stupid. Arriving at my little pond, I stood for a moment. I seemed to be alone. Still my eyes remained wide, darting everywhere. I just could not find a place where I could hide myself kitty-corner in order to view everything around me. Even the pine trees, which once seemed so majestic, masked my moonlight. So many foolish thoughts filled my head from so many scary movies as a child. Then again, wasn't I doing exactly what most victims did? *Dumb, Becky, dumb.*

Standing there, wide-eyed and open-eared, I waited and I listened. The sounds of broken branches cracked noisily around me over the sounds of the brook. In the beginning, I was sure it was him. Or her. I felt like it was a him. Still, no one made their presence known. After a bit, I could make out the little chipmunks and squirrels scurrying along the ground, uncovering the food they had hidden for the winter and darting for the tree, which gently yet securely cradled their nests. Oh, how I longed to be sitting in one of those nests so that I could view my blind date from above.

The crackling sounds began to grow louder, and the shadow of a man emerged from behind a tree. I froze, just like the foolish girls in the horror flicks.

"Rebecca." I stood there, still frozen.

"Who are you and what do you want?" I said.

"I want to talk." The figure stepped closer. I stepped back. "I have a lot of explaining to do, and if you'll listen, you'll understand." He took another step. I stepped back again. The voice seemed familiar. "Don't be alarmed. Listen, I know there is some type of attorney-client thing that ensures that whatever I say to you as an attorney stays between us."

I began to relax a little bit, but still retained my guard. "Yes, that is one way of putting it." *Actually, it is a bit more detailed than that,* I thought to myself. Those evidence classes sure do a number on someone. What if someone were spying on us? What if the voice told someone else? I wouldn't have broken the privilege. He would have broken it. *Stop, Rebecca. This is not an evidence or an ethics exam.* Furthermore, what kind of client would demand a meeting in the dark in the middle of the woods? There is more to an attorney-client privilege than just keeping secrets. There is an element of honesty and trust far beyond what some view as a type of confessional. My voice grew stern and authoritative. "You have to tell me who you are."

The figure took one more step, and I saw the reflection of his face in the pond, partially illuminated by the moonlight. My heart skipped a beat. "Charlie?"

"Hi, Rebecca." His eyes were wide, and his face seemed sincere. "I'm sorry to meet up with you like this." The rush of adrenaline was overwhelming. I was staring at Charlie again, in person, and not a repeat visitor to the court's criminal program out for revenge because he decided he didn't like the outcome of his case.

"It's okay, Charlie. I'm glad to see you again, and in one piece." I paused for a moment, took a deep breath, and rethought my last statement. "No, actually, it's not okay. It's not okay, Charlie. What is going on here? You come back to your widowed father after a number of years, meet up with me, only to disappear again without telling anyone. Do you understand that your father isn't getting any younger? And what is this—leaving messages on my machine like some sort of freak? I thought we had something." Charlie's eyes narrowed. I gulped, forcing tears back. He wasn't worth it. "And how dare you interfere with my work by the way!"

For the next couple of moments, I thought to myself, did I *really* know this man? I mean, I had spent hours with him driving around Vermont—learning the area, meeting the people, and treating his father like my own. Maybe, just maybe, he really was some sort of psycho. I could be dead in the woods in a matter of minutes, never to be found again, with the exception of wild animals who would naturally take care of my return to the cycle of life.

"Becky, listen." Charlie came closer, and I stepped back. "I'm sorry. Let's sit down and talk. I think you'll understand everything if you just give me a chance. I know this has been somewhat unusual, but believe me, it could only be done this way." Charlie sat down on a rock by the pond. I decided to sit and listen, albeit from a distance. If this was to be my last story, it had better be a good one.

"Before I begin, Becky, you must ensure me that you will not tell another living soul what you are about to hear. Understand?" I smirked. Not quite an affirmation, but he didn't seem to notice. Charlie took out his wallet and flipped it open. "I am an agent with the Central Intelligence Agency."

"The CIA?" I grabbed the wallet for a second look.

"Yes, the CIA. I work undercover on several secret projects in the New England area. Years ago, some of the people I hung around with also worked for the agency. After a while, they told me that I had what it takes to be an agent, and I joined. Coming from such a small town like this, of course, I couldn't tell anyone, even my family. Everyone would know in as little as an hour, and my cover would be blown. It hurts at times, but I do love my job. It's incredibly exciting. The only regret I have is not having attended my mother's funeral. I was on a classified project at the time and finishing up a section of training and just heard too late. My father would never understand. I think you being an attorney, though, and understanding how the government works, could understand what happened."

The entire time he spoke, I just sat and stared into Charlie's eyes. One thing that I had come to learn is the art of getting information out of people. People have a natural fear of silence. All I had to do was remain silent and attentive and hope that he would continue speaking.

Another thing I had learned is that most truth tellers are able to hold a stare without darting their eyes. Here Charlie held his stare and didn't seem to be babbling. In fact, his entire demeanor appeared relaxed. I began to find his story quite fascinating, and my initial anger began to subside. I even began to feel bad for Charlie. "So when you left, you left because you—"

"Got a call."

I nodded slowly and looked at my feet. "Okay. So why are you here? And why now? You could have said you were CIA. I wouldn't have said anything," I said.

Charlie got up and sat next to me, careful not to touch me or move too fast. "I know, Rebecca. That's why I wanted to explain. Anyway, I'm here because I'm working."

My curiosity took over. "Working? What are you working on? Will you be here long?" And since when did he call me Rebecca? He had to have been serious.

"I'm investigating Financial Investments." Shocker. "You could be in serious danger soon, if you're not so already. I need your help." My heart skipped another beat.

"Charlie, listen. Not that it's your business, but I gave up that client. Well, no thanks to you. Do you have any idea what I have been going through?"

"Actually, yes. But you have to trust me. And I need to know that I can trust you. I can only end this swiftly and in the safest way possible if you help me."

I took a deep breath, threw a rock into the pond, and stood up. My face grew even more serious as I watched the circles in the water grow larger and larger, like the trouble I felt myself getting into, aside from the fact that I had to worry about attorney-client privileges. "What is it exactly that you are looking for me to do, Charlie?"

CHAPTER THIRTEEN

I T WAS quarter to one in the morning when I strolled back to the house. I had offered to take our conversation into the house, but Charlie said it would be best that we stayed right where we were. Naturally, I rechecked all the doors and windows to ensure that they were locked. They were. My heart was racing, as was my mind. All I could picture was Charlie's soft brown eyes looking down at me with such concern as he detailed every last piece of the Financial Investments puzzle. Strange, I thought: I hadn't dated anyone since Frank, my last winner in law school. Perhaps I had realized a girlish crush on Charlie simply because he was around my age and in the neighborhood. Everyone else in Deering was either of retirement age, a repeat customer of the criminal session, or a client I had represented sometime in the past. *No*, I thought, *there was nothing wrong with him. We definitely had a connection.*

I began to wonder: if things worked out with Charlie, how would he treat me in the future? As we grew more comfortable, I quickly learned that Frank was not a big fan of my mother's wardrobe, much of which I had been wearing, and of course, that affected my self-esteem. What also affected my self-esteem were the anger issues. Would Charlie ever grow angry with me? Would he be physical? Would he yell? What would he do?

At the end of my relationship with Frank, we had been dating long enough to argue freely, and I stuck up for myself pretty well. However, I only stuck up for myself for a short period of time, as Frank had a hot temper. If he was angry, he would slam the nearest door, punch the nearest wall, or throw whatever object was within reach. My mother was always a calm person, and I took her approach. The approach seemed to work well. Eventually Frank would hate my silence or my tear-soaked eyes. Eventually he would apologize. I, however, lived in the dream that he was a nice person and his temper was not so bad. He had faced difficult times as a child, some of which lingered into adulthood. I was determined, of course, to help him overcome his obstacles; and if we had wound up together, I would have made sure that our life would have been much different: a life that we both treasured and a life where he received the credit that he deserved but felt that he never got.

Like Frank, Charlie was extremely romantic, giving me cards on holidays or roses if I accomplished something at court. Still, we had yet to experience an argument. Charlie also criticized people easily, but could not take criticism from others. Then again, I had encountered many men who took that approach to life. At least Charlie didn't seem to have any violent tendencies like the guys in the made-for-TV movies. He just was a guy with a temper, and so far, I had yet to meet anyone without a temper. I had a temper myself.

What I occasionally wondered was whether Charlie also had a so-called sentimental side that not everyone saw. Frank had kept every card any girl had ever given him since high school. He also kept in his wallet a vast array of pictures of every girl. I thought that any other guy would have long since thrown those away. I had many friends who saved things, but most of those friends were girls, not guys. Originally, I saw nothing wrong with it. It was part of Frank's past. After all, I had pictures from proms. Perhaps if I had realized sooner that even I, being a girl, didn't keep pictures of all my "prom dates" at my fingertips, I would have saved myself a lot of grief.

I decided that given my past, I would have no choice but to be on guard with Charlie. My heart had been broken before, and it was the only heart I had. Hopefully, it wouldn't be too long before I decided whether I could ever trust him again.

Other than Charlie, the few men I met in Vermont whom I would even considered dateworthy complained too much for my patience. I just couldn't be in that type of a relationship. Not after Frank, and not after my chosen career, where I basically was paid to listen to and handle others' problems. I wanted a partner with whom I could sit and listen to his stories, no matter how happy or sad, without making mental notes about how each little fact affected him legally. Charlie seemed to be in that position, and that was a good start. He could make me forget the law. I also supposed that human nature was playing a factor as well: few girls could resist a hero, and Charlie's line of work was incredibly intriguing.

I changed into my pajamas and went to bed. Convinced that sleep was just about an impossibility, I thought of my mother telling me that as long as my eyes were closed, my body would appreciate the rest. Suddenly my thought turned to Ken. *How* was I to face him, knowing that I had seen his son? For a moment, I thought that I could avoid him. Then I remembered my latest version of Murphy's law—he had my cat.

I wasn't surprised when I awoke to find my digital clock reading twelve noon. For a moment, I wondered if the events were just a dream. Reality hit when I realized Miranda was not curled up in her usual spot at the bottom left corner of my bed. It was a good thing that I had no morning court appearances—I would have slept through them all.

I stayed in bed for a few minutes, planning my outfit for the day. I didn't need to get up and rummage through a drawer. I knew what was there. Eventually I decided to go with khaki pants and a lavender blouse. After I gathered my things, I took a nice long bath. Closing my eyes, all I could see was Charlie. Over and over, I relived the events of the evening.

Talking with Charlie gave me a great sense of relief. All he wanted me to do was give him copies of the Financial Investments files and take a statement. Simple enough. I already forwarded Allan an itemized bill for services rendered. One more letter severing contact, and I would be all set. But shouldn't I ask for a subpoena? I still had an attorney-client relationship. I would have to play everything according to the books while at the same time respecting the agency.

The office would have to wait. After all, I was the boss. Instead of the usual coffee and bagel on the fly, I'd make myself french toast with powdered sugar, coffee, juice, and some bacon.

After brunch, I made my way to work. I would pick up Miranda after dinner. Ken would enjoy the company, and Miranda would enjoy a new place to explore.

As I climbed the familiar stairs to my office, I suddenly smelled the scent of cologne: the same strange cologne I had smelled earlier. My pace slowed as I approached the door to my office.

My eyes darted back and forth, but my brows remained crinkled. The only visible sign of any trace of fear was my heavy breath, which I carefully filtered through my nose as best as I could.

Fishing for my keys through the black hole otherwise known as my purse seemed to take forever. I acted frustrated, only to mask my nervousness. I suppose deep down, I was frustrated with myself for being so nervous. Seconds later, my keys appeared. I opened the door and stepped inside, glancing around the room, which seemed untouched. Certain that I was alone, I closed and locked the door.

I stopped and stared at my conference table. Scattered on top were piles of Financial Investments paperwork, which I quickly began to gather together. Oh, how I wished Charlie was there so that I could rid myself of the paperwork, take the foolish statement, and get on with my life. Still, my situation remained unsettling, and I did begin to rethink giving up the paperwork. Surely the CIA had other ways, even though it may not have been as easy as to go through me.

Photocopying the last ten pages, I began to question my trust in Charlie. After all, I had only known him for so many months. Sure, his father was a good person, but every family had hidden secrets.

At that point, I decided that my participation in Charlie's "project" would not end with photocopying and a statement. Why did Charlie have to pressure me? Worse, what if *he* was in fact involved in illegal activity? What if Allan Richards was right about Brent? What had I gotten myself into, and how would I get out?

My thoughts turned to Judge Haley. He could help. But then again, I wouldn't want to risk him having to recuse himself from any potential cases in his court or, worse, dragging him in as a witness.

Judge Haley was a fine judge. I had never heard of him rendering an unfair decision. I wished that there were more judges like him.

It always bothered me that the general public expected every judge to be perfect. *Perfect* is such a subjective term. At the very least, judges should keep in mind that they serve as role models, mentors, teachers, and friends, both inside the courtroom and out. A common problem facing many judges was that they become caught up in the "this is *my* courtroom" motif. A courtroom is a place of respect (ideally more respect than intimidation), and respect is a two-way street. True, some criminal defendants benefit from some intimidation; but when it comes to courtroom communications with counsel, unless an attorney is acting with utter disrespect and is completely out of line, there is no room in our system for Napoleonic judges.

If fate decided that I someday would be honored with the robe, I would vow to act as a teacher, mentor, and friend. Judge Haley always welcomed members of the bar into his chambers no matter what time of day. He constructively criticized each lawyer at the conclusion of trial without embarrassment and made his courtroom a learning experience for the juries, most of whom entered the courtroom with the negative notion that their call to service was somehow a personal punishment. I would laugh at my criminal clients who used to complain about jury duty and then wind up having to make a decision to elect a jury trial if the trial judge was threatening to his case. Each defendant was challenged to imagine what would happen to them if there were no such thing as an impartial jury. It was disheartening that the only ones as of late who ever spoke highly of our jury system were the elderly with nothing better to do and the naturalized citizens who appreciated the system so much more than people born in this country.

Packing up my photocopies, I placed them in a box and carried them to the storage closet in the basement of the building. Before Charlie was to get hold of anything, I was determined to find my own answers. The last thing I wanted to do was to put Financial Investments into the wrong hands if Charlie was somehow not legit. And if I was to be directed to hand over the documents while Financial Investments was still considered a client, I would do so only after I had covered all my bases, and in accordance with what was required of me by law.

I began to reminisce about my days at Trenstaw Law. So many times the professors had said that if there was anything that law school would do for you, it was to teach you how to research. Trenstaw was right. It was time for me to play private detective for a while.

I went to my desk, pulled out my Rolodex, and dialed Allan Richard's number. "Financial Investments, may I help you?"

CHAPTER FOURTEEN

F ORTUNATELY, ALLAN and I were still on good terms. The last time I had seen him was at dinner, and that had been some time ago. Lunch was scheduled for the following Wednesday. Even though this had now become a personal priority, I had to attend to my other files, which had been neglected for quite some time.

The next few days passed without incident. On Friday morning, I found myself in the clerk's office of the courthouse, filing some paperwork, when Tyler walked into the room.

"Hey, Counselor!" Tyler exclaimed. "What are you up to?"

"Tyler!" I exclaimed with a big grin on my face. "I'm just filing some discovery motions here. How are you doing, sir?"

"Fine, just fine. Listen, are you busy?"

"Not really," I replied while the clerk handed me back a copy of a docket sheet. "What can I do for you?"

"Well, our fine court is currently blessed with the presence of a couple of new customers downstairs in the lockup. Actually, four need a lawyer, so I thought you'd like to pick up the extra work." I glanced down at my gold-and-silver watch—a present for my law school graduation from my brother. "Sure, I'll go downstairs and talk to them. Can you tell the judge to hold them over for a second call of the list?"

"Sure. It's Judge MacIntyre this morning."

"Okay, Tyler. Thanks again."

I really wasn't terribly interested knowing the judge of the day, although others just had to know as they passed through the metal detectors at the front door at eight-thirty each morning. I understood that some judges were more favorable to the prosecution and others to the defense. Some judges paid more attention to the rules of evidence, and others to their own opinions. Some judges at times even seemed to have no clue as to what was going on in the proceeding. Who cares? was my general opinion. Like I could "change" the judge of the day if I wished. Well, I supposed in some instances, with legal maneuvering, I could—but seriously, folks? My new clients were only being arraigned, so I didn't have to give things much thought at that point. The only reason I showed any interest in the judge of the day was so that I would show up in the right courtroom.

After I finished my business with the clerk's office, I made my way down to what was lovingly referred to by courthouse personnel as the dungeon. I always hated going down there. Even though the courthouse had security cameras and someone at every turn, I always felt as though I was down there alone. The echoing of my heels on the cold cement floor made me feel like I was in Alcatraz, not a little old courthouse in a little old town.

As I approached the line of cells, I could hear the prisoners milling about. One was talking to himself. Another was yelling at some court officer, and the other two were telling each other war stories. As I turned the corner, they grew quiet. "Shh . . . someone's coming. I think it's the lawyer," one of them whispered.

My first stop was at the court officer's desk. Lawrence Jones was his name. "Hi, Larry," I said. Larry, who was about five feet ten inches tall and 230 pounds of pure muscle, was working on a crossword puzzle from the daily newspaper.

"Hey, Counselor!" said Larry, putting down his pencil. "Are you the lucky winner today?"

"Yeah, I just met up with Tyler upstairs. What do we got?" The prisoners began whispering amongst themselves. "Hey, it's a *girl*," said one.

"She looks too young to be a lawyer," said another.

"Can you get me outta here?" yelled the third.

"Shut up!" barked Larry. Larry always made me feel so safe.

"I didn't do it," said the fourth. Larry rolled his eyes at me, and I smirked.

"Hey! Quiet! All of you!" shouted Larry. "Else you *all* will have lost your right to a speedy trial!" Larry turned back to face me. "Now the one that just commented on your femininity is George Newburry. He's thirty years old. Got busted last night for possession of Class B." George was about five feet six inches, had black hair and beard and hazel eyes. He wore faded blue jeans, a lumberman's shirt and black boots. *Great*, I thought. Possession of drugs. With any luck, he was selling and not taking: that way I could have at least some chance of a somewhat intelligent conversation with the man.

"The second," said Larry, "who thinks you're too young, is a fellow by the name of Michael Decotin. He's fifty-two years old and was busted on a third drunken-driving offense. Also has a couple of out-of-state warrants." I glanced at cell number 2. Mr. Decotin had silver-gray hair, was around six feet two inches, and about 210 pounds. Big boy. Clean-cut and slippery-looking. Well, maybe part of that was the alcohol he was sweating out.

"The third lucky winner is Shawn LaRue. Shawn was busted for attempted burglary at an old cottage on the eastern edge of town. Unbeknownst to Shawn, the cottage wasn't a vacation cottage, and the Pumpkins were not thrilled. Shawn will be taking care of a few similar charges in New Hampshire as well. Shawn is twenty." I looked at Shawn, who had blond hair and green eyes. He was about five feet eight inches and 140 pounds soaking wet. Shawn appeared apologetic. I rolled my eyes. "Pumpkins?" I inquired, looking at Larry.

"Yeah, Will and Esther Pumpkin," he replied.

"How cute is that?" I whispered, picturing a little elderly couple who had been married for over sixty years, boasting twenty-two grandchildren.

"Uh, Becky," Larry continued, "don't take anything from the name. The name's the only cute thing about that couple. The DA would most likely want to put in a motion to change their name to Mr. and Mrs. Jack O. Lantern if the case goes to trial and they have to testify."

"Oh," I replied, glancing over the police report. "So they don't look much like victims, huh?" Good.

"Anyway, Shawn's dad, Syd, is here to bail him out after the hearing," said Larry. "Syd's a good guy. We go back some."

"Okay," I replied. "Good to know."

"And finally, we have door number 4. Another attempted burglary. Nathanial Pickering. Nat is the one wearing a pair of faded Levi's and white tee shirt. Nat is twenty-two years old and lives with his widowed mother on High Ridge Road. This is Nat's second offense."

Larry was clearly enjoying the ethically challenged group of the day. I supposed that spending every hour of the day with the element in the dungeon required at least a sense of humor. Actually they weren't all that bad. When I first became a lawyer, it seemed as though all my clients were guilty—at least guilty of something. As time went on, I took the approach that every defendant required at least one person in the world to stand next to him and speak on his behalf, even if there weren't many positive things to say.

I interviewed everyone on the question of bail, gave each a business card, and prepared them for the hearings. Unfortunately, they weren't exactly dressed for the occasion, and the shackles didn't help. As always, I hoped that my new clients would adhere to my words and not grimace at the presiding judge or say anything in court unless I gave the okay. Most did as I asked, but once in a while, a client would make the occasional outburst and stick his tongue out at the judge, whom he was always destined to see at some point again. Not smart.

The arraignments were rather quick, and each entered a plea of not guilty. George Newburry was released on personal recognizance so that he didn't have to post bail. Michael Decotin was kept basically to sober up. Shawn LaRue and Nathanial Pickering were held, but their bail was reduced significantly. Syd bailed Shawn out within the hour. I gathered up my belongings and returned to the office.

Back at the office, I grabbed four manila folders and separated the paperwork. Shawn and Nathanial intrigued me, I supposed because of the mysterious footprints in the snow that I had found earlier around my cabin. *Then again*, I thought, *maybe Charlie was checking up on me*. At that point in my life, it would take a lot to surprise me.

On Wednesday morning, I prepared for my lunch meeting with Allan. I was much calmer than when I left at dinner the last time. Perhaps even more confident.

Lunch went well. I scrutinized Allan's every word, every action. While we were drinking our coffee, I asked him if he wanted me to return his paperwork. He laughed and declined. "Thanks, Becky, but I gave you photocopies. Besides, I know you are a good lawyer. Attorneys always keep photocopies for themselves, right?" I laughed. *Actually, I have two sets,* I thought. *In fact, I had one set shipped into a storage unit in New Hampshire just in case.* "Look, Becky. I feel that we may have gotten off on the wrong foot. I sought your assistance to investigate an employee of mine. Your sole purpose was to see if my company had grounds to fire him. You found none. Now we both know I get bad vibes from this guy, but that has nothing to do with you. You did a fine job."

"I'm glad you think so, Allan."

"Look, I still want to be able to refer cases to you as they arise. And if anything comes up with Brent, I'll run it by you. Is that okay? If nothing comes of Brent, we are in Vermont. Slips and falls seem inevitable in the winter. I can kick those to you too, right?"

"I would be delighted to review anything that you send me," I replied. There, that was good enough: noncommittal but accepting. Good lawyer talk. Part of me loved the idea of more business and not what Charlie's opinion would have been.

Allan and I had lunch a few more times in the next few weeks and coffee quite often: definitely more than I had originally planned. Charlie hadn't contacted me in a while, so I figured I was in the clear.

I enjoyed getting to know the employees at Financial Investments, particularly since most were people who lived in the community. One woman I saw each time I entered the building was a housekeeper named Marie LaValle. Marie was from Canada, and French was her native language.

Easter finally arrived, along with my family, for five very relaxing days. Although Charlie lingered in and out of my mind, I still invited his father to dinner. Ken rather enjoyed himself. My time with him had decreased significantly since my meeting with Charlie, as I didn't dare drag him into the situation. My family seemed to like Ken. I think they found it comforting to know that there was someone older in the community who was watching out for their little girl.

It was nice to take time off of work and play daughter with my family again. We enjoyed strolling through the Vermont woods behind the cabin each morning after breakfast and shopping at the area's unique country stores in the afternoons. My dad actually began to take to living in my little log cabin. He even said that perhaps if he and my mother retired, they would consider purchasing a similar home for a summer place.

My mother, as usual, expressed her hatred with me living so far away. In a moment of weakness, I made the deadly mistake of telling her that I handled criminal defense cases as part of my practice. She worried about me far too much. Good thing I kept the Financial Investments issue to myself. Otherwise, she'd drag my sorry-ass self back to Boston sooner than Judge Haley could strike his gavel.

The guy scenario was a completely different issue. I attempted to dodge the topic as best as I could, but my mother had already heard about Charlie from the beginning. Being my mother, she sensed that I still had feelings for him, although our status had obviously changed.

The Easter holidays ended, and my family returned to Beantown. A part of me wished I could be a little girl again: I wouldn't have to work or think about bills; if I was hungry, I would go to the refrigerator, which was never low on milk or junk food. My meals, always prepared by my mother, would be well balanced, and I would eagerly eat every last bite, whether or not I was in the mood. If I heard a bump in the middle of the night, my dad would be the one to investigate. Just hearing him get out of bed was comforting enough to make me return to dreamland. On Saturdays in the fall, I would sleep late under layers and layers of blankets, surrounded by pillows. As a little girl, it seemed that it would take forever before I graduated eighth grade. My only problems were deciding how to fill my spare time. Looking back, I thought that no matter how bored my friends and I thought we were, dinnertime and bedtime always came far too soon.

It seemed ironic how my childhood prepped me for lawyering. Summer days of secrets with my best friend: secrets still hidden or long forgotten: secrets that, unbeknownst to me, were practice for the famous attorney-client privilege / confidential-communications" doctrines.

Despite my desire to turn back time, I looked forward to my life ahead of me. Law school was over, and so were two state bar exams. It was time for me to face my fears and play by the rules. Success was within reach, and losing was not an option.

CHAPTER FIFTEEN

*E*THICS. IT was so hard for me to believe that a six-letter word would make such a difference in my profession. The Confidential Communications doctrine was churning all the juices in my stomach. First of all, there was Allan and me. Everything that I discussed with him as attorney and client was privileged. I had a duty to keep quiet. It was generally up to Allan to spill the beans if he desired.

Then there was Charlie and me. Charlie was a CIA agent, and I—well, we both, were expected to uphold the Constitution of the United States. I was an attorney. I took an oath. Was it ethical to tell all I had even to the government during an investigation? People over the years had been arrested and held in jail for withholding information. I had read and studied those cases. But then again, didn't those actions result in the rest of us being able to enjoy certain rights?

If I did give up my information, I would certainly lose the trust of Allan and who knows how many other clients if Allan spread rumors that I couldn't keep a secret. What if it was the local district attorney's office investigating my civil client for a criminal offense? Would I tell? No. I couldn't. I still had a duty to keep quiet. The college debate team seemed so easy compared to the resolution fate had thrown at me.

Technically, I had not given Charlie a real answer as to whether or not I would cooperate and he had no documents. I was just "at the ready." I was not a risk taker by any means, but my desperate desire for my own answers was tempting me to perform my own investigation. So against my better judgment, I made the quick decision to somehow *invest*. Within the hour, I pulled together some of my savings money and called Allan from the courthouse.

"Hello, Rebecca!" said Allan. Ah . . . the melodious sounds of a salesman.

"Hi, Allan, hi. Listen—"

Allan quickly interrupted me, apparently enjoying the sound of his own voice. "How have you been, Becky? What's new with you? It is so good to hear from you!"

"Listen, Allan. I was looking to speak with you about your company." Allan paused. "Oh, really?"

"Yes, really. I'm interested in investing."

"You're kidding, right?" Allan queried, his voice now serious.

"No, Allan. I had some extra money I was saving for a rainy-day fund, and, well, working with you a bit made me have a change of heart. I thought that perhaps putting extra money into some type of mutual fund or IRA or something might be better for someone in my position."

The salesman was back. "Well, Becky, Becky, Becky. I am quite shocked. But certainly, we would be honored to have another customer such as yourself."

"Thanks, Allan." I hoped that my awkward breathing didn't give away my anxiety. "Would it be okay for me to come by today and speak with someone?"

"Sure. I'll set you up with Mike Petoli. You can come in whenever you like."

"Thank you, Allan. I'll be down soon." I hung up the phone and breathed a sigh of relief. I then grabbed my keys and drove to Financial Investments.

My meeting with Mr. Petoli was fairly uneventful. He reviewed the various types of risks I could take and how my investment would be affected. He explained what would happen if I wanted to withdraw funds, transfer funds, or borrow against them. After about one hour, I told Mr. Petoli that I wished to invest my funds in several different accounts but still "needed sometime to think before signing on with the company." Mr. Petoli gave me a number of brochures to look over and said to take all the time I needed. After our meeting, I eagerly returned to my office with a series of new documents to review.

My next move was to place a call to the *Wall Street Journal* and order a subscription. I was determined to learn about investing real fast.

It was then that the telephone rang. "Hello?" I said.

"Hello, Becky. It's me, Mrs. Fitchmier." *Identification is not necessary, Mrs. Fitchmier,* I thought before answering her. "Hello, Mrs. Fitchmier. What can I do for you?" I pictured Mrs. Fitchmier sitting on the same old-cushioned rocking chair at the front window of her house, her gray hair pulled up in a bun, with whisps of white sticking out in the rays of the sunshine. Her glasses would sit on the tip of her nose, and a crocheted shawl would be draped across her lap. She would be talking to me on the only telephone in her home: an old-fashioned black rotary-dial phone. The not-so-pleasing aroma of mothballs would drift outside, down the cement steps in the front of her home.

"Well, I wanted to know if you would draw up a will for my friend Wanda."

"Sure, I could do that. Just have her give me a call."

"While you are at it, I actually have a few more friends who are interested in wills from the senior citizen center. Do you think I could give your name out to them?"

"Oh, Mrs. Fitchmier, I'm flattered. I would be more than happy to speak with your friends. Thank you." I slowly began to feel guilty that I dreaded Mrs. Fitchmier's calls.

"You're welcome, deary. Oh, some of them might be a little more complex than mine. A couple of them have a lot of money. In fact, those kind people at that new company that does investing for you . . . the one that had to do with you in the paper a while ago?"

"Yes?" I strained my ears as much as I could. Deep down I knew what was coming.

"They come down and visit us once a week to give us free financial advice. A lot of my friends have been going through those stocks and bonds. So it might be a little complicated." I smiled. "I think I can handle that, Mrs. Fitchmier." I was beginning to think that I could handle anything.

As soon as I hung up with Mrs. Fitchmier, I grabbed every file pertaining to wills and codicils, which I had drawn since my arrival in Deering. I then went home and began to reread and take vigorous notes on each. Next, I reviewed the paperwork pertaining to stocks and bonds from Financial Investments. Fortunately for me, my new clientele had all the information I was searching for. I would not have to invest my own funds at that time with Mr. Petoli. Looking back, my move was wise. I would probably have been risking my ticket. Plus, the Charlie element was still at large. Phew. *Close call, Becky.*

For the next two months, I slept little. I spoke with my mother once and saw Ken only when I needed bread or milk. Even Miranda began to give me a well-deserved attitude. I was so wrapped up in my work that I gave her virtually no attention.

At that point, I would wake up in the morning, make some breakfast, and read the paper. I documented the investment section for each and every file I had, as well as my personal investments, which were few and unrelated to Allan's company. My time with the daily paper increased each day as I began to draw wills for the senior citizens referred by Mrs. Fitchmier. It was amazing the number of townspeople that were involved with the company. Of course, those at the senior home loved my visits and would talk for hours while I learned the company from their perspective, inside and out.

My afternoons were dedicated to other files, unless I had an appearance in court. If that was the case, my evenings were dedicated to my newfound hobby.

Four months went by, and there was no change. The investment reports related to Financial Investments were completely accurate. Feeling that I had exhausted my seemingly brilliant idea, I decided to rent a movie and spend the evening with the television and my cat.

About ten forty, there was a knock at the door. I was half asleep at the time, curled up in my pajamas and fluffy robe. For a minute, I thought I was dreaming, until I heard the knock again. It was Charlie. "Oh, hi, Charlie," I said, nervously. Charlie pushed his way through the door. "I thought I told you to stay away from Financial Investments."

"What is that supposed to mean?" I said.

Charlie was extremely upset. "Look, don't play so coy with me. I saw you go see Mike Petoli, and I see you are getting mail from them—the consistency of mail, which indicates that you are doing business with them."

"Listen, Charlie. What I choose to do is no business of yours. And for your information, I am not doing business with them. Have your boss pull my bank accounts if you like. Now is there something you need? It is almost eleven at night."

"You know what I am looking for, Becky. I am looking for the Financial Investments information." My heart began pounding, and I was in desperate need of a drink of water. "Where is it, Becky?"

Charlie began to pace around the room, eyes darting everywhere. Miranda raced upstairs. "Oh, I apologize," I said. "It has been really busy at the office, you know?" Charlie stopped and looked deep into my eyes. Not the kind of deep stare that a high school girl dreams about. It was a cold stare, and a mean stare. I began to rethink my decision to live in the woods. "Look, Charlie," I said, adjusting my robe partly because I was cold, but more so because I was nervous. "While you are here, I have a problem. Now I have no doubt that you work for the FBI or CIA or whatever you said. My problem is the work-product rule. Now in order for me to keep my ticket, I need you to get a warrant or subpoena or whatever your authorities wish so that I do not violate any ethical rules, understand?"

Charlie's eyes softened. "I'm sorry, Rebecca," he said, approaching me and taking the liberty to retie my robe. He then sat down. "It's the job, you know? There have been so many times when I have been forced to go retrieve files and pieces of evidence and in order to do so, you become almost robotic, you know?" *Funny*, I thought. Most of my criminal clients did complain about the way they were treated when the police arrived to execute warrants—and to think that I usually brushed off their complaints.

Miranda soon returned, and Charlie picked her up, stroking her gently. "Whenever you get around to it, okay? But the sooner the better. I'll tell my guys that you need to go through the hoops. It is perfectly understandable, and I don't think there will be a problem. Consider the request on hold." Charlie smiled. When Charlie smiled like that, I wanted to melt. He was just doing his job. Oh, I wish he just worked with his dad. I would have a lot less meals alone. "Penny for your thoughts?" he asked.

"I was thinking that it was a shame you had such a low-profile job."

Charlie stepped closer. "You're right. I take my position for granted. I can find you anytime I want. Do you have any wine?"

I blinked. "Uh, yeah. Just a second, okay? Have a seat." Strolling into the dining room, I pulled a bottle from the wine rack. Of course, I had the "Kittery, Maine, special" wineglasses since I lived alone. Perhaps one day I'd be married and have beautiful stemware. Oh well. For now, Kittery outlet glasses would have to do.

Perusing the kitchen cabinets, I found some crackers in the cabinet and carved some of Ken's Monterey Jack cheese. Charlie was looking through my CD collection when I returned. "A little music, perhaps?" he said.

"Sure," I replied. "Whatever you like." Charlie picked out a CD, and soon the voice of Harry Connick Jr. filled the room.

"Nice choice," I said, raising an eyebrow, painfully aware that my pajamas were mismatched.

"You have good taste in music," Charlie replied. "Care to dance?"

Suddenly I forgot about work, about my family, about Financial Investments, about my pajamas, and about my fluffy robe. The room completely disappeared. Charlie and I danced and danced until the wee hours of the morning. We shared childhood war stories and sipped wine. We shared dreams of vacationing in Europe: taking trains through wine country in France and gondola rides through Venice. My Charlie was back: the Charlie with whom deep down inside I was falling in love.

CHAPTER SIXTEEN

I AWOKE the next morning in Charlie's arms. Tiny specks of dust particles danced in the sun's morning rays, in a world where time stood still. Birds chirped outside the window, and Miranda perched herself on the sill to watch. I began to think what an incredible evening had just taken place and decided to make Charlie an old-fashioned breakfast. After all, he had been on the road for quite some time. Surely he would appreciate some french toast with powdered sugar on top.

Playfully feeling that I had earned the right, I tossed on Charlie's shirt and sauntered downstairs. As I pulled out the milk and the eggs from the refrigerator, I heard the soft pitter-patter of kitty feet, and Miranda soon appeared in the kitchen. I was amazed at how relaxed and happy I had felt after so many years of tension stemming from law school, bar exams, and work. It was Saturday: I could stay up late and sleep in the next day. Better yet, the man of my dreams was upstairs in my bed. It was then that the cynical lawyer came out in me. Life was too good. When would it end?

"Morning." I almost dropped the bowl of eggs I had been mixing. "Do you always whip eggs with a fork?"

"You scared me to death!" I said, smiling and snuggling in for a hug. "Hey, it was within reach and accomplishes the same task. Besides, I don't have a dishwasher, and I really hate washing those whisks." Charlie smirked. "Anyway, good morning. I hope you like french toast."

"I love french toast. Tell you what, I'll make the coffee." *Wow*, I thought. *All this and a cook too. What would Mom say? Yeah, what would Mom say. I might have just made a huge mistake.*

"Sleep well?" said Charlie. His eyes were like magnets, and I couldn't help but melt. I just hoped that I didn't show it. "I slept okay," I replied, smirking slightly, eyebrows raised.

After breakfast, Charlie broke the news I sadly expected. "Listen, I have to go away for a couple of days." My heart sank. "I should be back by Thursday. How does dinner on Friday sound?" Nice save, lover boy. "Friday's good."

Charlie left just after lunch. I spent the day poking around the cabin, doing the laundry, dusting, and vacuuming. I then went for a walk through the woods and made myself a cup of chicken noodle soup. Later, as I was washing the dishes, I found myself gazing out the kitchen window into the woods. The task of washing dishes may not have been the ideal thing to do, but I did admit that I enjoyed the feeling of the warm water running through my fingertips. Suddenly I realized that I was washing one of the wineglasses from the night before. Was the wineglass in my hand the one Charlie had used? Suddenly I didn't want to wash it. I wanted to hold on to every savory moment as long as I could. Naturally, I changed my mind envisioning a green wineglass but felt better when I turned on the CD from the evening before, with songs that suddenly carried so much more meaning.

On Sunday morning, I decided to go to church. I arrived ten minutes into the ceremony and sat in the back pew on the right. Although I didn't go every week, I thoroughly enjoyed Mass in Vermont. The church was a simple small white church with an impressive large and meticulously landscaped front lawn in the nicer seasons. When I first saw the church, I wondered why they didn't replace it with a bigger one, given the amount of property they owned. But as time went on, I grew to appreciate the history of the town and its little church. Admittedly, I would rather stand in the back of a packed church for Mass than kneel in the middle of a seemingly empty one.

The church offered only three masses per weekend: 4:30 PM on Saturdays and 9:00 AM and 11:30 AM on Sundays. Deering didn't need more than three masses; the population of the town was so small. As Father Joseph began his sermon, I recognized Marie LaValle in the second row. It appeared as though she was by herself. At Communion, I glanced over at her and smiled. She smiled back. *Bonjour, Marie.*

After Mass, I waited for Marie at the edge of the lawn. Father Joseph stood just outside the doors, shaking parishioners' hands and wishing each a good week. Marie caught my eye as soon as she exited the door. Smiling, she shook Father Joseph's hand and walked over to me. "Bonjour, Mademoiselle Lawson," she said.

"Bonjour, Marie. "Comment allez-vous?" I replied. It seemed strange to see Marie dressed in a fancy dress and hat, clutching a purse instead of dragging cleaning supplies.

"I am *fine*, thank you," she said.

"Marie, are you taking English lessons?" I asked. "I thought you could only *parlais le Francais.*" Marie laughed. "No one knows, Mademoiselle. I do not feel comfortable to speak English, uh, *soulement.*"

"Your secret's safe with me, Marie. If you need any help, let me know, okay? I know a little French. Perhaps we could teach each other. Bien?" Marie seemed pleased. "Thank you, Mademoiselle. I would love that. I have no family in this country. I come from northern Québec. I began working for Financial Investments on the day that it opened here. I saw an advertisement in the paper for, how do you say . . . housekeeper? The pay was good, and I thought it would be a chance for me to move to America and travel a bit. Oh, I loved living in Canada. But I always wanted to live in America. My husband died when I was thirty-one. I have one daughter and one son, both married. They don't need me much anymore. Life is too short, Mademoiselle. I want to learn English on my own, without my family and friends watching me. They all learned L'Anglais in school, and I am afraid they would judge me. This way, I can take my time."

"Good for you, Marie," I said. "So you've known Allan for a few years, n'est-ce pas?"

"Ah oui. I have watched the company grow bigger and bigger. They don't talk to me much or invite me to their Christmas parties, but they pay well and are nice to me. Plus, they set me up with accounts, which I am leaving to my children and any children they and their spouses may have. In fact, they just take the money from my paychecks so I don't have to think about it each week."

"What a nice idea. Do you understand the stock market?" I stated.

"Oh no, Mademoiselle. That is why I am so happy to have Financial Investments. They are doing so well in this area because many people do not watch the stock market. They know what it is, but they don't pay attention. They want to cash in the money when it is their time. That is all I want to do. Financial Investments is very helpful." I could feel the wheels in my mind turning. "What do you mean by *helpful*, Marie?"

"Oh, Mademoiselle, I have seen this many times. The first question that they ask a customer is whether or not they understand the stock market and investing and such. Most say no. They then send them to one of the representatives in the company for a meeting in the board room. The meeting takes as long as the customer needs to understand and pick an investment type. The investment is then set up, and a file is created for the customer."

"Do all the representatives meet with the customers?" I asked.

"No. Just a certain number of them. Usually the new people. The big executives generally do not meet with a customer, unless they are businessmen who fully understand the way the market works."

"Do you know anything about their background?" I asked.

"Oh sure. All have degrees. Allan would not hire anyone as a representative unless they had a degree. They hang them in the walls of their offices. So many degrees."

"Hmm," I replied, still listening attentively. "What about internships?"

Marie rolled her eyes. "You mean have someone work for Allan for free? You would think that he would love to have an employee work for free. But no. He wants complete dedication. He feels that the students would tell their professors all inside information about the company, and he wouldn't get ahead in the area. He calls it something that sounds like the board game Monopoly."

"Monopolize, you mean?" I asked.

"Oui, mon-o-po-lize," she replied.

"Well, that is interesting," I stated. "Say, Marie, have you had breakfast this morning?" Marie's eyes opened wide. "Well, no. Not yet. I was planning on going home and getting something to eat."

"Tell you what, breakfast is on me. Where would you like to go?"

"Well, there is a nice place not far from here that serves a good country breakfast. It's in Littlefield."

I smiled. "I'll drive."

Marie and I had a nice breakfast. We talked a lot. She explained to me in the most basic of terms how the company was structured and her perception of how Allan really worked.

"So how does Allan choose the high executives?" I asked.

"Sometimes the new executives are promoted as they gain experience and Allan's trust. Only the hardest-working executives will move up the chain, and spaces open only as needed. There are very few at the top," said Marie.

"What do you know about Brent Thompson?" I asked.

"Oh, Mr. Thompson. He has put in the most hours any new executive has ever worked. He has degree after degree and a long résumé. He speaks so many languages. I am surprised that he doesn't have his own company, let alone work at the top floor with Allan. He has never seemed to win Allan's respect. He is like the others," she continued. "But perhaps he works too much?"

I was thrilled with all the extra information. Marie was a very observant individual. But then again, I sensed that she was very lonely. I noted that loneliness served as a fine catalyst for inspiring detailed observations from people: observations from a multitude of interesting angles. "Marie," I asked, "what happens if someone were to decide to cash in their investment?"

"Oh, Allan would be very upset. As for the first level, a whole new level of executives, the next level higher than the original executives . . . you know . . . the next floor above . . . they would meet with the customer and convince them to either stay with the company or try a different type of investment. If they still questioned the investment, even higher executives would be called into the board room. Few customers actually walked out of the company having cashed in their investments. Normally, they were those who got the account through a will after the investor had died, leaving it to them."

After breakfast, I hurried home to my computer and drafted a five-page memorandum of my conversation with Marie. Although I had made a new friend that morning, I didn't want to lose such interesting information. I printed three copies and e-mailed the memorandum to an e-mail address at Trenstaw University Law School. I then deleted the memorandum from my computer and placed a call to the law library. "Law library. How may I help you?" answered a female voice. *Quite perky*, I thought, *for a Sunday morning*. Surely the voice did not belong to a student. "Yes," I said. "Would Joshua Tameron be working today?"

"Sure, just a sec," said the voice. *Oh great, bad music.*

"Hello, Joshua Tameron," said Joshua.

"Hey, Josh! It's Rebecca." I replied.

"Becky? Becky Lawson? How goes it, girl?" he said. "I heard you moved to the boondocks."

"I'm great, and it's Deering, Vermont. By the way, no one refers to Deering as the boondocks when ski country hits. Suddenly it's 'Hey, Rebecca! Let's get together sometime! Maybe do some skiing?' Such turkey vultures. Listen, I got a favor to ask."

"Anything for you, honey. As long as you invite me up to Deering . . . during the *spring* . . . and I'll buy you dinner."

I laughed. "You got a date." I wondered if that comment would be considered cheating on Charlie.

"I e-mailed something to you about ten minutes ago. Can you take it off your screen, seal it up in a manila envelope, and hold on to it for me at your apartment? It's completely confidential. I'll pick it up later."

"Ooh, big case huh? What is it—the secret document?"

"No, it's work product, and I just need you to hold on to it, okay?"

"Sure, Becky. You know you can trust me. Now tell me, what has been going on in your life?"

I knew that I could trust Joshua. He was one of the few people in law school, and in life for that matter, that I could trust. I spent hours in the library during school and studying for the bar exam. He was extremely helpful. He would fetch me coffee when I didn't think I needed it and water when I thought I needed the coffee. He'd send me home when I thought I was on a roll with studying but truly too tired to concentrate and walked me to the train when he decided it was too dark. Joshua had light brown hair and soft blue eyes. He was tall and fairly muscular as he spent a lot of time in the gym. Joshua also held a law degree and passed the Massachusetts Bar Exam two years before me. He loved working in the library, however, and did very little lawyering. He was a true researcher and wrote a number of articles and books on various topics of law. He also made guest appearances in local schools, discussing law and society. Joshua was a good guy.

I thought back to the time when I first encountered Joshua. It was my first year of law school, and I had arrived for my first class. Although I was excited to be in law school, I was extremely intimidated by the intelligence of those around me and wondered whether I would last. The professor asked a question that may as well have been in a foreign language as far as I was concerned, but Joshua raised his hand. Joshua sounded very intelligent, well spoken, and seemed to know exactly what he was talking about. In fact, the professor was impressed as well, as they conversed for about five minutes. I, on the other hand, sunk even farther in my chair as I took copious notes that I knew nothing about. The voice I was hearing was the voice of a man who would surely send me to the bottom of the class. The voice I was hearing was the voice of a man who would graduate number one while I would not graduate at all. Was I not ready for law school? Eventually I turned around ever so slowly to see his face.

Joshua was seated two seats behind me. Directly behind me was a girl named Nicole, whom I had not yet met, but thankfully, she looked confused as well.

"And your name, sir?" inquired the professor.

"Joshua Tameron," he said, staring instead at me with his big blue eyes, smiling slightly. He had two big dimples, one on each cheek, and thick brown hair speckled with a few grays. Surely he knew he was beyond law school material. I turned back immediately in complete frustration. Great. He's good-looking too. Naturally, I was depressed for the remainder of the class. Thankfully, however, my brand-new book was highlighted as I had learned to "read with a pen." I may not have answered and I may have looked confused, but it was clear that I had read the words on the printed page.

The next day, while walking through the windy streets of Boston, I decided to start over, determined not to let one class assignment get me down. In fact, I would make it a point to forget about Joshua (as if I could) and enjoy the rest of my classes.

I took the elevator (albeit reluctantly) to the twelfth floor. I hated elevators. When I was young, my father would jokingly jump up and down in elevators, telling me what to do if the cable were to snap. The last thing I needed to do was go up an elevator in a high-rise building, but I was not about to walk with all my books. I could have rented a locker, but I had classes in several buildings and would rather spend my time in the various lounges in the library finishing my homework early. Everything I needed for the day would always be within reach.

As I took off my coat and prepared to sit down, Nicole introduced herself. She seemed like a nice person, and we had a lot in common. Fortunately, she had already met a few other people and started to introduce me to them. I was happy to have some new friends. They joked about class the day before, which made me feel a little better. I clearly was not the only one dazed and confused.

As the professor walked into the room, Nicole tapped me on the shoulder again. "I have someone else for you to meet," she said. "This is Joshua. He'll be joining us for lunch today."

Apparently, I had not perfected my poker face, as Joshua's familiar grin, with the big Irish dimples, turned into a look of confusion. Or at least I noticed it in his eyes. "Nice to meet you," he said, extending his hand.

"Nice to meet you too," I replied, accepting his hand. Thank goodness, the teacher was beginning the class. I couldn't bear talking to *him* any longer. He was the competition. *Then again,* I thought, *Perhaps I should attempt to befriend him. Maybe we would all be in a study group, and I would eventually understand where he is coming from. Maybe then he wouldn't seem so threatening.*

In between classes, the lounge became the hub of the universe. There were ten people in my new circle of friends, most from various honors programs, at least in college. Together we passed hours chatting, snacking, doing homework, or people watching.

As time went on, Joshua and I were the ones who spent the most time in the lounge. Although he would graduate before me, we had similar schedules and arrived at just about the same time each day. I grew to like him as a friend, and in fact, we had the most in common of the entire group. My relationship with Joshua was completely platonic, however, as I was of course in love with and dating Frank. Joshua, soon after, began dating another girl, and we, as couples, double-dated often. Joshua eventually came to know everything about me, both good and bad, and was there during the best of times and the worst of times.

Talking to Joshua from Vermont, I couldn't help but think about autumn in Boston. The first crisp day requiring a sweater on the way to school was always so refreshing, especially after a hot summer. I supposed that part of wanting the cold weather for school was simply so that I did not feel as though I was being robbed of my summer. Joshua loved the fall as well. I could still see him strolling into the lounge with his red duffel bag and his off-white Irish knit sweater.

Ironically, because of Joshua, I began to love school. Well, at least hanging out in the lounge. I enjoyed my friends' company very much, and Joshua and I would share stories for hours, as we were both magnets for the strangest of situations.

Autumn in New England did not just bring the cool, crisp air; the apple picking; the hay rides; or the foliage. The season also brought hurricanes: some hurricanes which were, in fact, movie-inspiring and hurricanes which, for us, would prove to be good story-telling material.

Trying to snap out of my daze, I began to think about *our* hurricane. "Hey, Joshua, do you remember our hurricane?"

"Wow, do I ever! In fact, that's the first thing I thought about when you called," he said, chuckling. "Good times, good times—"

As with any other day, I had arrived at school just before 7:00 AM. That morning, I was grossly disappointed as the deli close to the school was closed. I knew that a bad storm was to hit that day, but Trenstaw hadn't been closed when I had left home. So I continued to walk to the lounge with my backpack, now desperately craving a cup of tea and a grilled bagel with cream cheese.

The neighborhood and the school were deserted. Still, the doors were not locked, so in I went and sat on one of the usual couches in the corner. It shouldn't have been long before I had some company from our group of friends to commiserate with, and hopefully by then, I would be enjoying that nice cup of tea.

Within about twenty minutes or so, Joshua arrived. My smile turned to a frown as I noted he was not carrying his usual cup of black coffee and one sugar. He reciprocated with a sarcastic grin as he sauntered over to take his place next to me on the couch, obviously reading my mind.

At least I had company, and the company was Joshua. Joshua always made me laugh, and our Irish Catholic backgrounds were so strikingly familiar that our bond grew stronger every day. In fact, I could count on one hand the number of days he was absent from the lounge: it just wasn't the same when he wasn't with us to give us his dry-witted but intelligent thirty cents on our topic of conversation. Joshua and I were convinced that we were the only two at school not to rent the $10-per-year locker because we both determined the lockers were inconveniently placed and did not enjoy forgetting books. We did pledge early on as others mocked us that we would join a physical therapy rehabilitation program together after graduation due to the unnecessary lengthening of our right arms and herniated vertebrae.

Many times we shared the lounge alone, but the conversations were never strange: well, at least never uncomfortable. I was still in a serious dating relationship, as was he. I had no interest in Joshua romantically, nor did I ever feel any pressure from him. We were simply best friends and shared everything with each other: from issues with school, work, or home; crazy stories; or people watching. Despite our platonic relationship, we would get heat occasionally from our significant others (mine short-lived, of course). We just ignored the allegations. It wasn't worth the argument. We were more like family who got along and who had known each other for years.

That particular stormy morning brought conversations surrounding how wonderful it was to attend a commuter school that rarely canceled a class. We just could not understand how someone could look out a window, and if they observed no snow or perhaps only light wind, classes would not be canceled despite the Doppler radar. I mean, really: it was a *commuter* school. As a result, students simply had to make their own judgments to either skip classes or risk a potentially dangerous commute.

Joshua and I were commuting from different areas but arrived at pretty much the same time every day. The day of the hurricane, we were the only ones who had arrived, unaware of the extent of the forecast. By 11:30 AM, after attempting to attend the second class, which was missing only a cowboy whistle and some tumbleweed, we both decided to call the game.

Leaving the lounge, we found, to our great surprise, a piece of paper taped to the glass window of one of the outside doors. Joshua opened the door for me, and we both peeked around the corner to read the sign. All classes had been canceled due to the inclement weather. Apparently, even school security had stayed home; otherwise, they would have seen us walking around the empty school or hanging out in the empty lounge. Great. By then it was pouring sideways, and dangerously windy.

Joshua walked me back to the train, as he often had. In fact, he was my personal escort everywhere in town, job interviews included. I was about five feet three inches and about 110 pounds, with a strong tendency to blow into the street with the slightest gust of wind. That being said, Joshua was always there to grab the back of my backpack as my other friends often had, or let me grab onto the back of his as I walked behind him into the wind. Joshua was a fabulous bodyguard. After all, the bigger the town, the stranger the people.

So onto the back of Joshua's bag I clung, and we made our mutual ways home to grab our mutual cups of tea and coffee with mutual ridiculing families. Naturally, we both skipped classes on the next nice day just on principle alone.

Joshua and I reminisced for a few more minutes on the telephone, as I didn't want to tie him up at work. He promised to keep in touch and come up to Vermont for a visit. I promised both him and myself to give him a call if I returned to Massachusetts to visit my family in the coming months.

CHAPTER SEVENTEEN

S INCE I didn't expect to hear from Charlie for the next few days, I decided to catch up on my criminal files. My law practice was happily picking up again. I received a few more calls for private representation on criminal cases, a few wills, and also a few personal injury cases. As long as I outlived my clients, managed not to get myself arrested, and didn't get hit by a car, I would survive just fine.

Of all my *morally challenged* clients, Shawn LaRue had many more personal issues than the others and called the office quite a bit. He, unlike most of the criminal defendants I had dealt with, seemed to be truly apologetic and thankful for my help. He just needed a bit of guidance and structure in his life. People like him encouraged me to continue taking the occasional criminal case.

Despite the quick turnaround, criminal matters taught me the most about the law and about human nature. It didn't matter whether the case was drunk driving or assault and battery. The criminal mind, or lack thereof, was nothing less than intriguing to me. The defendants were not bad people: they just tended to think in different, more creative ways and—well, of course, were lacking a bit of judgment.

It was my nature to get into the mind of my clients: I needed to find out exactly what made each and every one of them tick. As a result, my creativity increased to the benefit of future clients. I was always convinced that in order to adequately represent a client, I needed to keep an open mind and think creatively. Otherwise, my arguments would not be compelling, and both the criminal and civil clients' cases would be detrimentally affected. Of course, as much as I always try to get into the minds of my clients, I always make sure I get out as soon as I can.

As time went on, all my criminal matters drew to a close. George Newburry was as guilty as sin, but he insisted on his day in court. He knew he was going away at some point but wanted to delay the case as much as he could. It was his hope that the six witnesses who were to testify against him would have moved, died, or forgotten the incident by the day of trial. We gave George his day in court. He was found guilty on every charge, but I did manage to have one reduced from an original possession of a controlled substance in a school zone to simple possession.

Michael Decotin pled guilty but also received a reduced sentence, and Nathanial Pickering pled guilty with a reduced sentence.

Shawn LaRue was actually found not guilty after a two-and-one-half-hour trial. He did continue to call the office on occasion to say hello and fill me in on how his life was turning around for the better. I didn't mind.

Talking to Shawn one afternoon, he told me that his father, Syd LaRue, used to work for Cipcorp—a company that managed Buns on the Run, one of the biggest fast-food chains in the nation. Syd worked in the investment department for five years. Ironically, despite the fact that Shawn had this curiosity and jealousy of other people's belongings, his family was quite wealthy. Mr. LaRue had invested in Buns on the Run when it first started and was quite versed in the investment arena. As I sat at home obsessing about Financial Investments, I decided to pay Mr. LaRue a visit. He originally wasn't too pleased to see his son get off so easily in court, but since Shawn was making the attempt to stay on the right path, we began to get along famously. I dialed his number and set up an appointment for the following week.

It was amazing how I often viewed the families of criminal defendants. Their being labeled defendants made me think, although I wished I didn't, that they were somehow beneath me. I just could not imagine putting myself in a situation where I would intentionally break the law.

Although I had worked on enough criminal matters to feel like I was almost an expert, I sadly found myself often ignoring one of the most basic principles of the system: innocent before proven guilty. The second principle I found myself often violating was the notion that one cannot be found guilty by mere association. It seemed that I looked upon anyone sporting the same last name of any of my criminal session clients with a scrupulous eye. It was so hard to remember that my clients, whether guilty or innocent, had family members that could be normal, rich, educated, and moral. It would take some time and a conscious effort while practicing criminal defense before I could properly rewire my thinking. I supposed that Charlie probably thought the same way (perhaps even more strongly), given his line of work, although he wasn't exactly in the position to rewire himself anytime in the near future.

CHAPTER EIGHTEEN

ALTHOUGH I did not see Charlie as regularly as I had preferred, he did make it a point to visit me when he was "home." Ken was rarely blessed with a visit, as Charlie felt that his father would only monopolize his time and disrupt our time together. I felt sad for Ken, but my love-struck, selfish self was not about to interfere with Charlie's decision.

I did understand Charlie's other reason: he was protecting his father as well as his job. For the first time in a long time, I felt protected as well. I felt comfortable with our relationship. And even though our time together was now more sporadic, we continued to see each other. Charlie could leave at any time for who knew how long, but he always did make it up to me. Sometimes we took long walks through the woods, spending hours just holding each other at my little pond. Other times, we rented movies and ate popcorn until the wee hours of the morning.

My favorite times were those when we hiked the Vermont mountains and picnicked along riverbanks. It was surreal to scale a somewhat-unfamiliar mountain and then gaze down into the sweeping valleys below. At home I felt as though I should always be working on a file. It was as though Deering couldn't get along without me. Taking breaks was nothing more than a waste of valuable time that I could have been spending working on a case. But being so high up in such a majestic and quiet place, breathing in the fresh mountain air, and surrounded by nature in its purest form, I realized that I was only as important as I had decided I was. I could take a day off, or perhaps two. Heck, perhaps the world needed the occasional break from me. Naaw.

One of my biggest problems was that I was always insulted to witness attorneys who "slid by" their entire professional careers. They made it a habit to make as few appearances in court as possible, pleading out all their criminal clients and settling every civil case for figures much lower than the case was actually worth. Such behavior certainly was not the "zealous advocacy" that I learned in law school, and most of my professional colleagues turned a blind eye. To my delight, others who also frowned on such lazy behavior helped the bar associations to enforce what became known as "The Snitch Rule," requiring the reporting of ethical violations to the Board. I vowed never to let that happen to me. Additionally, I would prevent others from the temptation if I could, so long as I was a lawyer. I would be a lawyer until nature decided against it and until someone else, someone with new hopes and new dreams, moved into my little log cabin. I also vowed to try to work on sparing myself from the guilt of my own occasional vacations.

When Charlie was away, I continued to study investing and tediously followed in the papers the investments of each of my senior-home clients. The first time I ever looked at stocks in the papers was in the sixth grade, as part of a homework assignment. At the time, the assignment was so far beyond me. I stubbornly declared to my parents that I would never become involved with such boring material again. Surprise, surprise: the "boring material" was actually quite useful.

My visit with Syd was invaluable. Syd was kind enough to invite his cousin, a financial advisor who had been working in the field as a broker for twenty-five years. Timothy Taristo was his name. Mr. Taristo, who was sporting what appeared to be a very expensive suit, was considered an expert. He had been invited to hundreds of seminars on subjects relating to investing and was often a guest speaker at the request of various Ivy League universities. Even though I was invited to call Mr. Taristo by his first name, his presence, which was almost palatial, simply wouldn't allow me.

The three of us spent the entire afternoon discussing in layman's terms the various ins and outs of the stock market. Class A stock, Class B stock, options, futures, long trades, short trades, mutual funds: so many foreign terms were finally becoming familiar.

It was amazing to consider the number of different hands through which money traveled, and how many people affected the market on a daily basis—unsuspecting consumers shopping at Christmas, Labor Day, the Fourth of July, or any other given day of the year affected the market. Others affected the market as well, whether it was by hoarding oil, responding to devastating virus outbreaks in livestock, or filing claims against restaurants for finding foreign objects in their food. Depending on the world scene, stocks were bought and sold in a matter of minutes.

Everyone was affected, whether they understood the intricacies of the stock market or not. People affected the market just as much as the market affected the people. Jobs depended on the market, federal benefits depended on the market, and international relations depended on the market. I found it most interesting how even the average person with limited market experience became upset when the news reports stated, "The Dow Jones is down . . ."

After my meeting with Syd and Mr. Taristo, I began to spend a great deal of time in Deering's public library. Unfortunately, the library was small (and extremely dusty), and I was limited to a select number of old books and mostly outdated magazines. Still, I learned more about the market and its philosophy, and some of the newer magazines did make me consider investing. That is, until reality hit: I was still a starving attorney.

A field trip to nearby Conifer Community College (home of the Bobcats) was much more valuable, as they offered an endless supply of information from which to choose. Conifer also offered several introductory courses (ironically taught by first-level employees from Financial Investments), which covered the topics I was interested in, so I ventured over to the bookstore, purchased the introductory books (and a stylish CCC sweatshirt for myself . . . hey, cut me some slack—I love cats), and spent a little time in their library researching on the Internet.

It was strange yet comforting how I no longer worried about Financial Investments. Instead, I was becoming obsessed with the market. Charlie found my interest humorous and questioned me about it often, particularly since I found it difficult to put the books down the next few times he was home. He was right. I was obsessed.

"Becky?" he called out one evening from the living room. "Why don't you come out here and watch a movie with me? We could use some quality cuddle time. I could start a nice fire with those cool rainbow logs that burn in different colors."

I just wasn't feeling the pot of gold at the end of the rainbow logs. "I'll be out in a bit. I have all my stuff spread everywhere on the kitchen table. It's just too hard to set up camp and read comfortably in there. I have to read this stuff while I am in the mood to, or else I'll never read it at all. I have a general practice. I need to know about all the laws affecting our town. I already have some banks considering bringing me on for refinancing, and some of this is related." Charlie sauntered into the kitchen and grabbed himself a beer from the refrigerator, his eyes traveling all over the papers and notes that I had written.

"So what's the scoop with Financial Investments?" he said in a tone that was more aggressive than I preferred.

Suddenly I shuddered. Something about the way Charlie said the name of Allan's company brought back the great fear that I had felt when I received the messages on my answering machines. "What about it?" I replied, tapping my fingers nervously on the table.

"Did you think I'd forget? You were going to give me information about them, remember?"

Now feeling threatened, I glanced around the room. For the first time, I realized that Charlie had basically moved into my home. His clothes were upstairs in the bedroom, his toothbrush and razors were in the bathroom, and his briefcase was in the hallway. He could strangle me to death with his belt in the bedroom, sever one of my arteries in the bathroom, or strike me in the temple in the hallway with the corner of his briefcase. That was, of course, if he chose to use one of his things. "I thought we were over that," I replied.

Charlie shook his head and pursed his lips. "No, we really haven't visited the subject in a while. What's going on?"

"I don't represent them, Charlie. And as an attorney, I can't give you anything right now, which I may have collected from them. I am bound by an attorney-client privilege—a confidential communication if you will. Now there are two ways that I am comfortable with that would allow me to give you anything you need without breaking my client's privilege." *Please don't bring up my almost having invested in the company*, I prayed. My senior citizen clients should be safe. Would he have checked them out too? Were they safe? Maybe he had no idea about them unless there was some form of audit or something, and he didn't indicate that he was at that stage yet. I wished I knew what he had.

Charlie attempted to egg me on. "And those would be . . . ?"

"Well, I could ask permission from them to hand the files over to you."

Charlie showed a nasty look in my direction as he began to pace back and forth, toying with the label on his beer bottle. "And that would be real prudent."

"Or you could get a court order."

Charlie ran his hands through his hair in frustration and slammed the bottle on the counter. "You know we are still investigating this, Rebecca. I am not ready to do that yet. I will say that you are interfering with a *federal investigation*." Charlie, quite proud of his last statement (or, in my opinion, threat), stopped and stared, eagerly waiting for my response.

"Well then, you can get some documents from the proper authorities, which would grant me some form of immunity, or permission. I am a new attorney, and I may be wrong. But right now, I have a former client to protect, and I won't talk."

Charlie stormed around the kitchen table in a huff, picking up papers, quickly glancing at them, and tossing them down. "What are you really doing?" he said furiously, his eyes wild.

I was beginning to feel extremely unsafe, but I kept my cool. "I am an attorney, Charlie. I have work to do," I replied. "Now step back and leave my things alone!" I said, straightening up the mess that he had created.

Then with no warning whatsoever, Charlie charged my side of the table and placed his hands forcefully around my neck. As he squeezed, I started to fall to the left, slamming my head on the edge of the kitchen counter. Fortunately, I was able to free myself and took a few steps back, shocked.

"Keep your hands off me!" I shouted, protectively holding my neck and lightly touching the now-throbbing side of my head for wetness. "How *dare* you touch me like that!" I stormed out of the room, fast and furious. My eyes filled up as I fought back tears. I could not believe what had just happened. *I handled it fine*, I thought. But why that type of stress, and why had it escalated to that level?

Charlie followed me to the front of the house. "Oh God. I'm sorry, honey. Please . . . please forgive me. Are you okay? I was wrong."

Unbeknownst to me, a giant red mark had formed on my neck. At the time, I was more focused on the wet lump that had taken up residence on the side of my head. Fortunately, it was under my hair: concealable. In my foolishly love-struck heart, I had already forgiven him: he was stressed. I took an ibuprofen earlier when I felt a headache coming on; it thinned my blood. Plus, I bruised easily to begin with. That part was not his fault. But then again, why was it that I was so easily able to picture him hurting me? Surely healthy couples didn't envision such horrific scenes. Did I subconsciously sense a different, more dangerous side to Charlie, or was it all in my head?

I was certain that once the Financial Investments issue had resolved, our stress level would decrease. Still, looking back to the past few visits, Charlie had begun to act as though he was depressed, and he angered easily. I gave him beer when he needed it and left him alone to watch television more often than usual. Then again, I had work to do, so that was fine with me. He had stopped wanting to go out or out to dinner, yet he had the nerve to criticize my cooking. He compared it to five-star restaurants where he dined with people from work.

If my refrigerator ran low on beer, he would be angry that it wasn't restocked, despite the fact that the house was mine, not his. The truth was, I felt uncomfortable buying beer. But to avoid the argument, I would eventually suck it up and purchase some wine for myself at the same time. With the amount of liquor I'd buy, I must have looked like a closet alcoholic.

Charlie had also begun working out in the small garage attached to the cabin, having brought in some of his own equipment. The workouts lasted for hours after dinner. On some occasions, he would punch his bag like a boxer, nonstop for twenty minutes at a time, to the point where the walls cracked in my living room. I began to grow frightened of him but supposed it was part of the training he may have had when he joined the agency.

It was my romantic belief that once things were settled, our relationship would return to normal. I missed Charlie's once incredibly romantic side, where he would every once in a while give me something special like flowers or jewelry. But it was fine. I didn't need material things. As I said before, I always practiced law with an open mind so that I could figure out every argument there was to a case. I kept an open mind in life too. If someone hurt me in some way, there must have been a reason. Charlie must have had a reason. He wasn't the Charlie I fell in love with, but I was determined to find him and bring him back.

Charlie followed me to the front door. "Becky, are you going to say anything? I said I was sorry."

Skirting Miranda aside, I opened the front door. "Get out."

"But what about us?" Charlie said.

"*Get out!*" I was hurting, more from my broken heart than my bruised neck and pulsating, bleeding lump.

Charlie spent about ten minutes gathering his things and left the cabin. "You'll be sorry, Rebecca Lawson! You'll be sorry!" The door slammed behind him.

Charlie sped away in his rental car while I collapsed on my couch and cried, my hands gently caressing my neck. He was right. I was already sorry.

CHAPTER NINETEEN

WEEKS WENT by, and I soon resumed my normal routine. I had not seen or spoken with Charlie since he peeled off down the road after our argument. Still absorbing the situation, other than seeing clients every once in a while or appearing in court, I pretty much kept to myself. I took long walks in the woods and long bubble baths in my old-fashioned tub. Charlie had not only assaulted me physically, but he had also insulted me both personally and professionally. In fact, I came to the conclusion that he was using me in an attempt to gain information, when he certainly could have accessed it by another route. My problem now was that my stubbornness prevented me from wanting to give Charlie anything, but my conscience wanted to honor the federal government's request, as well as my ethical obligations as an attorney. The only person I really saw with any frequency was my new friend Marie.

I met up with Marie in Ken's Country Store one Friday afternoon while picking up some of the ingredients for a scrumptious peach cobbler. Ken had come over to say hello, as I hadn't spoken with him in a while. I supposed that a part of me was avoiding him, most especially after the string of events with his son. I introduced Marie to Ken, and they seemed to get along right away. In fact, Ken not only spoke to Marie in French, but he also tuned his old-fashioned radio to a nice country music channel (that is, after he dusted it off).

Before I left, I invited Marie over for dinner that evening. "I would love to," said Marie, still swooning over Ken. "Can I bring anything?"

"Oh no, Marie. Just yourself. I bought a pot roast, which is really too big for just one person. See you at six?"

Marie laughed. "À six heures." Ken waved good-bye to me from the rear of the store, pulling off meat from the shelves.

"Don't work too hard, Ken," I shouted.

"I wouldn't if the meat industry would pay a little more attention to their work."

"What's up?" I asked, worried about my pot roast.

"Oh, it's just the hamburg and a couple of steaks today. What a waste."

Relieved, I sighed. "People aren't perfect, I suppose. If it's not that, it's something else. Did you hear about the oil spill off the Gulf of Mexico the other day?"

Ken nodded. "Refer to earlier 'waste' comment. But they can afford it, right?"

Marie and I laughed all evening. When it was time for her to leave, she promised to call me the next day to make plans for church on Sunday. We would go to brunch afterward and were thinking about bringing Ken along with us.

The next morning, at about ten thirty, I was still in bed with Miranda at my feet. I swore she sensed my sadness. Even though Charlie had hurt me so badly, I still sensed something missing from my soul with him gone. If I wasn't distracted, I wouldn't spend each day wondering where he was and whether he ever thought about me. Suddenly Miranda leapt from the bed and peeked around the corner in the hallway. I could hear the front door gently closing and footsteps coming up the stairs. Miranda scurried into my office. I froze.

"Hi." It was a forlorn and apologetic-looking Charlie.

"What the hell are you doing here?" I screamed, holding the covers up to my neck. I was furious with myself for not changing the locks.

Charlie raised a hand in the air, the other resting around the small of his back. "Hold it, hold it. Calm down. I'm sorry. I just came to apologize and bring you some breakfast." Before I could say anything, Charlie revealed his hidden hand, placed a single rose at my feet, and held up a bag of coffee rolls. "You have coffee in the house, I hope?"

Sighing, I responded. "I'll meet you downstairs in the kitchen. Let me get dressed." Charlie smiled and went downstairs to make the coffee. I was still a bit nervous, but he seemed sincere. *We'll see where this goes*, I thought.

I took my time getting dressed, determined to make him wait. I would not act desperate or overly excited to see him. Of course, he had conveniently gotten a haircut and shaved for me. His cologne permeated the house. Still, I remained on guard. We would just remain friends from that point forward. As far as I was concerned, the name Financial Investments had best not be uttered by his lips ever again.

"Cream and sugar, just the way you like it," said Charlie. Impressively he had set the table with some odd pieces of china left from the elderly couple who owned the house before me. The children didn't want it, and since I lived alone, I didn't mind a few odd place settings. Who was I going to entertain? My family was the only group who ever came to my cabin for a formal dinner. I certainly didn't have to impress them to secure future visits.

"Thank you, Charlie. This is quite the surprise." I looked at Charlie skeptically, as though I was interviewing a criminal defendant whose court docket numbers totaled more than the number of cases I read in law school.

"Well, I felt bad about the way things were left. Besides, I missed you." I cringed. Was this guy for real? Perhaps he was reading Dr. Gray's *Men Are from Mars, Women Are from Venus*. Charlie was clearly from Uranus.

Charlie continued. "Look, I said some nasty things and shouldn't have let things escalate as they did. I shouldn't have done that. I was sucked into my job. I wasn't thinking clearly. I just have a lot on my mind lately."

"Like?" I said.

"Like how I hate my job because I have to leave here at a moment's notice without you. Like how I have to be careful what I say to anyone so that no one hurts you or threatens you. Like how I cannot have a normal relationship with my own father because I have to protect him too. I lost my mother as it is. And did I ever tell you? He's not my real father." Ahh, at last an admission. "But that's a whole different story for another time. Oh, how I wish I could have had even thirty seconds to tell her that I still loved her no matter what she thought of my line of work."

I supposed he sounded legit. His job was challenging. *Okay, I'm convinced. One more chance, but watch it.* "I'm sorry you feel that way. Look, no more fighting, and no more talk about work. How is that?"

"Deal." Charlie smiled, pulled a vase stuffed with two dozen red roses from under the tablecloth, and placed it in the center of the table, gazing lovingly into my eyes the entire time as though nothing ever happened. *Please let this last,* I thought. Suddenly the phone rang.

"I'll get it," said Charlie as he reached for the phone. "Hello? Who is this? Who? Hold a moment, please." He held out the phone to me with a concerned look on his face. "It's for you." *It's my house,* I thought. *Boy, master of the obvious.*

"Hello? Oh, hi, Marie. Sure, church will be fine. No, I'll pick you up. Is Ken coming too? Great! I'll see you tomorrow then. Bye." I handed Charlie back the receiver.

"Who was that?" Charlie said.

"Oh, that's my friend Marie. She comes from Canada. She's a good friend of mine. Goes to church Sundays. We're taking your dad to church and going out to breakfast after."

"Oh. Isn't she a little old for you?" said Charlie.

"Well, she is actually about ten years younger than your dad, but she is very nice. We have a lot in common, and they seem to be hitting it off."

Charlie strolled over to the hutch and picked up a picture of my mother. "I think you miss your mom."

"Of course I do. But Marie doesn't replace my mom. She is just a friend."

"What does she do for work?"

Uh-oh, I thought. "Well, she is a housekeeper. Maintenance. She is not educated. She actually is quite friendly with your dad. Who knows? Maybe we'll have a wedding to attend in the future."

Charlie brushed off the wedding comment. "Oh. Well, if you're so lonely, why not join some local clubs and meet some ladies your own age?"

Charlie realized too late that he made a gross mistake posing that question. "You don't understand, Charlie. Law school changes you. *Forever.* I am so used to waiting for someone to get to the point during a conversation that I have a terrible time listening to others at all. Not that *I* get to the point. You see, lawyers purposely detail conversations. They have to treat each listener as a jury member: someone who was not a witness to the incident. Lawyers are forever trying to convince others that their position is right, no matter what the position, even though every good attorney knows that there is an argument for everything. What happens then is a soliloquy—like in a Shakespeare play—since who wants to listen to a lawyer babble, right?"

Charlie's expression dulled as I continued to talk. "Some of worst conversations I have are the ones where a random person—realizing I'm a lawyer—has to tell me all his life's problems. I am paid $135 an hour—sometimes more, sometimes less—to solve problems that I listen to *all day*. I have listened to so much that I can no longer talk to someone in person, or on the phone, like most females my age for hours about gossip or dating dilemmas. I need intelligent conversations. I am *off duty* when I am not in the office or in court. At least *I try* to be. When I decided to become a lawyer and took the oath, I agreed to be a lawyer twenty-four hours a day, seven days a week. I can no longer listen to anyone or read anything without analyzing the situation legally. Sometimes I hate myself for that. I cannot explain how tiring it can be. In fact, many times with new people, I don't even mention that I practice law.

"Most of the time, when I listen to problems outside of work, I think: I have seen or read worse. And as much as I hate to say it, I'd rather speak to someone who's educated or who's really lived an interesting life. I'm easily bored if I am speaking with anyone else. I can't spend hours filling my brain with useless info. I'm sorry. It's just me. I'm burnt." A tear began to roll down my cheek. Charlie handed me a tissue.

"Then . . ." Charlie took a deep breath and sat down, his eyebrows arched and his eyes widened as I continued on. "I have the hypocrites who only want free legal advice, not friendship, and use me to second-guess the attorneys they already hired. These hypocrites constantly try and get out of jury duty but are *the first* to demand their day in court. What would they do if we didn't have juries? We have only so many judges, some of whom may tire of the same types of claims these people bring day after day, or tire of seeing the same persons over and over. How could we ensure a fair trial then? The people who worked so hard to form our judicial system must roll in their graves."

"Are you okay?" said Charlie. I laughed. "Yeah, sorry. I know I'm babbling. I'll get off my soapbox now. It's just that sometimes this business gets to me. I do get lonely. The only other ones who understand are other lawyers, and I can't hang around them in my spare time. I don't want to hear their exaggerated war stories all day. I just need intelligent, interesting, optimistic nonlawyer friends." Charlie placed his finger over my lips. "How about me?"

I smiled. "You'll do just fine." And with that, we were okay. Charlie led me upstairs, picked me up, and carried me to my room. Everything was perfect. Either that or I was caught up in the moment and Charlie's romantic charm. We stayed in bed all day, dozing on and off.

Suddenly, just when the crickets were chirping their best, I awoke with a start. Charlie was on top of me, both of his hands forcing the bulk of his weight against my shoulders. His eyes were wide open, but with a blank and determined stare. "What are you doing, Charlie?" I said sternly, but clearly confused.

Charlie placed his finger over my lips, but not romantically as he had earlier. "Shhhhh," he said in an authoritative voice.

I desperately tried to wiggle him off me, terrified as I knew that he wasn't even using any protection. "Charlie! What are you doing?" I said.

"Shhh!" he repeated. "Don't you move!" he said in a voice both authoritative and stern, lips almost completely closed, with three more angry thrusts.

Charlie had the strength of a thousand angry men and was really starting to hurt me. Desperate to put a stop to the incident, I thought back to Trenstaw. "Charlie! I am an officer of the federal court. Get off me now!" Saying nothing, Charlie moved aside and rolled over.

With Charlie's snores resonating the room, tears streamed down my cheeks while I replayed the incident over and over again in my head. Was I just raped? I was just raped. Frozen, I stared out the window. *Oh my God*, I thought. *I was just raped*. I had to remain calm. Some people are plagued with night tremors or sleepwalking. Given what I knew of Charlie's life, maybe he needed counseling. Frozen, I hugged the side of my bed with my legs crossed as far away from him as I could. The only thought comforting to me was he was again scheduled to leave for a few days, guaranteeing me much-needed time alone.

CHAPTER TWENTY

S OMEHOW I eventually was able to drift off to sleep for a few minutes, as the next morning, I awoke to the slamming of my front door—the angry sound echoing throughout the house, which felt as though it was shaking off its foundation. No "I'm sorry." No "Good morning." No kiss good-bye. No explanation. Not that I wanted Charlie to touch me in any way, shape, or form, but something: a word, a look; some explanation would have been nice. Instead I pulled the covers around me as close as I could and continued to tremble. My aching legs would not stay still, my skin crawled, and my heart felt as if it had been ripped into pieces like junk mail.

Glancing at the clock, I suddenly realized what day it was. Marie. Church. I took a long hot shower, sobbing while I scrubbed and scrubbed. As much as I wanted to cancel church, I figured that I could use all the divine intervention I could get and the distraction from being in the company of true friends. I just hoped that overly observant Ken wouldn't make me give up my game face. Marie picked me up, and we met up with a very happy and well-dressed Ken at church. Marie wore her best dress, and Ken wore his powder blue bow tie that he routinely wore to dinner at my house.

After church, we all went out for breakfast. Marie and Ken got along very well. It turned out that Ken spoke French fluently. He had been to Canada many times skiing in his younger years.

Marie was intrigued with Ken's stories, so much that I felt as though our meal should have been a candlelight dinner for two rather than Sunday brunch for three. It was difficult to fight the feeling that I should not have been there at all, and I secretly wished that I had instead driven myself to meet them at church. It wasn't that I was trying to escape their company while blocking out the events of a mere few hours before with Ken's son, but because the powerful connection between him and Marie made things a little awkward. At least being in the company of my rapist's family didn't bother me after all. Although I could not take a deep breath without my lungs trembling, I decided that Charlie's bad genes must have stemmed from his real father.

After what seemed like the eternal breakfast, a clearly love-struck Marie drove me home, only to see Charlie standing on my front porch looking at his watch. Trying to mask my trembling and not entirely certain what to do, I said good-bye to Marie and walked up my front stairs. For a minute, I was thankful that Ken had not been in the car. A shiver electrocuted my spine. "She works for Financial Investments, doesn't she?" said Charlie.

"Yeah, so? I thought we were over that," I replied as my blood began to boil.

"We are. I just told you that I did not want you to have anything to do with that company."

"Look, she is a friend. Nothing more." I fished for my keys and unlocked the front door, although I desperately wanted him to leave and wished Ken had been there after all. It was all too obvious that to Charlie, the events of the prior day had not occurred.

Charlie was persistent. "Has she told you anything?"

I sighed as I took off my coat, questioning whether I should have even opened the door to my house in the first place. Note to self: *always keep your car keys with you, Rebecca.* "If it makes you feel any better, no. She hasn't told me anything, and I don't care. Now end of conversation." Charlie turned toward the front door again. "Are you leaving?" I said.

"Yes. Actually, I had dropped by to say good-bye." My heart sank with emptiness and confusion. Why would he say good-bye now? Because of the way he abruptly left earlier? Where had he gone anyway? Maybe he remembered church and was avoiding his father in case Ken showed up at my house with Marie. I had almost hoped that he would bring up what had happened, especially given the sadness in my eyes, which was evident. "Where are you going this time?" I asked, my mind switching to autopilot.

"Not sure. I'll find out when I get there." He came back and kissed me gently on the forehead. "I'll see you soon. Take care of my dad for me okay?" A tender kiss? Was it his way of avoiding admission but halfway provide me with an apology? Or maybe he was avoiding the whole thing and instead wanted to skip to the part where things were magically all better and back to normal. Did he honestly expect me to wait for him? Oh, I see: *He gets to do what he wants, and I'd always be there to come home to. Stupid son of a bitch.*

Three weeks went by without so much as one word from Charlie, as I now paced my once-secure home, constantly feeling that he was lurking in every shadow. One Saturday morning, I sat in my office reading through some files when I heard a knock at the door. It was Marie, in tears.

"Marie! Oh my god! What's wrong?" I sat her down on the couch.

"Oh, Becky, I have been fired."

"What?"

"They said that I haven't been doing my job. They said I was slow and not up to *par?*" Her head fell onto her hands.

"What has been going on at work?" I said.

"Lots of meetings. Closed doors. Men from out of state coming in. I dropped one of my earrings my great-grandmother gave me in the trash barrel in the conference room the other day. It's so tiny that I had to move a couple of pieces of paper to get it out. The next thing I knew, Allan was standing over and screaming at me. 'Marie! What are you doing?' he says. 'I dropped my earring,' I said. 'Marie! You are to clean and throw away all the trash. You are not to read anything. What is not shredded you put in the incinerator. That is all. Now give me those papers.' I gave him the papers, and he stormed out of the room."

I sat at my desk and began to write feverishly. "Did you see what was on the papers?" I said.

"They were faxes from South America. I don't know from where. I didn't get a chance to read it. Not that I would be interested. I just wanted my earring." Marie began to sob, and I offered her the box of tissues from the corner of my desk.

"Okay, Marie. Calm down. Do you remember anything else? Do they always get faxes from South America?" I asked as I reached for a fresh package of manila folders from a bag of office supplies leaning against the wall.

"No. They get a lot of faxes from New York. I don't know what they pertain to because I don't understand that business stuff."

"Have you shredded documents before for Allan?" I asked. "In other words, was it part of your regular duties at work?"

"Oh yes," Marie replied. "That is, until he realized that I was learning English."

"Do you remember any phrases?" Opening the package of folders, I took one out I and began to place my notes inside.

"Some," she replied, fidgeting with the handle on her purse. "I remember New York City, the main office, always letters to Ron Peters. He is a landlord of a building that the company owns out there."

"Anything else about Ron Peters?" I asked, underlining Mr. Peters's name.

"There were faxes of an account with his name on it as owner."

My adrenaline was pumping. "Can you remember anything else? Anything at all? Take your time, Marie."

"No. Sorry."

"It's okay. Where does Allan keep the shredder machine?"

Marie began to focus. "It's in the basement. Near the incinerator." *Now that makes sense,* I thought. I hadn't recalled ever seeing a shredder machine during my visits to Financial Investments.

"Who will replace you at work? Do you know?" I continued.

"Jacqueline. She has been working with me for three months. She speaks very little English. Mostly French. Nice girl. She is from Québec too."

Later that day, I drafted a memo regarding my conversation with Marie and immediately mailed it to Joshua in Boston.

Two weeks later, I received a call from Syd requesting a meeting with Mr. Taristo. *Strange,* I thought, *but okay.* We agreed to meet at an out-of-the-way coffeehouse a few towns away. "Ms. Lawson!" exclaimed Mr. Taristo, extending his hand. "Pleasure to see you again."

"Pleasure's all mine, Mr. Taristo." Turning to Syd, I extended my hand. "And how are *you* today, sir?"

"Very well, thank you. Please have a seat," he said, extending his hand toward the booth they had already been assigned.

The waitress brought us some coffee, and Mr. Taristo began to talk. "I have colleagues associated with several big companies that are undergoing huge layoffs: the Greenery, who provides leafy foods like spinach and lettuce, as well as some prepackaged salads. Another is Fruition Nutrition, maker of organic juices; the Conifer Meatery; and Energec Oil. The rumor is that high-level executives are taking trips to unknown places and coming back with tans. They think South America and the islands."

"This is interesting information, Mr. Taristo," I said, "but what if they are just taking vacations? What is wrong with going south?"

"Apparently, these trips are taken regularly, Rebecca. And it appears as though a lot of the employees from different companies were 'paired up,' if you will. They would meet at an airport in Florida and fly out together to their destination place. Then they would fly back to Florida when they were through and separate from there. There may be a link. In case you ever decide to invest or if you'd be interested in representing my friends, I wanted to tell you. Then there's that attorney-client thing. We're not involved, of course. But someone needs to check this out. And since my cousin's son here has been in trouble with the law in the past . . ."

Syd rolled his eyes but smiled. "You know, Rebecca, my son has had enough dealings with the criminal courts for me to realize that sometimes it's better for the attorneys to investigate before the authorities muck up, hide, or destroy the information. And when you think about it, how many white-collar criminals expect attorneys to be investigating them? They're looking for people with badges."

"So you didn't want to go to the authorities," I replied, thrilled with the new information and potential new clients. *Wow*, I thought, *so this is how you build a practice. I may be able to pay off my school loans someday after all. Maybe even furnish my house. My folks would be thrilled.* "For the record, Syd, that's not exactly the way it always works. Only a handful of bad investigators spoil the reputations for the rest. Same as attorneys: it only takes one bad attorney to ruin the reputation for the rest of the profession. Anyway, I truly appreciate the information. I'll see what I can do. Keep in touch, okay?"

I rushed home as fast as I could and grabbed my files. All stocks I had been following were issued by major companies: the same companies Mr. Taristo spoke about including the Greenery, Fruition Nutrition, the Conifer Meatery, and Energec Oil. Was there a connection? Could it be a mere coincidence? How could I have gotten involved in such a situation? Little old me in a little old town.

Then it happened.

CHAPTER TWENTY-ONE

E ACH MORNING, my routine included a careful comparison of the stocks to the paperwork given to my senior home clients, paying particular attention to the names Mr. Taristo mentioned, alongside a grilled bagel and a cup of coffee. Despite my battling of the posttraumatic stress that stemmed from the incident with Charlie, I had in fact begun to heal. I was extremely thankful that I was not pregnant, and a trip to the doctors confirmed my continued health.

Six weeks passed, and at last Allan slipped: the stock information in the papers had not matched the information provided to my clients for two days in a row. The following week, a mismatch occurred on three occasions, albeit not in a row. Someone was clearly getting sloppy, and things were getting interesting. Excitedly I placed a call to Mr. Taristo.

After speaking with Mr. Taristo, my next call was to Joshua. Joshua had a friend who worked as a claims adjuster in a large insurance company in Boston. Most insurance companies used private investigators who were able to gain access to bank account information. Joshua's friend was kind enough to do some digging on Financial Investments, Allan Richards, Brent Thompson, and Allison Hatchfield. It could take time to receive the information from the national and international databases, but I would be patient.

To my delight, a package arrived three days later, and I immediately began to pour through the findings. Allan had several bank accounts listed in Vermont and New York. A Louise Richards was listed as having accounts in both Deering and in New York City. The accounts showed balances of $90,000 and $250,000, respectively. Interestingly, no Louise Richards ever lived in Deering, and the only Louise Richards of New York City died in 1969. Naturally, I would have to do more digging to find out whether or not Louise was related to Allan. The addresses on the accounts were both in the vicinity of the offices in Deering and New York City.

Brent was listed as holding a bank account in Deering containing approximately $55,000. Such an amount seemed fairly high. But then again, he did work all the time. What could he possibly spend the extra money on other than trips? Hmm. Maybe he was just one of those people who still "owned the first dime he earned." Still, he could have been involved with something. *Yeah, nice vague observation, Rebecca.* Perhaps he had been taking client funds and depositing them in his own account. I felt I was getting closer, although with Brent, I had nothing more than a bank account.

Allison had an account in Deering as well containing about $30,000. Perhaps Brent was dumping funds into her account. Then again, perhaps he wasn't. How frustrating.

Obviously, the problem I had was proving any hypotheses. I wondered if I should consider approaching Allan. Were my findings on Brent and Allison even billable? I could have matching silverware. No, I did not have enough information yet. I had just gotten started. Besides, the investigation was mine alone. I couldn't possibly reveal to Allan that I had hired a private investigator, let alone the fact that he too had been investigated at my request. Even Mr. Taristo had limited information from me as we only discussed the companies he mentioned. After all, I still had a duty to protect Financial Investments. Why was it that every move I made had to be analyzed like a bar exam question?

Suddenly I was struck with an amazing revelation, and I called Marie. She was just the person I needed to help me. The question was, could she be trusted? I had no other choice but to evaluate her as though she was one of my clients, or a potential witness on a case. Of course, with the way the investigation was going, I supposed that she would in fact be called as a witness somehow at some point by someone. Not in her own case, as she didn't want to pursue any wrongful termination claims with Financial Investments. But little did she know that if things went south for FI, people would call a prior housekeeper in a heartbeat.

People like Marie were funny when they were clients. Either they told me too much or they told me too little, and their friends and family were even more difficult. Like all clients, the expectation was that they would call if anything significant happened with respect to their case. Oftentimes, it turned out that they had been communicating with the other side, answering questions without informing the opposing party that they were being represented by an attorney. Other times, they outright waived their right to counsel during a recorded conversation as they enjoyed what they thought was a perfect opportunity to vent. Other clients were better at following directions and avoided the other side, but they never seemed to rest. Instead, they would needlessly dwell on their case to the point where they became obsessive. They saw nothing wrong with calling the office eight times a day to have the same conversation, hunt their attorney down at the courthouse, and eventually call them at home if they were able to obtain the attorney's private unlisted home number. Those cases, of course, always seemed to be the ones that were not major cases by any stretch of the imagination. Even if they were wise enough to keep quiet, it always seemed that they eventually told some close friend about the case, destined to be called later at trial by the opposition for impeachment purposes.

My plan was to invite Marie to my house that evening for dinner. She was extremely upset the last time we had spoken in my office, and I hoped to get to the bottom of the whole situation in short order. Marie answered the phone on the second ring.

"Hello?" said Marie.

"Hi, Marie. It's Becky. How are you?"

"Oh, Becky! I am fine. Actually, I can't talk right now. I am on my way out."

"Good for you, Marie. You are sounding better. Are you going anywhere fun?" I asked.

"Well, actually, I am going to dinner with Ken."

My heart skipped a beat. "You're kidding," I replied.

"Oh no, Becky," said Marie. "We have been meeting for coffee and talking a lot on the telephone. It turns out that we have a lot in common, and we enjoy spending time with each other. And we have *you* to thank."

I was so happy for Marie. Although I was a little lonely myself, I was pleased that I had earned my angel wings. In fact, I could almost hear the bell ringing in the background.

"I am even working in Ken's store part-time now," continued Marie. She was gloating.

"Well, good for you," I replied. "Listen, I don't want you to be late. Have a great time, okay?"

"Thank you so much, Becky. I'll call you soon."

Even though he made me angry; scared; hurt; confused; and, worst of all, used, a part of me missed Charlie. He hadn't called or written, and I began to understand exactly how his mother must have felt. Where was he at that exact moment? Where had he been? Did he ever think of me? Craving company, I decided to get a cup of coffee at Mr. Becker's coffee shop. Reading the *Wall Street Journal*, I heard a familiar voice call out my name. "Counsel!"

"Good morning, Judge Haley," I answered with a big smile.

"Where on earth have you been? We've missed you around the courthouse." Mr. Becker handed Judge Haley his coffee. "Your usual, Judge," said Mr. Becker.

"Thank you, John," replied the judge, accepting his coffee. "New cups, I see?"

Mr. Becker was thrilled Judge Haley noticed. "Why, yes, as a matter of fact, they are. See the name on the side, written all fancylike. What do you think of the colors? Brown and gold: very coffeelike." Mr. Becker was beaming with pride.

"Looks great, John," replied the judge. Quickly he turned his attention back to me. "So, Becky, may I join you?"

"I'd be honored, Your Honor." We both laughed, and Mr. Becker rolled his eyes as he disappeared into the kitchen.

Judge Haley took a seat. "So what have you been up to?"

"Oh, just tying up old cases and doing some research. I'm trying to get a handle on business litigation."

The judge caressed his chin. "Big case? Are you still representing Financial Investments?"

"Actually, no. I ran into some roadblocks. I gave them an opinion on some things and performed some research, but I haven't done any real work for them in a while. Actually, they prompted me to learn stocks and bonds on my own."

"Now you *do* like a challenge. I never enjoyed following that bologna until I invested myself. Of course, my investments are old. A lot older than Financial Investments."

"How do you like being a judge, Judge Haley?" I asked, comforted that he hadn't invested.

"I love it. You will too someday." He smiled.

"Me?"

"Yeah, you. You have the spark." Judge Haley admired his cup once more and sipped his coffee.

"Well, we'll see. Sometimes I feel like I have enough burdens on my shoulders."

"It is a tough job, but my dear Atlas, you'll love it. I would never think of doing anything else. You are a lot like me, Becky. You spend hours trying to police the system while representing clients at the same time. You get frustrated because you can only take the policing so far. I have the same problem."

"That is the most frustrating part of this job," I said, sighing. "Ethics. I never thought it would be a problem. It's common sense, really." I looked down and reorganized the complimentary packets of sugar in the container on the table.

"Listen. We judges can't do it without the lawyers. Lawyers can't do it without the judges. Everyone plays a part. Clients too. Frivolous claims are filed, and some lawyer is always willing to take them on. Everyone has a right to a lawyer, but some take that privilege much too far—they forget that you need a claim with merit."

"I love talking legal politics with you, Judge. You always make me feel better."

Judge Haley patted me on the shoulder and grabbed his coffee. "Listen, I gotta go. Come down and visit us soon, okay?"

"Okay, Judge. Thank you."

"You're welcome."

Judge Haley was just the breath of fresh air I needed. He always seemed to know when something was bothering me and was always there to give me that extra push to keep going. As the esteemed judge said good-bye to Mr. Becker and walked out the door, I made the conscious decision to see my investigation straight through to the end.

CHAPTER TWENTY-TWO

L ATER THAT day, I ran into Marie at Ken's Country Store. Ken had presented her with a locket containing their picture inside, and she was walking on air. I had to admit that they did come across as a very cute couple. They weren't dating; they were "courting," the old-fashioned way.

Marie told me that she was meeting Jacqueline for coffee later, and she invited me to join them. Naturally, I was all too delighted to do so. "So are you enjoying your new position, Jacqueline?" I asked through Marie, who was translating. While my French had come a long way, I wasn't willing to risk any misunderstandings during this meeting.

"Oh yes, Ms. Lawson. But I do miss working with Marie." Marie smiled sheepishly.

"That is some set of keys that you have there," I noted, looking at a huge set of keys on the table.

"Jacqueline was reissued my keys to just about the entire Financial Investments building," Marie sadly replied.

"Oh, I see," I said. Jacqueline then informed us that a big meeting had been scheduled for the end of the month with the top executives, and Jacqueline was to make herself available as a lot of paper was expected to be shredded. Allan called it an "audit." Hmm.

Almost at the point of salivating, I wracked my brain in a search for a way to access the trash before it was destroyed when no one was around. That is, unless I could prevent the actual shredding. On the way home, I had an ingenious idea and called Allan from my cell phone.

"Hi, Allan. It's Becky."

"Becky! What a nice surprise! How are you doing?"

"Fine. Just fine," I replied. "How have you been? I haven't seen you in a while."

"Great. Business is great. Say, why don't we have lunch tomorrow?"

"I would love to. Meet you at the office at one?" My plan had worked so far. He was always all about doing lunch.

"Sounds great, Becky. I'll see you then."

The next day, I met Allan for lunch. He reiterated that business had been going well, but he wanted to focus on more creative advertising in the community. I was relieved that he didn't mention my having not invested in the company.

"Why don't you get the kids involved?" I suggested, trying to keep the twinkle in my eye as innocent as possible.

"How so?" said Allan. He seemed very intrigued.

"Well, perhaps if you gave a speech to the kids at Deering High School about investing at their level of understanding, and offered a few jobs for a week, you could get the word out to their parents. I'm sure the papers would be all over it." I could tell by the look on Allan's face that he was taking the bait.

"What a *fantastic* idea! I will do just that. Student internships! Brilliant! Thanks, Counsel!" Allan was beaming with delight. "I should sign you up with the company. You're great at marketing."

I laughed. Yeah right. "Actually, Allan, I have no problem helping you out with the project if you like. I participated in a similar contest back when I was in high school. Besides, the bar associations always encourage community service projects. Perhaps I can help round up the students for you when you are ready?"

"Sure, Becky. You are definitely more organized than I am. What do you say? Maybe about ten kids for the project?"

"Sounds great." I was actually thinking five. Ten is even better. "How about we choose which ones by having them submit essays?" I suggested.

"Fantastic!" he replied. "And perhaps my company can kick them $500 each to start them on their own portfolio? I could get a tax write-off, I'm sure. I'll speak with my brother." Great way to kill the mood, Allan. A tax write-off. But whatever. *There's no turning back now, Rebecca. Please, God, let this plan work.*

"I was thinking actually U.S. savings bonds would be best," I replied. "You know, something in their hands. They're just kids after all. Go, USA, right?"

"Oh, right. Sure," said Allan. "I guess that would work too."

By the end of the week, everything was in place. I spoke with the principal at Deering High School, who was ecstatic about the project. From there, we picked some dates, and I marked my calendar. The students would have two weeks from the time Allan gave his speech to submit papers, which I would review. Allan would announce the ten lucky winners. The following week, the internship would take place: *just* in time for the big executive meeting.

Allan's speech was a success, and I picked up the essays personally when they were ready. The winners consisted of six boys and four girls.

Tyler ran each student's record for me at court. All were clean. In fact, their immediate families were clean as well. The group consisted of ten bright students, each fairly active in the community. The only two that I questioned were Patrick Carone and Joseph Farraca.

Patrick and Joseph were considered class clowns. They loved a good scheme and did anything for a laugh. Although they were partners in crime, they had no criminal records and did not frequent detention. Patrick was the oldest of three, and Joseph was the oldest of four. Always itchy for excitement, Patrick consistently staged schemes, which resulted in his brothers getting into trouble at home, while Joseph routinely made public his sisters' diaries. In gym, the pair always cut corners in organized games, but always successfully completed each challenge. Patrick and Joseph were, to my surprise, honors students, and just the two that I needed.

At home, I phoned Marie to schedule an appointment between Marie, Jacqueline, Joseph, Patrick, and myself. We would meet at Jacqueline's house.

I was extremely anxious about the meeting, and with good reason. As an attorney, I learned that trust is a gift, given freely by many but taken seriously by too few. Granted, the human race generally proceeds on faith. However, as an attorney, I thrive on facts and hard evidence: anything to lock in the truth. Faith to me resides in the realm of the unknown: a scary place where risks are taken.

I was never one to gamble, although it is inherent in my profession. Actually, the risks feel worse in criminal trials, where verdicts could go either way. Plus, the client's freedom is at stake. On the civil side, a risk does exist, and it does affect lives. Still, the civil attorney generally doesn't expect to see the client "escorted" to the lockup after trial.

The reason that I always detested the gambling aspect of my profession was I always allowed my life to be affected by whatever case I was working on at the time. I took all my cases to heart, putting myself into the client's shoes so that I would be better able to convince a finder of fact to side with my client's position. As a result, I was forever trapped on an emotional roller coaster. Oh, and did I mention? I always hated amusement parks. They never amused me.

We met at Jacqueline's house the following afternoon after school. Naturally, the students were interested in "the plot." They promised to be cautious and would do whatever they could to help. Their grades were very good, and both Patrick and Joseph were bright when it came to basic stock market principles, so I felt as comfortable as I could possibly be with them. As far as them spilling the proverbial beans, they were so involved in their roles that they became in their minds special undercover agents with only video-game training and lacking the cool props.

All ten students would intern for a week. Each day they would assist executives on a different level in the company, learning generally how the process worked. Patrick and Joseph would take extra careful notes and photocopy documents whenever they could to assist. They were not to create files for fear of getting caught, but instead, they would throw them in the barrel where Jacqueline would retrieve them daily. Marie drew a plan of the building for us and described to Jacqueline the places where Marie routinely hid personal items, not trusting any place of employment after a string of thefts in a place in Canada where she previously worked. Despite the fact that Allan had secured his building with video surveillance, he did cut some corners, and Marie knew just where each one was. Jacqueline could hide as much as she needed and retrieve them after hours.

The next decision I had to make was whether or not to pair Patrick and Joseph together. After some thought, I decided that my dynamic duo would remain a team, and the other students would simply intern. With any luck, Allan would never suspect his vulnerability to a pair of class clowns.

On Monday I would meet with all ten students at the school. Each day I planned to drive them back and forth from Financial Investments. The five teams of two would meet Allan in the first-level conference room to be briefed on their assigned levels. At the end of the week, all would receive $500 savings bonds. Being paid, of course, excited Patrick and Joseph even more. I was pleased knowing that not only would the students feel instant gratification but also, they'd be comfortable that their prizes would be legitimate. Mrs. Whitfield, of Deering Bank, who actually typed the bonds and loved to be the center of attention, would receive credit for her assistance in the project as well. Always thrilled to have her picture in the paper, she was more than eager to help. In fact, I could not recall one week when her famous purple-tinted beehive hairdo did not grace the local papers somewhere.

I made sure that my week was clear of court appearances so that I could be contacted at any time at the office. Marie had strict instructions to keep quiet, even with Ken. I would meet her on the weekend while Ken was at the store, unless things changed otherwise. At the end of each day, I would bring the students back to school and collect the notes from Patrick and Joseph. Jacqueline met me each night in the parking lot of a rest area off one of the interstate highways nearby.

On Monday I was extremely excited. I knew Patrick and Joseph would be too. I just hoped that the other eight students would not detect anything.

At my suggestion, Patrick and Joseph were placed at the introductory level. They would meet with clients and assist in filing initial paperwork. I suggested that Allan allow the pairs to rotate to a different level of the company each day. By suggesting the initial assignments, I was able to ensure that my junior secret agents would move up the proverbial corporate ladder in order. Allan took no particular issue to my suggestion, focusing instead on the community's reaction to Allan's student project. Some of the other students seemed to be more curious about the system as a whole, and I hoped that Patrick and Joseph would have an easier week gathering information. Allan took a liking to Patrick and Joseph as their quick wit apparently reminded Allan of himself when he was their age.

On Tuesday Patrick and Joseph assumed the next level. Again they were assigned more filing and photocopying, but this time, they were exposed to customers attempting to pull their business out of Financial Investments. Tuesday was a more important day for information gathering, and Patrick and Joseph would spend a great deal of time photocopying documents, which looked important to them. Cleverly they would photocopy the pages crooked, copy the pages twice, or copy partial pages. One would announce "Ooops!" and throw the paper in various barrels.

Jacqueline would later collect the trash and bring it into the basement for sorting and setting aside.

The remainder of the week was fairly routine for the boys, although gradually more interesting. They were the only two who began to enjoy daily lunch with Allan and were allowed complete access to meetings with the high-level executives for, if nothing else, comic relief. The two gave Allan the impression that meeting such powerful people was "cool" and the experience of a lifetime. At the same time, none of the students were well versed in the stock market, so Allan had no reason to suspect a thing.

All in all, the project was a success. On Friday the students and their families were invited to a party in the office. The office closed early, and the families arrived at 5:45 PM. I convinced Allan to order any unnecessary employees to go home early as he had invited the press to do a cover story. After all, it would look bad if Allan had his employees working late on a Friday night while a party was in progress. To my disappointment, Brent Thompson was not there. In fact, he was nowhere to be seen all week. Still, I was eager to analyze what Patrick and Joseph had found.

Friday morning's clouds were breathtakingly ominous, guaranteeing a dark and rainy evening. Although frightening at times, the beauty of life in the mountains was that the storms were quick, nasty, and sometimes extremely loud. While the party was continuing upstairs, Jacqueline quickly sorted through the remainder of the collected documents in the dark near the incinerator and hid them as she had done all week per Marie's instructions. I suggested that Allan have the door leading from the first floor to the basement locked so that no wandering family members had access to injuries. It was in his best legal interests. Having just completed his big executive meeting, he secured the door himself without hesitation. What made things even better was that the security cameras inside the building were also turned off during the party. The monitors were in Allan's office, and he thought it best to turn them off for just those few hours in case anyone walked by. Phew. One less worry for me.

Jacqueline again had the keys to almost every door in the building. After turning off the lights in the parking lot, she unlocked the exit door from the basement.

Jacqueline had to work fast, so Marie, at my request, met her outside; and together they pulled out bags and bags of documents in the torrential rain, storing them in the trunk of Marie's car.

I, of course, remained at the party, keeping a close eye on Allan and the windows to the lot. Although I knew that the thunder would mask any noise outside, my heart was in my throat with each flash of lightning that illuminated the area, revealing Marie and Jacqueline scurrying below. How I desperately wanted to join them and send the two on their way. Allan was under the impression that Jacqueline had left hours before. If he ever saw her car . . .

As the evening went on, I informed Allan that my side hobby was photography and offered to take some pictures for him of the children and their families at the party in addition to the pictures that were taken by the press. Allan, of course, loved the idea of memorializing the project (more so the praise) and suggested putting together a plaque for the wall of the main lobby.

Just before the evening was over, at approximately 9:15 PM, Patrick interrupted a conversation between his mother, myself, and Allan. "Mr. Richards, can Joseph and I take a picture with you together in your office?" He glanced over at me still holding the camera and winked.

"Why, Patrick," said Allan, "I would be honored. Follow me, boys!" We followed Allan into his beloved sanctuary, and there I took several pictures with Allan sitting behind his desk; the boys flanked him at either side. I also took some pictures of Allan and the boys in the conference rooms and of the boys with their parents.

By the time the last of the guests had left, Marie and Jacqueline were long gone. I met Marie at the now-all-too-familiar rest area, transferred the documents to my car, and drove home, keeping a careful watch in my rearview mirrors the entire way.

Pulling into the driveway, I began to dread the publicity that I was destined to receive working on the project with Financial Investments. Charlie most certainly would not be pleased. Then again, I did have other entities involved, like the school and the bank. Plus, the project was for a good cause: the children.

What was worse was the sinking feeling that I felt in my stomach, wondering how to safely transfer my highly anticipated reading material into the cabin. I just could not risk anyone watching. I hadn't heard from Charlie in a while but did not want to risk taking any chances. That being said, I did the next best thing: I put together an overnight bag and called Joshua.

That night I drove straight to Boston with everything that I had collected that related to Financial Investments in any way, shape, or form. Joshua's apartment was the only neutral and safe place I could think of, away from Vermont and away from my family. Plus, Joshua was smart and naturally very interested in the situation. Most importantly, I knew that I could trust him. At times it seemed that he was the only other trustworthy person in the world.

CHAPTER TWENTY-THREE

WITHOUT HESITATION, Miranda was appointed to ride as my copilot. Even though she was not exactly thrilled to be held hostage in her little plastic crate for four hours, once we arrived at Joshua's apartment, she immediately seemed to forgive me. Joshua was pleased to see Miranda again, but it did take some getting used to having what he considered to be a sneaky animal creeping about his home.

I was flattered with how thrilled Joshua was to see me. He had been eagerly looking out the apartment window—like a little boy searching the sky for Santa's sleigh—when I arrived and made it down three flights of stairs of his old Beacon Hill brownstone to greet me at my car before I had even fully parked. I guess I was just as eager to see him as my gaze was toward his apartment and not on a parking space as I finally approached his home.

I had barely pulled the keys from the ignition when Joshua yanked me out of the car and threw his arms around me in a big-bear hug. "Joshua!" I said, laughing, clinging to his neck as he spun me around and around. I was admittedly just as thrilled to see him. "Now, Rebecca," he exclaimed, "see what can happen when you drive with your window down? Some crazy old best friend of yours could just yank you right out."

"Okay, Officer Safety, I'll be more careful next time," I replied as he carefully placed me back onto the familiar cobblestone sidewalk.

"Come on," he said, grabbing the handle to Miranda's crate and one of my bags. "Let's get you inside, and then I'll come back out for the rest of your stuff here."

After I caught up on a few hours of much-needed sleep, Joshua insisted on spending the first day traveling around Boston, riding the duck tours, and gazing down at the city from the Hancock Tower. Later that evening, we dined at a little restaurant in the North End and took some time strolling back to his apartment on the hill. It felt good to be back.

Once inside, I stared out the oversized windows at the busy city while Joshua made us some cappuccino. "So, Rebecca Lawson, now that we've had a chance to catch up on everything else, what exactly brings you back here?"

"Business, my dear friend," I replied, sipping my drink, yearning to tell him everything about Charlie. Joshua was always so great at relationships. It would be just like the old days. Yes, I had survived an extremely confusing incident that would forever haunt my soul, but Charlie was so different than Frank. Sure, Charlie had his issues with the way I folded towels or ironed shirts. But everyone has their nuances. Especially under stress.

Joshua carefully placed the tray of drinks on the coffee table as though he was a private English butler and then jumped onto the couch, amazingly landing cross-legged. "Okay, let's talk," he stated. "Smooth!" I exclaimed in delight.

Joshua smiled, showing off his familiar dimples that I hadn't seen in what seemed like forever. "You know, random—dinner was so perfect tonight except for the salad. I wasn't overly impressed until dessert, of course. Man, do those people make a good cheesecake!"

I laughed as I dragged over my bankers box full of files, all color coded. "What salad?" I replied while Joshua grabbed an extremely disorganized array from two trash bags collected from the previous week. "Seriously, Josh," I continued. "It figures with our luck, they had to pull the salads because of a bunch of bad lettuce. I mean, really. Who goes to an Italian restaurant and isn't offered salad? But I will admit, the chocolate cream cheese cannoli were a pretty tasty treat too." Joshua handed me an envelope that contained the documents I had forwarded to him long before my unanticipated arrival. "Well, looks like we are in for a long night," said Joshua. I smiled. He was such an optimistic soul.

Together we plowed through all the organized files, student papers, observations from Patrick and Joseph, items smuggled out by Jacqueline, newspapers, memorandums, and other documentation with information given to me by Mr. Taristo. Finally, we analyzed the pictures from the Financial Investments party, which we had developed in Boston earlier in the day.

"Nice pictures, Beck. So tell me, are these your little spies?"

"Funny, Josh," I replied, pursing my lips. "And yes. Well, in Deering, they are known as *interns*."

"Nice South American motif."

I stopped looking through the pictures and glanced up at Joshua. "What do you mean by that?"

Joshua began running his finger delicately along the pictures. "The paperweights, the pictures, the cigar box . . . all that junk hiding whatever paperwork is on his desk. Why are we looking at these anyway?"

"Mr. Tameron, I am shocked—shocked, I say, that you haven't picked up on anything," I replied with a silly, sarcastic English accent.

"Okay, Miss Casablanca," he responded with a smirk. "Let's have it."

"It's not just the South American stuff. Look at the window behind the group. Look at the picture frames angled behind them on the credenza. See anything?"

"Ahh, clever, Counsel. Documents on his desk. What is that anyway? Bank statements?"

"Yes, sir. And the list of phone numbers on his direct dial. Also, look at Patrick's eyes. I told him to look at the desk."

"Very amusing, Rebecca. Yet another version of the documents on the desk." I had to admit, now that I had distanced myself from Deering, analyzing everything with Joshua was not only productive but a lot of fun.

"It worked perfectly," I said as I began to describe the festivities. "The party was at night, and the weather was horrible, so it was incredibly dark. I had Allan sit behind his desk for a photo for the newspaper. Then I positioned the boys so that there would be spaces behind the window to pick up a reflection, while Allan positioned the picture frames of his family behind him on the credenza so that he'd look more like a *family man*. Finally, Patrick looked down so that I could pick up more reflections on his glasses."

Joshua was impressed. "How presidential, Beck. He's just missing the blue tie and the flag pin."

"Right," I said. "Now pay attention. The other pictures that you see here are pictures with some of the other students near fax machines and other telephones in the conference room. More phone numbers for us to check out. I figure we could dial them in town from a public phone and get some names verified. Then I guess we can figure out what to do with them."

I looked up at Joshua who was proudly displaying a grin from ear to ear. "This is great. Now at the library, we can definitely get a search going for the property in New York and maybe even get some more info on those bank accounts."

"Not necessary, sir. I have information on the property and the bank accounts from Syd LaRue and Mr. Taristo already. I think we need to verify the numbers, though, first thing in the morning. Speaking of which, do you mind if I check my machine?"

"Oh, not at all. There's a phone over there in the kitchen."

"Thanks." I walked into the kitchen and dialed Vermont. A couple of seconds went by, and I heard my voice: "Sorry, I can't answer the phone right now. Please leave a message, and I'll get back to you." After the beep, my stomach dropped. Four messages. All from Charlie. "Where are you, Rebecca? I thought I told you to stay clear from Financial Investments. Your life and your bar ticket is on the line here. I *will* be in touch. You'd better make yourself reachable."

How did he know? The pictures weren't in the newspaper yet. And why was he so angry? I could hear Joshua growing restless in the other room. "Everything okay in there?" he asked. I walked back into the living room and smiled. "Everything is just fine." I was grateful that Joshua wasn't looking directly at me to see my response. I could never keep a poker face with him. Although I did plan to tell him the whole story, it was extremely complicated. He could only ingest one piece at a time. Besides, the Charlie factor would be tricky. I'd have to present it the right way to him or else risk having him go big brother on me.

"I'm glad you came down to visit me, Becky."

"Me too, kid. I've missed Boston."

"So how's the dating scene?" He *had* to ask. I swore sometimes that Joshua was a closet psychic.

"Well, turns out I met somebody," I replied with a smirk. Unfortunately, my smirk hid a horrible picture of Charlie forever implanted in my memory. The unforgiving hands pressing down on my shoulders. The wild, angry eyes. And me, the one who thought that she was the strongest person in the world. Nothing would ever happen to me. I began to understand how frustrating it must have been for some to hear: "You need to get over it. Move on with your life. Forget about what happened." How? How could one forget something like *that*? The statements were nothing more than other ways of saying "I'm sorry about what you went through, but I really don't want to talk about it anymore. Let's forget that anything happened and do something else."

Joshua continued. "*Really?* Do tell me about him!"

"Well, he's really handsome and smart and works for the CIA, as a matter of fact. Pretty exciting stuff, although he can't tell me much about what he's working on, of course."

"Of course. So you're *here*, why?"

I sighed. "Well, some things are just better dealt with in private, you know? I don't know that it's a good idea to involve the CIA in this. I just have to double-check things first. I'll explain as we go along. I promise."

Joshua was obviously disappointed but, thankfully, accepted my answer. Well, to a degree and for the time being. "You know, not for nothing, but a part of you seems sad. And it's not just this foolish case you dragged down here. You forget, Rebecca. I know you." Oh yeah, he definitely suspected something with Charlie.

I pouted but didn't reply. Instead, I yawned—exhausted from the drive, the day's events, and the relaxation I had felt in Joshua's familiar company again. Unfortunately, listening to my messages had summoned my anxiety once more.

"Okay," he said, "listen. You talk when you're ready to talk. In the meantime, you'd better get some sleep. You can fill me in on your man later. Besides, we've had quite the long day, and there's a lot of work cut out for us tomorrow. You can take my bed. I'll sleep out here on the couch." He then gently stroked my hair. "You sure you're okay?"

"I'm fine, Josh. Look. Let me sleep out here," I said. Honestly, I needed to curl up on the couch; the couch was a small area. My back would be hugged, and I fit just right lying down. My head and my feet would be bordered as well. A much safer feeling in my opinion than lying loose and free in an open bed.

Joshua stood up and playfully placed his hands on my shoulders. I tried desperately not to wince, although I was convinced that he noticed that too as he playfully stroked my arms and slowly stepped back. The flashbacks were just too powerful. "I insist. It's a done deal. Listen, I'm still awake from the cappuccino. I'll familiarize myself with these papers, and we'll both get to the bottom of this mess. Miranda will fill me in on any details as needed so I won't have to disturb you." His face then grew serious. "If you get lonely in there, come on out, and we'll chat. Okay?"

"You always were an avid reader, Josh." Fighting back tears, I gave him a hug and kissed him on the cheek. "Thank you."

Joshua turned me around toward his room. "Good night."

"Good night," I whispered.

As I lay in Joshua's bed, I watched the headlights from the vehicles on the streets below dance across the walls and the ceiling of the room. It was comforting to know that I was no longer alone, even if it was temporary, and my fellow Bostonians were awake too. The silence of the Deering woods was all too deafening when one was frightened and alone.

I did begin to feel slightly awkward at the number of sleepovers I had partaken in as an adult in recent months. But picturing Miranda weaving in and out of Joshua's ankles as though she'd been living in the brownstone for years, I couldn't help but smile. Joshua was the first person that I called when I adopted Miranda from the animal shelter. She loved him since day one and clearly remembered him when we arrived from Vermont. Drifting off to sleep, I thought about drawing up a will at some point for myself, making sure to leave Miranda to Joshua if, God forbid, anything ever happened to me.

CHAPTER TWENTY-FOUR

T HE NEXT morning, Joshua and I had breakfast in a cozy little French café we had frequented for years on Newbury Street. I was reluctant on wasting what I considered to be valuable time, but Joshua insisted that we should begin work on a full stomach and let the businessmen become engrossed in their projects before we started crank-calling them. He figured that it would be best to catch them while their minds were elsewhere, and least suspecting our calls. I complied, relieved to feel somewhat normal again, and took my time savoring my french toast sprinkled with powdered sugar and strawberries while sipping on a fresh cup of absolutely perfect coffee.

Joshua was pleased that I was enjoying my breakfast. "Wow, Beck. A penny for your happy thoughts?" he asked.

"You know when you get that perfect cup of coffee?" I replied, holding up my cup as though I was a priest at Sunday Mass.

Joshua smiled. "Yes, there's nothing like that perfect cup," he replied.

"Yep," I continued, savoring my last sip. "I'm ready. Let's rock!" Joshua laughed and gratuitously left enough money for the bill and a tip on the table, and we left the restaurant.

It was a sunny day, and we walked the familiar serpentine paths through the public gardens that we had enjoyed during law school, which seemed like a lifetime before. Walking over the footbridge (a perennial favorite for photographers and artists), we overlooked the swan boats carting people on peaceful twenty-minute rides for a dollar on a pond surrounded by majestic weeping willow trees. Joshua even playfully engaged a bunch of children in a game of leapfrog with the famous Make Way for Ducklings statues, which created quite the stir from the unamused mounted park police. Joshua always did find creative ways to make me feel better about the status of the world.

At around 10:30 AM, we made our way over to Downtown Crossing, another busy yet less-expensive shopping district than Newbury Street. The only problem we faced there was finding public payphones. That being said, we went to Filenes Basement, then Macy's, and finally ventured underground to the Orange Line train station. Despite my lingering concern that my CIA boyfriend of sorts should be able to find me just about anywhere in the world, our quest had actually become quite fun. Joshua, on a dare, even made our final call on a train passenger's cellular phone.

"Hey, Beck, remember when you fell under the fire truck at school?" Joshua asked, still laughing uncontrollably from the successful fulfillment of his dare. "Ahh, a fine day that was," I replied, shaking my head. "I will admit that I have not looked at a fire truck the same way since . . . or come as close to one for that matter."

It was winter in Boston. I was always fascinated with the first snowfall, and given the fact that I was on the top floor of the law school when the snow began, I just couldn't help but glance out. Unfortunately, my professor did not share my idea of beauty.

"Excuse me, miss?" he said with a voice that made him sound as though he was the host of a talk show. I had the sinking and sadly accurate feeling that he was referring to me. "Yes?" I replied, ready for the obviously unavoidable debate. Fantastic. The clock would now slow down, and class would seem like four hours instead of two. "Tell us the holding of the next case, please," he ordered, carefully checking my name on his all-too-anal-retentive seating chart.

Luckily, I too was anal retentive. I was one of the few at graduation that could actually say that I had read every case in law school, including the squib notes at the end of each chapter assigned. Because, however, I was reading everything, it was virtually impossible for me to find the time to prepare my own handwritten formal "brief" on a legal pad as the first-year professors suggested. Instead, I "book-briefed," having "read with pens" for years.

While formulating my answer, I thought about the last time that I had been caught looking out a window. It was during an ethics class with Joshua. Ironically, our teacher was far from ethical. Even though I would occasionally look out the window, I always listened in class and was fully aware of what was going on. The professor had me so angry that particular day, as the little ethical principles he quoted were quoted incorrectly. At my wit's end, I gazed out toward the golden dome of the statehouse. "Would you care to share with us what is so interesting outside?" Professor Unethical queried. My anger somehow surprisingly (as I was always considered to be "the quiet student") turned to bravery. "I'm looking at the State House, sir," I retorted. It was then that the sarcasm took over. "A lot more is going on in that building than there is in this lecture hall."

"Well, then, okay . . . we'll go to the syllabus, since obviously we are in the presence of an unhappy student," he said. The class sighed. "How about you tell us what the concept of Original Sin is, Miss Lawson?" Joshua laughed. "Where would you like me to start?" I replied, grinning, thinking about how proud the Catholic nuns who taught my high school classes would be.

That ethics class had long since ended, and my current debate would not involve the concept of Original Sin. Still, after quickly glancing at my carefully colored book, I answered what originally seemed like a trick question with ease. Obviously embarrassed with my finely crafted answer and eager to turn the tables on me in front of the ninety-nine other students in the class, my unsatisfied professor stormed up to my row. "Book briefing?" he yelled, holding up my book for all to see as though he had found the Holy Grail.

"Yes, Professor, I had a lot of homework and did not have time to brief all my cases last night," I humbly replied. "I apologize. I am prepared for this class, however, and I assure you that it will not happen again . . . in this class," I continued, albeit reluctantly. His was the only class in which I would prepare all short formal briefs. No one ever collected them anyway.

Suddenly the fire alarm sounded throughout the building, and I was thankful to be saved by the proverbial bell. Snow had been coming down hard for quite some time, mostly mixed with grains of hail. Quickly I gathered my books and walked down the stairs with the rest of the students. Most students left their books and other belongings in the room, but I didn't dare leave a blessed thing. My precious notes were not going to be the ones that were stolen or burned if I could at all help it.

As I reached the bottom of the stairs, I was overcome by an overwhelming stench of burnt toast stemming from the cafeteria. Students outside were milling about across the street, laughing along with quite an embarrassed chef. Several fire trucks were lined up outside in front of the building and down the street.

I was the last person to leave the school, and as I prepared to cross the street around the front of the fire truck, my feet came straight out from under me on top of the grainy snow. Like a feather, under the fire truck I went.

Under the fire truck, I lay on my back, stunned. I could not believe what had just happened, let alone the fact that it happened directly in front of the entire law school community. And since I had been wearing sneakers, I could not get enough traction from them to push myself out no matter how hard I tried. Almost immediately, the wetness of the dirty, grainy slush began to seep through my jeans. "Uh, a little help here?" I yelled, choking on the truck's exhaust. "With the guy-to-girl ratio in my favor at this school, it would be nice if someone would be kind enough to come help me!" I mean, really, what did they honestly think I was doing? Making snow angels?

People were laughing in astonishment, and a few firemen came back out of the building, frantically looking under the other trucks. Just then, I felt myself being pulled out from under the truck by my book bag, which was still draped on my shoulder. It was Joshua.

"Thanks, Joshua," I said, shaking my head. I stood up and brushed off the clumps of slush from my jeans while he picked the rest out of my hair like a monkey. Once I collected myself, I became completely aware that the world was staring at me. I then turned and faced the professor: "I'm going home, now," I declared.

The professor wisely said nothing. No one would question me at that point. As they say in a popular children's book, I was having a "terrible, horrible, no-good, very bad day." Walking straight past the professor, I took the long route to the train. I didn't care. I just walked and walked, the snow and frozen rain dropping down my hair and face, dreading the next day when I would have to face everyone again.

I pondered whether to sit on a seat (if I was lucky enough to find one available on the train) in an effort to hide my wet behind (guaranteeing a miserable day for the next lucky winner to sit in my sloshy seat). My other option was that I stand and air-dry while everyone in the car sent me unnecessary rhetorical (and if they were wise, telepathic) comments such as "*You fell*, didn't you?"

Once I was safely on the train (now being stared at by a new and very colorful collection of gawkers), I realized that once I recovered from the incident, I would be reminded of my fall throughout the rest of law school as a box of grape juice inside my book bag had exploded when I fell, staining, of all things, my pocket legal dictionary. Ahh, what a nice shade of lavender that was.

Back in the apartment, Joshua and I compared our findings. Most of the names I had acquired from the night of the party on Allan's desk matched up with the layoff list that I was given by Mr. Taristo. Other names appeared to belong to high-level contacts from other major corporations including Aquicard, the Greenery, and Energec Oil. It was time for us to put some pieces together. "I don't think that this Brent guy or Allison for that matter are involved, Becky," said Joshua. "I don't see these two on anything we have here. What makes you think they're involved?"

"Well," I replied, "I got their names in the beginning when I first met Allan. He wanted me to investigate them—Brent, actually. Allison, I guess, was his girlfriend. Allan thought it was some sort of a front. Apparently, he doesn't trust either of them. Allan wanted to fire Brent. The problem was he didn't have a legitimate reason. I did have Tyler look them up though, and he said that their records came back clean. They have bank accounts in the area, but other than that, I have nothing on them. You know, random: is it really a big deal to have such high-level contacts from all these companies? FI is a big business, you know. I mean, every big business would ideally have deep pockets on their side, right?"

Joshua crinkled his brow as he perused the pictures of Allan's office again. "I hear ya. But you know? Humor me for a second. All this South American stuff: it is just like the movies. People hide things in South America. And then there's the dead lady: it looks like she's gotta be his mother or something like that. You know, there is a surprising number of people in this world that do not close out their dead relatives' bank accounts."

"Woah! Josh, do you really think that Allan is putting money into his dead mother's accounts?" I exclaimed. Joshua looked pensively in Miranda's direction, who was strutting around a fake rubber tree in the corner of the room. "Possibly. But we don't have any motive or connections to anything just yet. Now let's take a look at the business itself: Allan owns the building in Deering, but not the one in New York, right?" Joshua caught me off guard. "He doesn't?" I replied.

Joshua shook his head. "No. Looks like it's this guy named Harold Weston. But on these papers over here, it seems as though there's also another building in New York City for Financial Investments under some other guy's name. These two people don't appear to be partners. And you said that Allan's the only guy on FI, right?"

"Yeah, but wait a minute. What's up with Harold Weston? I'm getting confused," I replied.

"I don't know," said Joshua. "We should probably put this section aside and go over it again later. Mr. Weston had an apartment in New York. That's all I know. His name is on a lot of the documents, and even in the reflection of a bank account number scratched on a piece of paper on Allan's desk. It appears to be interchangeable with this other guy, Ron Peters. That's the guy I was referring to on that second building. There's Ron Weston, Harold Peters, Ron Peters, and Harold Weston. It is very confusing, but we'll hold it aside and see if the names come up again in this other pile o' stuff."

I took off my sneakers and began to rub my aching feet. "Huh," I said, biting my lower lip. "Everything otherwise appeared as though they were going by the books. I just don't get it. Now what I would like to know is why Charlie would want me to stay away from Financial Investments. I mean, it does seem sketchy looking at it now, but what is the real reason?"

"I don't know, honey," Joshua replied, grabbing my right foot. "You have gotten yourself into a big mess in a big hurry. I don't blame you for investigating before making any moves. I am just glad you decided to come back." I playfully looked around the room and leaned in toward Joshua. "Just don't tell my mom," I replied. Joshua laughed. "Like I would tell your mom and have her take my best friend away from me?" Tilting my head back, I gently closed my eyes. "Ooh, that feels good. You have a gift, you know? But seriously, no. Don't tell my mom I came to Boston and didn't visit her. She'll have my head." We both laughed.

Joshua reached for the stock certificates while I reluctantly took back my foot. "Even these look legit. I just don't know. Hey, listen. In the top drawer of my desk in the other room is a file with my own stock certificates in it. I should have a pretty recent one for Energec. Wanna grab those for me?" As promised, the file was the first one I grabbed in the desk. "Here you go, sir," I said, offering the file to Joshua.

"Thanks." Joshua replied, looking through his certificates until he found the Energec stock certificate and comparing it with the Energec certificate from Financial Investments. "Wait a minute." He put on his glasses. "What?" I replied. "The printing on this FI certificate is off just a tad. Geez, this really does sound too much like a movie. But you know, sometimes common sense answers these questions. I don't know, but I would think that stock certificates have to be uniform from a company—particularly since I received my stock certificate the same month that this copy you have here was issued. Look here," he said, holding it up to me. "It is even set up slightly differently. We may have something here. Put this aside when you are done looking at it." I grabbed the papers and began to compare them. He was right.

"Okay," I said. "Let's review this. Now what do we have here so far? We have several major companies where the names are repeated over and over on these certificates, and Allan has contacts in each. Plus, key employees that Mr. Taristo knows who otherwise had impeccable reputations have been getting fired."

"Right . . . right," said Joshua. "And we have Aquicard, Energec, the Meatery, Fruition Nutrition, and the Greenery."

"But wait: what do those names also have in common on the news?" I asked.

"The news!" Joshua exclaimed. "The food companies have had to pull food from the shelves. Some people died from food poisoning!"

"Yes, and . . . ," I said, coaxing him to continue his thought.

"Well, Energec has had their share of oil spills and some refinery incidents, but—"

"Yes, but lately, when have they been a big deal?" I asked.

"Mostly since . . . when . . . uh, maybe law school? Remember when Professor Roberts talked about it in that workers compensation seminar?"

I was smiling as the synapses in my brain fired away like a video game. "Exactly! Now when did FI make it big?"

Joshua froze for a moment and then grabbed another folder. "Woah!" he exclaimed, opening it up. "He was big about a year and a half before the first major oil spill down in the Gulf Coast! Oh my gosh, Rebecca. Could he be manipulating these things? Is that why he's in Deering?"

I stood up to stretch my legs and shook my head. "No, if he's hiding, he's doing so in plain view. Believe me. But seriously, focus. We're on a roll here. Now Allan's business is the stock market, right?"

"Investing, right," he replied.

"So he takes money from people and says, 'Here, I'll buy you a bunch of stock.'"

"Sure, I'm with you," said Joshua.

"Then the market crashes after an incident, and the stock's junk. Right?"

Joshua paused for a moment. "Well, yes. But they generally bounce back if you sit tight for a bit."

"But until then," I continued, "stock is cheap, right?"

"Yes," said Joshua.

"So if I'm Allan, I'm going to buy a whole bunch for I don't know . . . maybe myself then, right?"

Joshua was sporting a big grin from ear to ear. "Aha! Exactly!" he exclaimed. "The next question is what would you do if you *knew* that the stock would fall?"

I was all but jumping up and down on the floor at that point. "Sell while the getting's good!" I exclaimed, kneeling down on the floor next to Joshua. "And," I continued, "when it was low, I'd want to get more customers to invest in my own company . . . you know . . . so that they could take advantage of low stock that would almost definitely go up again with some patience."

"Right!" said Joshua. "Except little would these customers know that they were getting fake stock certificates. They owned NOTHING!" he yelled, putting both hands on his head.

"Oh my god, Joshua, I think we have something here. Something big. The question is, so . . . like . . . what do we do with this information? I mean, seriously, if this information ever gets into the wrong hands . . ."

Joshua began to reorganize the files. "Listen, don't panic. I think we should get on the computer right now and put some of this down in black and white. We'll be fine." I felt comforted. At least I wasn't alone anymore, and I had another brain thirsty for the same answers as I was. It was different being with Joshua in familiar territory, in the middle of a city that I knew like the back of my hand. We were the perfect family: the two of us and my cat.

Joshua booted up his computer and faced me. "It's all yours. Would you mind typing? You always did type faster." I laughed as he strolled toward the kitchen. "You know, Josh, you just may wind up taking back that comment that you're glad I came down here."

"Never!" Joshua exclaimed. "Hey, want something to drink?" he said, poking his head around the corner. I nodded, already typing feverishly. "How about some coffee?"

Joshua stepped forward and bowed his head with his hands in a prayerlike position. "As you wish," he said. With that, I continued to type.

CHAPTER TWENTY-FIVE

TWO HOURS and several drafts later, Joshua saved our data in three compact disks. It was three-thirty in the morning, and we were both exhausted, finally collapsing on the couch. "Seriously, Josh," I said. "People DIED here. Food poisoning, industrial accidents—"

"I know. We do need to dig just a little further, but it does look like Allan is staging everything. He did have the means to control the FI stocks, but is it really possible that he was behind all those recalls and disasters too?"

I sat back and ran my fingers through my hair. "And to think—all that money. He gets all kinds of money from unsuspecting clients, hides them in bank accounts, and lives the high-life living really off of the interest from this megaplex that he's created."

Joshua began going through his wallet and pulled out his credit cards. "See this? Aquicard. These guys invested with FI in the beginning. But they're getting screwed and don't even know it. He uses their name on his customer's fake stock certificates!"

"And the others too," I replied. "Anyway, it's getting late, and you have to work in a few hours. Let's call it a night."

"Okay, kiddo," Joshua sleepily replied. "Believe me, though, I'd call out if I could. I'll try to get home early anyway, okay?" Leaving the computer on, we both fell asleep on the couch.

At about 9:30 AM, I awoke to the sound of the computer buzzing. There was a note next to me on a yellow Stickie in Joshua's handwriting: "Gone to work—call me for lunch. As always, love, Josh." I held the note for a second. Joshua was always a thoughtful, intelligent person. I prayed that I didn't get him into trouble by keeping him so busy during his time off from work.

Making my sleepy way into the kitchen, the computer's persistent buzzing began to annoy me. Suddenly it hit me, and I dropped Joshua's teapot into the sink. Why was the computer active?

Racing into the living room, I figured out that someone had hacked into the system and most likely downloaded our data, which might still be saved somewhere on the hard drive through the Internet. *Please let it be Joshua*, I thought. I shut off the computer immediately and yanked the modem cord from the wall, sending Miranda in a panicked frenzy into the bedroom. I then immediately dialed the number to Trenstaw Law School. "Library please," I said frantically.

"Good morning, law library." Thank God. A familiar voice.

"Joshua?"

"Hi, darling. Rested?"

"Oh sure. Listen, are you on the computer at work right now?"

"No, kid. I am talking to you. So are you coming by for lunch or what?" Joshua's voice was so innocent and unsuspecting that I felt horrible knowing that I was about to ruin his day.

"Joshua, listen. I am not kidding. Are you on the computer?" My eyes began to fill, and I began to tremble.

"No. What's wrong?" he replied, his voice growing deeper.

Unable to keep still, I began looking out the windows and continued to pace the apartment. "Someone hacked into the computer, and they may have gotten the stuff from the hard drive. You know how sometimes the computers save things automatically? Like an emergency file that you can retrieve later?"

"A timed backup. Oh my god. Listen, Becky. Pack up your things. Everything. Meet me in the lobby of the law school right away. And get off the phone. Time to get you out of here. Take a cab or whatever, but leave your car. And be super careful, okay?"

I was becoming disoriented. "Where will I go? My mother's? I don't want to get you into trouble!"

"Just get off the phone and meet me. For all we know, someone can be listening to us as we speak." Aaaargh! I hadn't thought of that. Why didn't I just go directly to the school? Do not pass kitchen. Go to the school. Have your conversation in person. It was within walking distance, for crying out loud.

"Okay. I'm on my way." I hung up the phone and continued to pace. *What do I do, what do I do?* I thought. Suddenly I picked up the phone and called the operator.

"Hi. Can you trace the last phone call to this number?" I said.

"Sure, dear. Hold on just a moment." I could not catch my breath at this point and tried holding it so that I didn't come across as a pervert on the phone. "It is a private number, dear. But it is coming from Vermont." I slammed the phone and ran to Joshua's closet. *Dumb, Becky, dumb*, I thought. *Why did you call your house to get messages? Someone must have broken into the cabin and traced your last call. Dumb, dumb, dumb.*

Rummaging through Joshua's closet, I knew that he played roller hockey in his spare time and surely had one of those giant duffel bags. Every guy I knew had one. I could hide a ten-year-old child in one of those bags, and no one would know. Not that I would, but the point was the size. Heck, now that I was thinking about it, my stalker could kill me and put *me* in the bag. Then if I was lucky, some lobster fisherman would find my discarded unrecognizable remains years later at the bottom of Boston Harbor. Suddenly on the way out of the door I stopped, hearing a familiar sound. "Meow." Miranda was on the edge of the couch, sitting perfectly straight, her innocent big blue eyes looking at me with wonder and love.

My heart sunk. Still, I couldn't risk taking her with me. *Maybe Joshua could arrange for us to come back for her*, I thought. I couldn't possibly carry her and everything else at the same time. Dropping my bags, I picked her up, holding her tight. I must have gently kissed the top of her head a million times as she nuzzled into my neck, the familiar purr that I so loved. "Be safe, sweetheart," I said, scanning her bowls to make sure they were filled with food and water. "I'll be back as soon as I can, okay? I promise. I love you."

Within thirty minutes, I arrived in the law library, sickened after leaving Miranda all alone. She was like a child to me. Sure, she was independent, but I was still her caretaker, and she relied on me. I chose to adopt her, and she chose to unconditionally love me back. Joshua met me at the door and yelled to a girl behind the desk. "Be back after lunch, Sue."

"Okay," said the voice of a woman from behind a bookshelf.

Joshua and I ran to the elevator and took it to the top floor. He then led me through a series of corridors and down some back stairs to a connecting building that was part of the undergraduate school. As we passed our last series of old gray lockers, suddenly I could smell the pungent aroma of formaldehyde. Joshua grabbed the duffel bag and took me into a back room near the biology lab, where there was another series of lockers in the back.

"Your stuff will be safe here," he said.

"Are you sure, Josh? I don't know if I like this."

"Just for now. In the meantime I have to get us a room." Joshua grabbed my hand and pulled me back into the hallway.

"What do you mean a room? Can't we go to my mother's?" I really wanted my mother.

"No. It is not safe for you or your family. You don't know who you are dealing with Becky. We'll find a hotel on the South Shore and stay there for a few days. I have some vacation time anyway. I'll take it now."

"You'd do that for me? I don't have any money right now." My eyes saddened.

"You'll pay me back later. My buddy Dave is a travel agent here in the city. Right now, we are off to see him. He'll loan us a car too. He owes me a favor. Any requests?"

"How about the Cape?"

"The Cape it is."

A few hours later we found ourselves at a bed and breakfast close to the beach. The sounds and smells of salt water, seagulls and sand filled the air. I could breathe once again.

Joshua pulled the duffel bag and some other belongings from the car. Wisely, we stopped at a grocery store on the way and had some food with us, thinking it best not to leave the inn too often. It was strange: strange to be so far away from home, strange to be running from places I thought safe, and strange to be after all this time sharing yet another crazy life experience with Joshua. Not long ago I was just a young attorney trying to make my own mark in the world. Now I find myself and because of me, my best friend sucked into a major international conspiracy. It was certainly surreal being away, renting a room and sharing it with of all people, Joshua Tameron. Strange, yet comforting. He made me feel as safe as I could be. I had never gone away with a boy before in my life. Even though I was out of school, a grown adult and not in any kind of romantic relationship with Josh, the Catholic guilt still lingered.

Once we settled inside, we revisited the recurring question, who to tell? We decided that the FBI would be the ones. The situation was federal, and they would know what to do. I dialed the operator and had her connect me to a Special Investigations Unit. A female voice answered: "Can I help you?" she said.

"Yes," I replied, my voice quivering. "I need to speak to someone about a federal situation . . . uh . . . criminal situation . . . well, potentially criminal."

"Please hold." Her voice was ice cold, and she sounded bored. No, maybe annoyed. Well, I guess a little of column A and a little of column B. Immediately, I was placed on hold, and a computerized voice informed that my call was being recorded. After a few minutes, the live voice of a man answered.

"Yes, Special Agent Frank Mulcahey."

"Mr. Mulcahey, my name is uh . . . I am calling from . . ." I was so frazzled that I just wasn't sure where to begin. It apparently didn't matter, I suppose, since Mr. Mulcahey cut me off anyway. "I know. You think you found something criminal. What is it? We get a lot of these calls."

"I think that a company based mostly in New York and in Vermont is engaged in illegal stock activity, including embezzling client funds, and I think that some other major companies across the United States are involved. I don't know who to turn to."

"What is the name of the company?" Mr. Mulcahey sighed as though he was as bored as the original operator.

"Financial Investments Incorporated." Joshua sat next to me like a puppy dog waiting for a cookie.

"And the evidence you have, Ms. Lawson?" said Mr. Mulcahey, his voice having changed slightly.

"I have phone records, lists of names, pictures, documents, et cetera."

"And all this information is verifiable? Because we just can't put together a case based on a hunch. It is not our practice here. You should know that." Mr. Mulcahey laughed.

"Yes, I am familiar with the 'mere hunch is not enough' phrase." Since Mr. Mulcahey remained calm, I began to feel a little better. Joshua seemed more relaxed as well.

"Well, I'll tell you what, I would like you to meet one of my agents tonight at Castle Island in Southie. You know where that is, right? Give them everything you have. We'll take care of it from there. If we need you for anything else, we'll track you down."

The phone conversation did not last long. And even though I finally had a place to send my findings, something didn't sit right. In fact, I wasn't exactly comfortable with the idea of sending all of my paperwork out right away and kissing the case good-bye. I just did not feel safe.

"So what did he say that was so funny?" said Joshua.

"Oh, he alluded to the mere hunch principle in criminal law—you know, the search and seizure stuff." Joshua laughed while I continued. "He was a nice guy, though—not a very warm or fuzzy bedside manner, but he was polite enough. He got to the point, asked for the evidence I had, and that was it."

"Good. Are we going to meet them or drop it off at the Boston offices?"

Suddenly my eyes widened. I gazed out the window. My mouth dropped. "Oh no. Joshua, what do you know about FBI agents?"

"What's wrong. What about them? We'll be fine."

I got out of my chair and walked slowly over to the window. *He called me Ms. Lawson.* Joshua froze. "Do you suppose he traced the call? Are there records he was looking up to find out where I was calling from? How would he know my name? I never had a chance to tell anyone who I was."

"Sure. Don't panic. I would think that the FBI agents get thousands of calls each day with hypothetical scams across the nation. If someone were to fake an allegation on purpose, they could be prosecuted. We shouldn't panic. Listen. Instead of staying in, let's go out and grab something to eat. My treat. You'll feel better, okay?"

My body was trembling. "Joshua," I continued, gasping for air, "he wanted us to meet an agent at Castle Island. Tonight. In the dark. Why wouldn't we go to their offices?"

My thoughts turned to Charlie working for the CIA. Maybe I should have called them instead. What was the jurisdictional difference between the FBI and the CIA anyway?

Joshua took me to the car and, after driving around for a little bit, found a local restaurant. Joshua tried as hard as he could to calm my nerves (even waiting an extra forty-five minutes so that we would be seated at a private table in the back), but I just could not focus. "How about some wine, Becky? One glass?" he asked. I refused. "No, thank you, Joshua," I replied. "I don't think it's a good idea to drink right now."

"Okay, but promise me that you'll eat a good dinner, okay?"

I picked at my food the entire meal, but I did finish as promised. My problem was that I analyzed every person who walked in or out of the dining area instead of chat with my company.

Joshua seemed to take forever finishing his meal as well, mostly because he was trying to get me to slow down and relax. When we finally did finish, Joshua suggested that we walk the beach located behind the restaurant. As we began to walk, he took my hand in his. It was nice. I didn't have the heart to tell him I was still terrified. In fact, when we originally pulled up, I hadn't even noticed any beach.

"I always loved the sound of the ocean waves crashing over the rocks," I said as I stared off into the distance. "Tonight, though, they're just too loud. Don't you think? We need to be completely on guard."

"Let's go back," said Joshua, noting my increased anxiety. I immediately agreed without question, and we began to walk back to the car.

As we approached the car, I spotted a payphone at the edge of the dirt parking lot. Since the—well, for lack of a better term—*bad guys* obviously knew that I was in Massachusetts, I decided that I should check my machine once more. "Hey, Beck, why don't you use your cell phone?" asked Joshua.

"I have it with me, but I think we should save the battery for emergencies."

"I guess they'd trace that call back too, huh?" Joshua remarked.

"Exactly," I said. "They can always trace the call back to here if they had the right connections, but I feel better this way. Can't they trace us like a GPS thing if our phones are on anyway?"

Joshua paused for a moment, turning off his own phone. "Sometimes yes. I think it depends on where the cell towers are."

"Okay, well, I'll call real quick over here while you get the car started," I said, walking toward the phone. "Okay," Joshua replied, heading toward the car.

Approaching the payphone, I was startled when it rang. Loudly. I picked up the receiver. "Hello?" I said cautiously. The voice was familiar. "I told you to mind your own business."

"Charlie?" I was stunned.

"Who did you think it was?" he replied, his voice cold and assertive.

Looking toward the car, I could see Joshua playing with the radio. "How did you find me?" I said.

"Doesn't matter. What matters is that *you* are in a lot of trouble. *Everyone you touch* is in a lot of trouble. *Everyone that touches you* is in a lot of trouble. *Including* that little boyfriend of yours."

I glanced over at Joshua again, who was still futzing with the radio. *Look up, Joshua*, I thought. "What do you mean by that?" I replied. "I didn't do anything, and he is not my boyfriend."

"You have made the wrong decision once again, Counsel." Charlie was breathing heavily. "Now you, no questions asked, will give me all the papers in that car. Pictures included. *Now.*"

"Charlie, I am begging you. Please leave me alone. Besides, nothing is in that car." Turning to beckon to Joshua, something made me glance down at my feet. There was a brown manila envelope at the base of the payphone. A picture of Miranda was taped to the front.

My stomach dropped. As I picked up the envelope, Charlie began to speak again. This time, his voice was almost teasing me. "Go ahead, Rebecca, *open it.*"

Tearing open the envelope, I pulled out Miranda's faux-diamond-encrusted personalized collar. "MEEOOW," he said tauntingly. Charlie's voice was the voice of pure evil.

"Charlie, please. Please leave me alone!" *What has he done with Miranda?* I thought. *Oh, dear God. There's no blood on the collar. Or is there? Maybe he's just toying with me? Please let him be toying with me. Maybe it's a fake. It has to be.*

"Motion denied. And yes, the collar is real." Charlie had read my mind. I immediately dropped the receiver and began running toward Joshua when suddenly, I heard the revving of a very loud engine behind me. Charlie was at the wheel of a black Suburban, cell phone in hand, the outline of a woman appearing suddenly in the seat next to him. To my disgust, he made a motion as though he was zipping up his pants. At the same time, she wiped her face with her forearm. Charlie threw on the high beams, and the truck started toward me at racing speed.

I had almost reached Joshua when something was tossed out of the moonroof of the Suburban. The sound of the waves was suddenly muffled by the familiar, albeit terrified, call of my precious cat. Landing with a hard thud off the hood of the truck, Miranda bounced lifeless to the ground and succumbed to the Suburban's left front wheel as Charlie continued to drive in my direction. Blood spattered everywhere with a horrible loud pop.

I froze. Joshua, still in the car, revved his engine and floored the accelerator, ramming directly into Charlie's Suburban. My blood pressure dropped, as did I, to the ground. Charlie sped away, and Joshua jumped out of the car, rushing as fast as he could to my side. "Becky! Becky! Oh dear God, Becky! Honey, are you all right? Talk to me!"

"What?" I was dazed and dizzy.

Joshua cradled my head. "Are you hurt, sweetheart? Tell me you're all right. Who was that fucking no-good son-of-a-bitch psycho?"

"Just get me back to the room, Josh," I whispered. "Let's get our things and leave."

"Okay. It's going to be okay."

"I feel sick. Oh my god, I feel sick." I said, still clutching Miranda's collar as it began to rain.

CHAPTER TWENTY-SIX

JOSHUA DROVE us back to the bed-and-breakfast in silence, taking unpredictable routes down foreign streets without headlights as much as possible, as he was determined to ensure that we weren't being trailed. Joshua suggested in the beginning that we report the incident immediately to the local police, but quickly reconsidered when he realized that we had been unable to fully trust any agency, let alone any local authority just yet. A steady stream of tears flowed down my cheeks, glistening in the moonlight as the rain began to subside. When we arrived, Joshua guided me out of the car, and we cautiously started toward the house. "Let's get you in and dried off, honey," he said, whispering in my ear. "It's going to be okay. I promise. We'll get to the bottom of this." I continued to sniffle, but began to take control of my tears, painfully aware of the fact that we were still in danger.

"Let me ask you one thing, and we can drop the subject for a while: was that the guy you have been seeing in Vermont?" I was ashamed, but too emotionally and physically drained to care all too terribly much. "Yes," I replied. "So what do you think? Cute?" I thought that maybe a little bit of old sarcasm could break the ice at that awkward moment in time.

It was then that I felt the weight of Joshua's body pull away from me, and the next thing I knew, he was facedown on the ground in the dirt. "Oh my god!" I screamed, my horrified gaze darting all around us in the darkness. The adrenaline rushing through my body at that moment surely would have qualified me to fight alongside the most highly trained Navy SEALs.

Joshua slowly put his hands beneath his chest and began to push himself up. His eyes met mine with a look of pure innocence surrounded by a new crimson visage. "I fell," he said, grinning sheepishly.

"Well, that's what you get for making fun of me with the fire truck," I replied, giggling in relief as I pulled him to his feet. "I just don't understand how Charlie could possibly find us so quickly," I continued, watching a nervous Joshua almost helplessly fumble with the room key as we approached the door. Suddenly Joshua froze. "Shh!" he whispered, placing his finger over his mouth as I heard the sound of odd scraping noises stemming from inside our room. Two muscular men, dressed entirely in black from head to toe, were in the midst of breaking in through a back window. "Stop! Police!" Joshua screamed in a loud, authoritative voice, pounding his fist on the door.

Hearing a very convincing Joshua, the intruders immediately stopped in their tracks and hastily abandoned their efforts without saying a word. As we watched them disappear into the darkness, we knew that we were obviously unsafe. There was no other option for us other than to leave immediately. Keeping with our new tradition, our next move was something that we had started to become very good at: we grabbed our bags and bolted for the car.

Once we were safely back in the car, Joshua quickly put the key in the ignition and fired up the engine as fast as he could. I fastened my seat belt and made sure all the doors were locked. "Tell you what," said Joshua as he sped away, the back wheels skidding like a big wheel in the dirt. "We stay in the car for now. I have an idea. We just need to stop at a gas station at some point. You try and rest. We'll talk later." Keeping an eye out for followers, I sighed, still slightly out of breath from our unplanned evening jog.

"I can't imagine what your apartment looks like right now, Josh. I am so, so sorry for dragging you into this," I sadly replied, my voice now soft and hoarse.

"Well, I'm sure that your house in Vermont isn't any better," he responded, gently stroking the hair on the left side of my head. "Now rest. I'm right here." Joshua still had no idea about the incident with Charlie in my kitchen, and more so that the area in which he gently stroked once displayed a prominent bloody contusion. "He hurt you, didn't he?" said Joshua, putting everything together. "Yeah, a little bit," I replied, closing my eyes as Joshua territorially shook his head. He didn't need to know every single detail just yet. Although it was a perfect time to explain, it was just not *the* perfect time for me. I wasn't ready, and did not have the energy. Instead, behind closed eyes, I started to relive every last rotten moment I had wasted with Charlie and, for that matter, Frank. No arguments would come from me on Joshua's suggestion to sleep. Emotionally and physically drained, I quickly drifted off, waking a couple of hours later to hear the sounds of music off in the distance. "Where are we?" I groggily whispered.

Joshua appeared to be quite pleased with himself. "Foxwoods, my dear. What do you think?" I chuckled, only to humor him, as I was still tormented by the horrible popping sound of Miranda innocently succumbing to Charlie's wheel. Joshua continued. "I thought that while we were playing the gambling game, we could escape in here for a while. It's open 24/7, right? Sometimes the safest place to be is in public. We can get lost in the crowds here if need be. Besides, we need to brainstorm." My expression immediately changed. *Great*, I thought. *Just what I wanted to do. Think.*

Joshua noticed my look. "Listen, Beck. I know that this is draining on you, and you would much rather hide out in some other country. But let's be serious. Do you want to keep running, or clear this thing up now?" Furious with his insinuation that I wanted to run away from my problems, and even more furious that what began as an investigation had turned into a test of survival, I fired back, "I strongly suggest that you take that comment back."

Joshua said nothing, but continued to drive, looking straight ahead in an angry daze as though I wasn't even in the car. "Joshua! Take that back!" I screamed.

Eventually Joshua broke his silence and slammed on the brakes, throwing us both forward toward the dashboard. Fortunately, we were still wearing our seat belts. "I will *not* take that back. You know, you are pretty damn lucky that you have me here right now, pal. Where would you have turned if you didn't know me? What would you do if I were working for Allan and you had no idea?" I began to cry again as I rubbed my neck. "Fine. Cry," he said. *Shut up, Joshua.* "Should I just drop you off somewhere, and I'll just go ahead with my own life? You must have all the answers, and I'm just the lucky winner you decided to bring along just for the fun. 'Cause I gotta tell ya, this is *real* fun, Rebecca." Cars behind us began to honk, and the situation began to grow extremely uncomfortable. On top of everything, Joshua and I had never argued. *Ever.*

"Are you working for Allan?" I said, wondering whether I could trust anyone anymore. I couldn't even trust myself for getting wrapped up with Charlie in the first place. Stupid, stupid, stupid.

"No," said Joshua, changing his tone. I just stared at him, while I sarcastically credited his intelligence for calling attention to our car before we had even parked at our proverbial safe house. "I mean it, Becky. I'm on your side."

Cars continued to honk in frustration, and an elderly woman behind us started to yell. "Hey, move it buddy, will ya!" Joshua rolled down his window and stared back, seemingly hexing her with a look of death. "I'm going! I'm going! Hey, riddle me this—how lucky are you feeling now, lady?" Our frustrated neighbor responded by throwing her hands up in the air, vigorously rubbing her forehead, and then slamming her hands back down on the steering wheel with a sigh.

Rolling up the window, Joshua turned in my direction. "Look, don't be mad at me. I apologize. I do. I shouldn't have said that. This whole thing is just making me crazy, and I need you to keep your head too. Sometimes I think I can deal with you better when you're mad than when you're sad."

"Forget about it. Just change the subject," I replied, stretching my back and neck after my uncomfortable nap and abrupt stop. "And for the record," I continued, "I wouldn't be stupid enough to skip the country. Don't you think that Allan would be two steps ahead of me no matter where we were? He has allies everywhere. I don't have to tell you that. I think that it has become painfully obvious. Hey, we may as well save ourselves the trouble and call him. He'll tell us where we're off to next."

Joshua smiled. "You are a smart kid, Rebecca Lawson."

"I know. And when this is all over, I'll be even smarter," I said, beginning to feel vengeful. Joshua had successfully completed his mission: as always, he talked me off the ledge and made me choose the mind frame he thought was most beneficial to the situation.

After sometime, Joshua finally found a parking space fairly close to the hotel adjacent to Foxwoods and rented a room on one of the upper floors accessible only by a limited number of guests who had been issued a special key in the elevators. Our new names were Mr. and Mrs. Crawfeld. When we arrived at our room, Joshua closed and locked the door. After a couple of minutes of making sure that everything was secure, I picked up the telephone, dialed a code so that the call could not easily be traced, and then dialed a number. A familiar voice answered. "Syd?" Joshua raised his eyebrows in approval, nodded, and disappeared into the bathroom.

Ten minutes after I hung up with Syd, the telephone rang, startling the both of us. Thankfully, it was Mr. Taristo. "Hi, Rebecca, Tim here. I'm back down in DC. Listen, I just got off the phone with Syd. I need you guys to get yourselves to the airport and take the first flight out to BWI Thurgood Marshall Airport in Maryland. I'll meet you there. It's about thirty minutes north of Washington DC."

"Uh, okay, Mr. Taristo. We'll do that," I hesitantly replied, beckoning to Josh to collect our things *again*. Joshua sighed, obviously growing tired of living the life of a nomad. "Listen, Becky. You should travel light. Plus, I don't trust the airports rummaging through your stuff. Ship everything you have pertaining to FI to my attorney down here. His office is right in the middle of the district. You'd be impressed, actually."

"Hang on a sec, Mr. Taristo, let me get a paper and pen," I replied, reaching for the hotel's complimentary stationary. "Okay, go ahead," I stated and began to take down the information.

In the next half hour, Joshua and I were the proud owners of a new set of luggage and began securing all the files that we had with us inside. While Joshua ordered our plane tickets to Maryland, I reluctantly released what felt like my life into the hands of a stranger—a common carrier who claimed that they would be traveling in the direction of DC. The rest of our documents (most of the more important ones) still remained hidden inside the locker at Trenstaw, although much of what we were shipping was the only copy we had. Plus, we had with us two of the compact disks that not even Mr. Taristo knew about. For now, that was enough. Joshua kept one and I the other, each labeled as if it was a burned CD of songs to throw off anyone questioning us, particularly airport security. Once we felt comfortable that we could trust the right agency, we would send for the rest.

Joshua and I locked the keys under the front passenger seat of the now-barely-recognizable beaten-up car at Foxwoods and took a cab to the closest airport. "Boy, am I going to have to make this up to Dave," said Joshua. "Who's Dave?" I asked. Joshua shook his head. "He owns the car." *Oh right, Dave the Travel Guy. Oops*, I thought to myself, lightly slapping my forehead. *Just another name for me to add to the list of all the people whose lives are being made miserable at the hands of Rebecca Lawson.*

Thirty minutes and an hour's plane ride later, we greeted Mr. Taristo at the gate. He quickly ushered us to a car, and we drove for what seemed like forever, en route to a hotel. Sensing our fears, Mr. Taristo broke the silence. "We're almost there, guys," he said as we entered Washington. "It always seems longer when you are unfamiliar with the area and your destination. Plus, I'm taking a slightly different route just to be on the safe side. We're almost there."

To our astonishment, Mr. Taristo pulled up to the front of the Willard InterContinental Hotel on Pennsylvania Avenue and waved to the doorman. Mr. Taristo had already reserved the Thomas Jefferson Suite for us under a false name. We took our carry-on luggage upstairs and began to unpack, which did not take long given the fact that we had traveled light. It felt better traveling light actually, as we were always faced with the threat of an abrupt exit. Mr. Taristo was kind enough to leave us a pile of touristy clothing he had grabbed at the last minute, knowing that we would be limited on our attire. The clothes weren't exactly red-carpet material, and probably would shrink with the first washing, but we were very thankful at that point to have something. Anything.

Joshua and I would share the suite, as Mr. Taristo enjoyed his own condominium in Georgetown, close to Georgetown University, where he frequently taught. It was incredible, really. The suite was approximately 2,800 square feet, with a red-and-gold eighteenth-century design scheme that replicated designs of none other than the White House itself. The foyer that welcomed us was decorated with a harlequin pattern of black-and-white marble, leading to a dual-parlor living room. The oval dining room seated ten with views down Pennsylvania Avenue to the U.S. Capitol. Then there was the master bedroom boasting a sitting area, which had not one but *two* bathrooms—one with a Jacuzzi tub.

Instead of exploring the suite as I normally would, I found myself first investigating the locking systems on every window and door. Even though the suite was exquisite, everything just seemed so big. Still, seeing the Jacuzzi tub with fresh towels hung neatly on warming racks, courtesy soaps placed delicately in an obviously expensive basket, and complimentary bathrobes brought my stress level down about thirty pegs. It had been a while since I showered and changed without being rushed. Our suite was one where really only heads of state and dignitaries had the distinct privilege of resting their weary heads. Never in a million years had I imagined that I too would experience such luxury. If only I was experiencing it at another time.

Once we were settled, we explained everything in detail to Mr. Taristo. After he heard our story, he made a telephone call while Joshua and I freshened up in our respective bathrooms. About an hour later, there was a knock at the door, and Mr. Taristo excitedly welcomed in a man and a woman whom I immediately recognized. Seeing the look on my face, Joshua instinctively rushed to my side. We were staring directly into the faces of Brent Thompson and Allison Hatchfield.

Mr. Taristo carefully locked the door and ushered Brent and Allison to the dining area. Seeing the fear in my eyes, both began to reach into the pockets of their suit coats. Joshua instinctively threw me to the floor and grabbed the oversized bouquet of fresh flowers from the dining room table. "Hey hey hey!" shouted Brent.

"Calm down! It's okay!" yelled Allison.

"Really! It's okay!" said Mr. Taristo. "These guys are legit. I promise you!"

Joshua, who was looking a tad bit pathetic as he struggled with the large floral arrangement, apologetically helped me from the floor while our new guests flashed badges and credentials. I barely looked at any of it. "FBI at your service, Ms. Lawson," said Brent.

I thought I would collapse. Allison, in fact, was the woman with the expensive compact in the ladies' room at Café Mirabelle. I had already spoken with Mr. Mulcahey at the FBI, and he wanted a secret meeting in Southie. With all the federal agencies in DC, surely Mr. Taristo could have come up with something else. "What do *you* want?" said Joshua. Noticing the blood drain from my face, Mr. Taristo tried to hand me a glass of water, which I refused. Actually, *refused* is not the correct word. I completely *ignored* his outstretched hand.

"Listen, don't be alarmed," said Allison. "We have been trailing these guys for quite some time. Mr. Taristo had us figured out once you left Deering. You should come work for us, Tim." I looked at Mr. Taristo, and then Joshua. Mr. Taristo was smiling. *Glad you're having fun, Tim*, I thought.

"How do I know that I can trust you, Ms. Hatchfield?" I stated, furious that they were in the room. "Yeah, you barge in here flashing your fancy badges and credentials, but I don't know what badges are legit or not. I'd have to go look it up or something. People have those things made all the time for illegal purposes. Those pieces of tin mean nothing to me." Joshua nodded in agreement, although I knew that he would have originally trusted them if it wasn't for my original reaction. "Yeah," he said, looking up at Mr. Taristo.

"You can trust *us*, Becky," asserted Mr. Taristo. "Jordan, Doug, and I go way back. Georgetown University undergrad. Right, guys?" Jordan and Doug nodded. "Anyway, after our conversations, I began to put things together and did a little checking myself. That's when I ran into these guys. Talk about a small world. The important thing to remember is that you have not—and I mean *never*—been betrayed in any way by any of us." Mr. Taristo was at least acting extremely serious.

Jordan continued, "Let me explain: we both work for the Bureau but are junior to the gentleman that you spoke with—Mr. Mulcahey. Mr. Mulcahey is one of Allan's cohorts. That information would have gotten you nowhere but probably dumped into the Boston Harbor if you had met any so-called agents in Southie. Mulcahey has been trailing you all along. Joshua's apartment, in fact, was already bugged while he was at work not long ago—right after the first time you contacted him, as a matter of fact."

Joshua's mouth dropped in astonishment while Jordan continued to talk. "Now Brent and I . . . well, Doug and I—actually, my real name is Jordan. We've been working with the Attorney General's Office in Vermont and various other states across the country, as well as down here in DC for quite some time now. They are planning on federally prosecuting everyone involved." Jordan looked at me. "Everyone. Including Charlie, who, by the way, is not CIA." *Shocker.*

Jordan continued. "We just didn't have all the documentation we needed yet, and Allan was becoming suspicious of Brent, uh, Doug." Doug chuckled and continued, "Until, that is, you, my friend, provided us with all the missing links."

"I—and I am not your friend yet, *Doug*—have provided you with nothing yet, and that includes you too, Allison, or Jordan, or whatever your name is," I retorted, making sure to keep the table between the alleged agents and Joshua and me. Jordan looked at Doug, who pulled a chair from the table and sat down on it backward. "Listen, we know how you feel. But believe me, you're safe with us. Warrants have already been issued and are being executed as we speak. Just know that you will be protected to the max throughout the entire prosecution."

Joshua, now a little bit more comfortable, took a seat as well. "Okay. If you are telling the truth, how long will all of this take?" he said, knowing that the answer was "until it's over." I rolled my eyes and faced Jordan. "So what happens after the prosecution is over?" I asked, now in my more serious "attorney voice."

"No need to worry. We have spoken with your employer, Joshua, and we will reevaluate the situation to see what your needs are, if any," said Doug.

"Yeah? What about me?" I said. "I have clients, private clients, some who have a right to a speedy trial!"

Jordan turned to face me. "Doug spoke with Judge Haley earlier today. He will be expecting your call first thing in the morning. If there is anyone in Deering who you would like to cover court appearances, it will be arranged through Judge Haley's clerk. We can also ship your files down here to you if you wish. However you are most comfortable handling things is fine. We'll make it happen," said Jordan.

Slowly I wandered over to the front windows and looked out toward the Capitol. Everything seemed so big and foreign. And here I was, in the middle of a sea of attorneys, me a new attorney myself. I was in a surreal suite, trapped in a surreal situation, looking out at the monuments I had only seen in pictures. "You don't understand. This is my life. I miss my clients. I miss my fucking cat. I miss my mother. I miss my friends. What about Ken and Marie? Are they okay? You haven't even mentioned anyone in Vermont."

"They're fine," said Doug. "They are all fine. Jacqueline, and Patrick and Joseph too. In fact, they were the only ones, it seems, who didn't get wrapped up in FI at all. The FI people were absolutely clueless about the real goings-on with the student internships and the party. Ingenious!"

"Thank goodness," said Joshua.

Doug continued. "Both of your families are fine. Neither of them were involved, and both have been updated as to where you are—well, not exactly *where*, but they know that you're safe in DC, and why. They'll be expecting calls from both of you later too. I know that I don't have to remind you to limit your discussions with them, though, okay? Don't discuss the case. Let them follow the news for now." I nodded. "What about my house?" I asked.

"Your house, Rebecca, is fine too. A bit messy, but fine. As I'm sure you can guess, Allan's lackeys tossed the place after you left."

"Shocker," I replied, raising an eyebrow and glancing at Joshua.

"Of course, we tossed your house too. Sorry. Uh . . . and your office." I nodded back with a sarcastic smile. "Hey, my pleasure. Hope you had fun."

Jordan excitedly chimed in, obviously thrilled that the investigation was nearing an end, and wanting Joshua and me to share in the excitement. "It turns out that every time you left the house, the sheriff tipped off Allan. Allan knew that with Charlie's help, you'd eventually be frightened enough to leave for a longer period of time—enough for Charlie to go through everything. Especially since he was already quite familiar with your house. And if it wasn't Charlie setting up things, it was the sheriff. Sheriff Patterson knew your place inside and out from the prior owners. Charlie stalled you many, many times, Becky."

"Of course," I replied with a pout, thinking back to our meeting at the pond. *And don't call me Becky*, I thought. *You haven't earned that right.*

"You know, you two?" said Doug. "You are both very, very lucky. People have died, you know." Joshua nodded in acknowledgment. "We know," he replied. "Don't order the orange juice, right?"

"No, Joshua. It's more than that. He's talking about murder," said Jordan.

It was then that it all clicked. "Mr. Peters! Ron Peters. The New York landlord!" I announced.

"I knew it!" said Joshua. "Woah!" he exclaimed, turning to me with a look of relief. "Good thing they are making arrests."

"Uh, that's not all, Joshua," continued Doug. "Ron Peters was murdered because he began to figure out Allan's scheme. Charlie McCabe was the one who had befriended Ron in New York City and acquired enough information for Allan's people to *take care of the rest*, so to speak. Like you, Rebecca, Ron lived alone, far from family and lacking close friends in the area. It wasn't his fault. He was lonely too."

"Oh my god," I whispered, placing my hands over my mouth.

"Ron was tricked or taken to South America after he confided in Charlie what he suspected Allan was doing. He never returned, Rebecca," said Jordan.

"Too bad it wasn't Charlie that didn't return," said Joshua. "Get it? Charlie? Who never returned? The song? 'He took the train in Boston and—'"

"Joshua!" I yelled, trying desperately to make him stop. "We know. We all know the song." Joking was the last thing that I needed to do. Doug, who had definitely enjoyed the joke, stopped humming and patting his leg.

After a few moments of silence, Joshua turned to me. "What were you thinking?" he asked. I immediately fired back a look. Joshua got the message. Doug chuckled, winning a similar look from Jordan.

"Right now, don't worry. You are both safe. Get some sleep. The pair of you have had a long couple of days. We'll take care of everything in the morning. In the meantime, there will be two agents detailed outside your door at all times for protection and two undercover ones outside with the doorman just to keep tabs on who's going in and coming out of the building. Anything else you need?" said Doug.

"No. I guess we are all set," I replied. "Unless the government is willing to compensate our services with an all-expense-paid trip to Paris when this is all over. I'd like to go somewhere where I can speak another language, eat as much chocolate as I want, and not be reachable on my cell phone for a while." Joshua smiled in approval as we led everyone to the door. "There's a difference between running away and getting away," he said to me under his breath. I winked back.

CHAPTER TWENTY-SEVEN

A S EXHAUSTED as I was, it didn't appear as if it was the sleep fairy's destiny to pay me a visit that evening. My mind and my heart were racing: everything that Jordan and Doug had said had completely begun to make sense. Still, how could I put my trust in two alleged junior G-men agents when their boss was still on the payroll, supposedly working with the proverbial criminal mastermind? Then there was the connection with Mr. Taristo. I supposed that any good friend wouldn't dare give up someone else's cover. Still, a big concern of mine was that even if Joshua and I did put all our trust in Mr. Taristo's, Doug's, and Jordan's good intentions, I wasn't sure that even they could completely guarantee our protection either.

No one left with any documentation or formal statement that evening from us. As far as I was concerned, everyone and everything would be verified, and we would work pursuant to my terms, and mine alone. After all, if they were secretly on Allan's side, of course, they would be able to explain away any sensible theories I offered and do so in detail. I would gladly make my information available only in a real court setting with a real judge, and pursuant to a legitimate subpoena.

"I just don't know if I can trust them, Josh," I whispered in the darkness at the early hour of three, platonically lying in Joshua's arms in the queen-size bed. At least that felt right: we fit. Best friends who could just be. "There haven't been many so far that we have actually been able to trust. I question everyone. Even Mr. Taristo sometimes. He always knows where we are, and so do everyone connected with Allan and this incredulous scheme of his."

"Don't worry, Beck. Mr. Taristo is perfectly reliable, and we are in an extremely public place. We'll be fine. They specialize in security down here. The District of Columbia is like one big security office." Joshua turned to lie facing me on his side as he rested his head on his arm. "You know how it is in the mornings. Would you like one or two secret service agents with your mocha latte?'"

I smiled, glancing up toward the windows at the lights of the planes traveling into and out of Reagan International Airport in the distance. "I'll feel better only when I see those clowns in nickel-plated shackles secured to belly chains on their way to federal prison. Leg irons too—thick ones that resist picking, drilling, or anything else. And both the special bracelets and anklets would have a unique key system: only one key, with real strong rivets." Joshua laughed while I continued on with my rant. "And even then, we don't know the extent of people who are involved.

We just started this thing. What if Allan sends people out on a revenge mission? His connections are endless. I mean, seriously: remember the sickos who tainted the baby jars last year? Pretty creative and those bastards never got caught. Just imagine what Allan's guys could do to us."

Joshua began to gently stroke my hair, and I will admit, I was beginning to love when he did that. "Well, I don't think you have to worry about the handcuff issue, Beck. Generally, they are all that durable. Let me throw this out at you though: is it still the thing to wear silver jewelry when you walk into nightclubs to let people know that you're single? Now *that's* a statement to make on the way to the clink!" After that comment, Joshua had me giggling to the point where I was wiping away tears. The *clink*. I mean, really, when was the last time I had heard anyone reference prison with that name? I loved the way he framed things sometimes. He had such great comedic timing. "Listen," he continued, "we have to focus on the present. It's only natural for you to try and place yourself two steps ahead of these guys. It is the nature of your profession and the nature of your personality. Right now, though, you are in a position where you could quickly lose focus. We can't do that here. Not here, not now." Feeling a little better, I slowly drifted off to sleep.

The next morning, we awoke at nine thirty. Joshua grabbed a few complimentary cans of soda from the suite's refrigerator and turned on the television. Neither of us was hungry and, having watched too many movies in our day, didn't trust room service just yet. At 11:00 AM, the telephone rang. Joshua was just finishing his shower so I answered the call. "Hello?" I said, expecting to hear perhaps Mr. Taristo's voice.

"Hello, Ms. Lawson?" It certainly was not Mr. Taristo. It was the voice of some woman.

"Who is this?" I replied, wishing that I had not answered the telephone.

"My name is Margaret Rinaldi. I am an attorney working with the Attorney General's Office down here."

"Oh?" I replied, remembering that Jordan and Doug did mention that we would be squaring things away today.

"I'm sorry to have disturbed you, especially if it is too early. But we need to get together to go over everything."

"Oh yes," I replied.

"We'll meet with other prosecutors and federal agents in my office. But as you know, people have been arrested, yet the streets are still not safe. I'll meet you at the lobby of the hotel and escort you myself to make sure that there are no problems. Have all your documents ready to bring with us okay? I'll be there within the hour."

While I was listening to Attorney Rinaldi's instructions, my eyes became fixed on the windows overlooking Pennsylvania Avenue. The reflection of the television was depicting a live press conference at the federal courthouse, where the defendants would be prosecuted. A well-dressed woman was standing at the microphones, surrounded by reporters and officials behind her, discussing some event that had just transpired that morning. The name *Attorney Margaret Rinaldi* flashed at the bottom of the screen, identifying her to everyone watching.

Joshua emerged from the bathroom with a towel wrapped around his waist, just to make sure that all was okay. I placed my hand over my mouth in shock and pointed to the phone, then to the television set, and began to shake my head—partially in fright and partially in disbelief. Joshua quickly turned down the volume of the television and began to scroll through the other channels. Seeing the expression on my face, he turned off the television, threw on his clothes, and gathered our things yet again. He had become quite the professional packer, although this time, he didn't have much to pack other than a few cheesy T-shirts and sweatshirts that Mr. Taristo had purchased for us from the vendors on the sidewalks below (because that was just what we wanted—five-dollar T-shirts which read FBI). Ah well, it's the thought that counts.

"Attorney Rinaldi," I said, "we just need to get cleaned up, but sure: we'll meet you in the lobby in an hour. We look forward to meeting with you." I was proud that I kept my composure before hanging up the telephone. Then again, Joshua and I had certainly aced our unscheduled crash course in survival skills by the time we reached DC.

As we made our way past the agents stationed outside our door, one of them stopped us. "Uh, where are you guys going?" he said. I was frozen, naturally questioning whether or not he really was an agent. "Oh," Joshua replied, "they've called us to court. We'll be back. Thanks."

"Uh, okay. We'll have a car meet you downstairs," the second agent replied as he radioed the undercover detail outside on the sidewalk.

Carefully making our way down the back stairs of the hotel, I leaned in toward Joshua, "Josh, we don't even have documents in the room, and this chick was expecting us to bring them downstairs," I whispered, my voice shaking. "I know, I know, Beck. Come on. This isn't the time to chitchat," he replied, breathing deeply as he began skipping the last few steps on each landing and swinging himself around the banister to land on the next level.

Steering clear of the main lobby as best as we could, we made our way outside through a side door, walked around the corner, and summoned a cab directly across from the treasury building at the Hotel Washington. "Federal District Court, please," Joshua wisely instructed the driver, in the event that anyone within our vicinity was listening.

Two blocks later, I told the driver to change destinations. "Will you please drive us to the Supreme Court instead, sir?" The cab driver shrugged his shoulders without saying a word.

Despite the fact that our direction had not changed too terribly much, the ride, which I assumed should not have taken long at all, instead seemed to take forever between the tourists and routine DC traffic.

"Maybe we should have offered this guy extra money to drive faster—like through some shortcuts somewhere or something?" I whispered, scanning the licenses taped to the Plexiglas behind his head.

"No, Beck. Let's just stay lost and act natural. It's best," Joshua replied.

I hated sitting in such a low car and longed for tinted windows. Plus, in all the traffic, with license plates representing nearly every state in the country, I couldn't help but envision Miranda's lifeless body under the wheel of every dark Suburban we passed (of course, in DC, it seemed that every other vehicle was a dark Suburban). Joshua, feeling the same, pretended that we were newlyweds and cuddled low and close to hide our appearances as best as he could without drawing too much attention.

At last we pulled up to the majestic four-story white marble building that housed the Supreme Court. Joshua paid the cab driver, and the two of us quickly made our way toward the side entrance. "Are we really going in?" asked Joshua.

"Yep," I replied, quickly losing my breath. "Keep walking." Joshua, who was breathing heavy himself, gazed up at the building in amazement. "Cool," he said in astonishment. "I really didn't think the building was this big! I mean, it seems like it's taking forever to get to the side door."

"It is impressive," I replied, getting my identification cards ready in order for the security guards to review.

Fortunately, the security check for admittance to the Court was not very long, and we were soon safely in the building. Even more fortunate was the fact that no one appeared to have followed us. At the security desk in the main lobby, I phoned Kathryn, secretary to Justice McNaught, while Joshua perused the statues and portraits of former justices on the marble walls nearby.

Justice McNaught was an old friend of the family, and I knew that if there was anyone in Washington we could trust, it would be him. "Good afternoon, Justice McNaught's chambers. Kathryn speaking," chimed Kathryn. "Hi, Kathy? It's Rebecca Lawson," I replied.

"Rebecca Lawson? Becky? How are you? I haven't spoken with you in years."

"It has been far too long," I said. "Listen, I'm downstairs with a friend of mine. If it's okay, we need to come up to Justice McNaught's chambers and see him as quickly as possible if he's around. I'll explain everything when we come up." Without hesitation, Kathryn instructed a U.S. Marshal to escort us upstairs.

Justice McNaught himself was waiting for us at the main door to his chambers, still wearing his robe as a session had just concluded. "Well now, Attorney Lawson. How are you? It's about time you paid us a visit down here! And good timing, might I add." Justice McNaught raised an eyebrow and looked over the tip of his glasses resting on the bridge of his nose. "Especially since you are now receiving mail at my office?" The U.S. Marshal ushered us all in, closed, and locked the door. I finally felt safe. The thick, exquisitely sculptured oak served as a great barrier between us and the evil outside world.

Joshua seemed just as perplexed as the Justice. "Uh, Josh," I said, "I didn't send our stuff to Mr. Taristo's attorney. I sent it here." If Joshua had been a cartoon, his eyes surely would have popped out of their sockets at that very moment.

Keeping our meeting serious, I turned to my old friend. "Your Honor, I am so glad to see you. First, let me introduce you to my friend Joshua Tameron. He's an attorney too and works in the law library at Trenstaw University Law School." The two shook hands, Joshua in complete awe, standing in the presence of a Supreme Court Justice and still taken aback about our temporary Supreme Court post office box.

"Justice McNaught," I continued, "we are in a lot of trouble. I don't know a soul other than you here in DC, and I know that I can trust you."

The Justice ran his fingers through his wavy black hair, wrinkled his brow, and invited everyone to have a seat in his private office. The office was as impressive as would be expected: rich, thick mahogany wood and high-backed raisin-colored leather chairs—absolutely flawless and almost a century-old. Once everyone had settled in their seats, I continued. "There is a high-profile, mostly white-collar criminal matter that is about to be brought forward by the feds, and I am involved in the investigation." Justice McNaught interrupted, holding up the palm of his hand. "Wait a second, Rebecca. Slow down. You're talking much too fast. You're safe here, okay? Let me digest all of this. Now please, continue."

"I apologize," I said. "I'm just nervous. Anyway, I'm involved as an *investigator*. Joshua here is too." Joshua looked up and smiled, thrilled that the justice was again looking in his direction. "Anyway, I, well now—*we* have been contacted by several people posing as government officials trying to get ahold of our evidence, including down here in the District as recently as this morning. These people are extremely dangerous. I just need to borrow some space somewhere in the building if it's okay and have the real prosecutors meet us here where we know that it's safe. I just can't risk our information getting into the wrong hands. There is simply too much at stake, Justice McNaught, and I myself can't believe that I'm about to say this, but . . . my fear, believe it or not, is that our national security will be adversely affected in a *big* way if something goes wrong."

"Oh boy," said the Justice, massaging his chin.

"Look, I think, as an attorney, that this is all I should tell you in the off chance that the case somehow made it to you. I would never want to place you in a position where you would have to later recuse yourself, or worse, drag you in as a witness too."

Justice McNaught folded his hands and leaned on the top of his exquisitely carved wooden desk. "Attorney Lawson, I am very proud of you. Of course you can use space here. Kathryn will help you get set up, and the Marshals here can secure background and identification checks for you. In the meantime, you both look starved. We were just about to order lunch when you two arrived, so I'll order extra."

"Thank you, Your Honor," I said.

"Yes, thank you," said Joshua.

"My pleasure," said Justice McNaught.

Kathryn called the Attorney General's Office and instructed them to send their lead prosecutor to Justice McNaught's chambers, giving no reason why. The real Attorney Margaret Rinaldi, the one whom we had just seen on television, arrived within the hour and met with Joshua and me in private over lunch. Our meeting lasted two hours. We were given assurances that all evidence would be properly subpoenaed and no ethics rules would be violated. She also assured us that Doug and Jordan were legitimate, and reliable contacts in Boston would retrieve the documents that still sat in the locker at Trenstaw University. Other agents would contact Joshua's friend Dave to gather information and take pictures of his car—that was, if it was still parked in the lot in Connecticut.

"Oh boy, I didn't realize the time," said Attorney Rinaldi, glancing at her watch. "I have to get to court. It's two forty-five, and the first group of defendants are scheduled to be arraigned at three thirty." Attorney Rinaldi grabbed her purse, suit coat, and briefcase and scurried toward the door.

Justice McNaught met us in the hallway, this time having hung up his robe. "I trust your meeting went well?" he asked. It was strange seeing him in just a business suit after sitting with him for so long in his formal Supreme Court attire. Of course it was probably strange for him to sit in his office for so long with his robe on, but he was so intrigued with our extreme situation that he apparently didn't think to remove it.

"Invaluable, Justice McNaught. Thank you for letting us meet here," replied Attorney Rinaldi, shaking his hand. "And thank you for lunch. That was a nice surprise."

"Anytime, Meg. Big case, huh?"

Attorney Rinaldi was beaming. "This is really big, Your Honor. Bigger than I ever would have imagined in a million years."

Justice McNaught was intrigued, although he knew enough not to question much. "So I take it you will all be meeting again?"

Attorney Rinaldi turned to Joshua and me. "Actually, yes. I meant to ask you that. Next week okay?"

Joshua and I looked at one another, coming to grips with the fact that we would remain in DC for a while. "Sure," I replied, anxious yet cooperative, and relieved to finally know who we could trust.

Justice McNaught gave me a knowing look. "Tell you what, why don't you continue to hold your meetings here in the courthouse conference rooms. In fact, you may want to consider securing any evidence you collect here through the U.S. Marshals. It has a better chance of remaining safe. Just make sure that you tell them to keep your stuff separate from Ms. Lawson's."

"Good idea, Your Honor," said Attorney Rinaldi. "I'll do that."

Attorney Rinaldi left quickly, and Kathryn turned on the television so that the rest of us could watch the continuing news reports—not that we had any other choices on television. It was the "big story" unfolding by the second. "I'm glad they didn't need us today," said Joshua.

"Don't hold your breath, Josh," I replied. "We're always on call. But you're right. Looks like Doug and Jordan had everything covered there, and they are good people."

Donnie, one of the U.S. Marshals, was watching the events unfold with us. "You may want to save your voices, guys. Sounds like you'll both have a lot to talk about at trial, not to mention the press, if they have their way." Spoken like a true comedian, that's Donnie.

Joshua turned to me as though he was surprised that we had more work ahead of us: "Heh?" Everyone in the room had a good laugh as we shifted our focus back to the television.

Allan and Charlie were the first to be arrested, Charlie additionally on several counts, not the least of which was rape of a federal court officer. *Clever, Meg*, I thought. Little did I know that you'd attempt to wrap that one in down here in DC too. Attorney Rinaldi said later, of course, that the formal rape charge did belong in Vermont and would be taken care of later separately there. But for now, a shotgun approach, which incorporated details of all the illegalities, would do just fine. When she was done, any other state (and there would be many) could extradite any defendant they pleased as they saw fit and seek justice in accordance with their laws.

The arrests of other high-level executives from the Deering office soon followed. Over the next few days, executives of major credit card agencies across the nation were arrested, many of the arrests covered by the news live from Sanford International Airport in Florida—the routine stopover for most of them on the way to Allan's South American paradise. Indictments would later be returned on several members of other industries, the biggest being the meat industry and the gas industry. Last but not least, a very embarrassed Mr. Mulcahey, of the FBI, joined the club.

Attorney Rinaldi was thrilled. The arrests had been prepared well in advance, and with my and Joshua's contributions, they were able to not only take each defendant by surprise, but to also take each straight to the courthouse without delay.

Wasting no time at all, Attorney Rinaldi's office arraigned each defendant on the heels of the indictments. No one was surprised when the judge held every last one of them without bail and sent them off one by one to the local prison to await trial. Escorted out of the courthouse in shackles, Allan and Charlie stared right into the cameras. Their eyes were cold and piercing. I felt as though they were actually looking directly at me. Joshua took my hand as I gazed toward the floor. I just couldn't bear to look at either one of them, especially Charlie. "Heellooo, Rebecca!" Charlie crooned into the cameras, sending one giant tremor throughout my body. Everyone in the room felt the same chill. Everyone, that is, but Justice McNaught. He was furious.

At the end of the day, or rather, later in the evening, Joshua and I asked Kathryn if she would recommend a safe hotel in the area. It had been a long day, and we knew it would be a long trial. While we were not expected to remain in the courtroom for the entire length of the trial but where we had put together so much information, Joshua and I were eager to do so. We wouldn't be seated with the prosecutors, of course, but we were allowed as attorneys to remain behind them in the area known as *The Bar*, which was separated form the general public. The decision was entirely ours. "You know, Joshua, this may be long, but if it goes, we'll have the best seats in the house unless someone decides to throw in a motion to sequester us as witnesses." Joshua's eyes met mine and agreed. "Oh, you *know*, I'll be there," he eagerly replied.

Justice McNaught disappeared into his office and picked up the phone. A short time later, the Donnie from the U.S. Marshal's Office dropped us off at the Hay-Adams Hotel, again under new names as per instructions of the esteemed Justice McNaught.

The Hay-Adams was another luxurious hotel. Though it was not far from our original hotel, it was far enough away and safe enough for us, with a much lesser chance of our whereabouts being leaked to the press (and ultimately, Allan's lackeys). The hotel was located across from the White House and St. John's Church (oftentimes referred to as the Church of the Presidents), and we were fittingly assigned to the Federal Suite. This time, we took in a breathtaking, panoramic view of the White House, popular Lafayette Square, and St. John's Church.

"You know, Rebecca, you may have almost ruined my life, but you sure are making it up to me living in the lap of luxury," said Joshua. "You make a great roommate."

"Hey, we deserve it, don't you think?" I replied with a real smile while I gawked at the decorative ceiling, ornamental fireplace, and elegant linens. Then there was the master bedroom, which was accessed by french doors and even had its own small private balcony with a direct view of the White House. Of course again, plush bathrobes and slippers greeted us in a gorgeously crafted bathroom. To make things even more perfect, Justice McNaught had arranged for a private detail from the U.S. Marshals outside our suite: two at a time. The pair that stayed with us the most went by the names Sean O'Hare and Matt Pocareo. They were great guys, who at last made us actually feel safe in public. "I'd take a bullet for you any day, Becky," said Joshua, referring to our new bodyguards. "I know you would, Josh," I replied. "But I'd rather you didn't, comprendéz?"

Joshua laughed and agreed. "You know, Beck," he continued, "I'd like to take a shower, but it seems as though every time I'm in a bathroom, something happens. Do me a favor and stay off the phone for a few minutes, okay?" It was nice to have Captain Sarcastic back again.

I playfully grabbed the closest pillow from the bed and threw it at him. "Oh, give me a break!" I replied with a smirk. "Get your ass in there and spare the rest of us! You stink!"

Joshua charged me and tackled me on the bed, tickling me to the point where I could barely breathe. "Okay! Okay!" I shouted, desperately attempting to wiggle myself free. "Listen, Josh," I continued, as Joshua refused to surrender. "I might kick you by accident somewhere that might feel very unpleasant. So if you ever want to have children with some lucky lady down the line, I strongly suggest that you stop!" Joshua, laughing himself, had a moment of weakness, which allowed me to grab a good hold of his earlobe, and he let up. "Who needs a shower now, little miss?" he said, giving up and catching his own breath.

"Go on, get in there," I replied, slapping his backside as we both alighted from the bed. "What on earth will our new bodyguards think?" Joshua was still laughing as he clumsily closed the door to the bathroom, chanting "Bawmchickabawmbawm" while I walked over to the window and peered down at the new sights below.

Once Joshua finished showering and we were completely settled in our room, we phoned Mr. Taristo, this time on my cell phone (again, punching in a code and hoping that the call would not be traced). Everyone knew that we would obviously be staying in the vicinity of the District, but this time, we didn't want to risk someone narrowing down exactly which hotel.

Mr. Taristo understood the turn of events entirely and actually had us figured out not long after we left the Willard. In order to further the charade, Doug and Jordan wisely detailed two FBI agents who had similar characteristics as Joshua and me to continue occupying the hotel room as decoys. Everyone figured that there was a strong possibility that some of Allan's lackeys might continue their efforts with the hotel for a while, at least until the formal prosecutions began. The fake Attorney Rinaldi never made it through the ornate lobby that day; she was instead immediately arrested and was escorted back down the red carpet to the back of a police cruiser out front with cameras flashing, while other officers surrounded her partners in a stolen Cadillac with tinted windows outside the hotel. How fitting.

My next call was to Judge Haley. "Rebecca!" Judge Haley exclaimed. "I'm so glad you caught me. I was just about to leave the courthouse."

"You're there late this evening, Judge," I replied.

"Yes, well, I don't like to sit on pending motions, you know? The docket just never seems to get any smaller. Plus, I was watching the news."

I laughed. "True, true about the docket. Listen, Judge, I'm sorry to call so late, but I have been wanting to check in with you forever and let you know that I'm fine. I can't talk about anything of course but make sure you keep an eye on the news—maybe I'll say hello to you."

Judge Haley laughed. "While I have you here on the phone, I want you to know that you don't need to worry about any of your court appearances. My clerks here have already put everything over for two months and contacted your clients as well as opposing counsel. Anything else that is pressing will be handled by Attorney Cohen." A wave of relief went through my body. "Attorney Cohen?" I asked.

"Yes, Rebecca. You work so hard. Of course I'd secure the next best person to handle your files. She actually approached me on the bench this morning and offered her services right away, no questions asked. You may want to give her a jingle at some point when you get a minute. On top of it all, she's actually planning to do all of this pro bono for you."

"Really?" I replied. I was incredibly touched, although I also wondered if she took the appearances for her own publicity. Still, she was an excellent lawyer who rarely lost. And without sounding too egoistic myself, my duty was to secure the next best one to me, especially given the current situation. "Well, listen, Judge, I'd better let you get home. I'll be in touch soon, okay? And thank you for everything."

"The pleasure is all mine, Becky. And listen, have Mr. Hatley give me a call so I can verify with him when Attorney Cohen will be by your office to pick up the files. He's such a nervous soul. I don't want to worry him. He's been through enough with people breaking into the building and all."

"I'm sure he has," I replied, feeling horrible to put so many people in harm's way, let alone the simplest inconveniences. "I'll have him give you a call."

I was both relieved and proud of myself that I had always been extremely detailed in my case preparation. A five-year-old could have tried each one by the time I was through. Since I worked alone, I always took the stance that I needed to prepare cases for someone else to try so that my client would be protected in the event that I had to withdraw. Hmm, maybe I had jinxed myself.

Enjoying our new surroundings, Joshua suggested that we actually take advantage of the situation and relax. "Hungry?" he queried, glancing over the dine-in menu. "We can call everyone else we need to tomorrow, right? It's getting late."

"Yes, as a matter of fact, I am pretty hungry," I replied. Knowing that my sugar was low, Joshua didn't even offer me a peek at the menu. Instead, he walked over to the telephone, which rested on a fancy desk and ordered us a nice, healthy, normal dinner.

Joshua instructed the waiter to set up a table at the windows that overlooked the White House. Just behind, the beautifully illuminated Washington Monument stood proudly in the background, glowing in a perfectly clear, star-filled night sky. Joshua tipped the waiter, and once we were seated, he raised his glass: "To us," he said.

"To us," I replied, raising my own and meeting his.

As we sipped our wine, our arms playfully entwined as though we were toasting at a wedding. We noticed fireworks off in the distance. A chill went up my spine. We weren't even dating, and it felt like he was going to propose. Joshua seemed surprised too. It certainly wasn't a holiday weekend. Why the fireworks? "Must be the dead relatives," I said jokingly. Joshua laughed. We had so many things in common that it had become a long-standing joke that we would wind up together at the playful behest of family members who had gone before us. "It's really nice to finally have some things going our way," I noted, looking out at the spectacular Southern (and given the location, patriotic) light show.

All of a sudden, out of nowhere, Joshua leapt from his seat. Standing over me, he gently grabbed my face and kissed me, passionately. Although stunned, I didn't fight him, shivers traveling up and down my spine the entire time. *Oh my god,* I thought. *Things would forever be different.*

"You have beautiful eyes, you know that?" he said. "They sparkle. It's nice to see that again." Joshua gently ran his pinky finger down the side of my face. "There are so many colors. I have always been amazed at how you will wear certain outfits and sometimes they look green, other times blue . . . you have even specks of gold in there."

I didn't know what to say. I just smiled. I felt like I had been dating Joshua for years, although the butterflies of a schoolgirl flickered in my stomach, and the kiss was so natural. After we finished dinner, we went to bed, again platonically, me nuzzled into his arms. "You, my dear, have a good night," he said, his beautiful blue eyes looking into mine.

"You too," I said, looking back. After that, we slept and we slept and we slept. Everything was right in the world.

The next morning, I awoke to the now-more-familiar sounds of the city—emergency-vehicle sirens, car horns, whistles, airplanes, and the occasional helicopter. As I slowly opened my eyes, I could see the rays of sunshine beaming through the windows in the next room. Life felt good, and I was completely relaxed, enjoying the comfort of the luxurious bed into which my body completely melted. For the first time in a long time, I had not thought of the rape. I had not thought of my cat. I could finally take a deep breath without my lungs trembling, and I could actually lie motionless for a longer period of time.

It was then that I glanced over at Joshua. Our relationship had changed. *Dramatically.* Oh, how I dreaded the thought of losing him as a friend. He was my best friend. We had been through so much together. Uh, guys? Yeah, you up there in heaven? A little help here?

At that very moment, Joshua leaned over and gave me a kiss. "Good morning," he said, showing off those famous dimples of his. Wow, what a greeting. The same shiver as the evening before at dinner electrocuted my spine. "So we're okay?" he said, already knowing the answer.

I mimicked Joshua's smile, lifting the corner of my mouth just a pinch, deepening my own dimple with ease, and looking at him with big happy eyes. "We're perfect."

CHAPTER TWENTY-EIGHT

WELCOMING THE opportunity to be lazy at least for a little bit that morning, Joshua and I ordered a big country-style breakfast to the room, again dining at the windows that overlooked the White House. "This is delicious, Joshua," I commented. "Have you tried the fruit?" Joshua was enjoying a rather large piece of a waffle at the time. "Not yet, but I will!" he mumbled, covering his mouth. "The produce down here is so fresh."

After breakfast, Joshua thought it would be a good idea to call our immediate families, who surely had long been anticipating our calls. Little did they know, the U.S. Marshals had been detailed to them as well, just to be on the safe side. Thankfully, Allan and his people, busy with other matters, had steered clear of the lot of them.

"Oh, Rebecca, thank goodness. Are they treating you okay?" said my father, answering the telephone on the first ring.

"Yes, Daddy, I'm fine," I replied, soaking in the warm Southern sunshine through the windows. "Crazy stuff, huh?"

"Sure is, sweetheart. We saw you on the news, but—"

"Dad, hang on a sec. Do me a favor. Don't discuss me or the case or the news. Nothing. With nobody. Just in case, okay? It is very important that we wait until this is all over."

"Oh, right. Right," he replied. "Sorry. I should have known better."

"No problem. Listen, is Mom around? I only have so long on the phone, and I want to make sure to say hello."

"Sure thing, honey. Hang on a sec. Nancy!" he yelled. I cringed as in his excitement he forgot to cover the mouthpiece when he called out to her. Joshua, who was on the other side of the room on his cell phone, looked up at me, obviously hearing my father's voice. I playfully stuck my finger in my ear, pretending to be in a great deal of pain.

It was difficult to keep any composure after talking with my father. Although it had not been very long, it felt like years since I had spoken with him. After all that Joshua and I had been going through, I was never really sure that I would ever have the chance to speak with him, let alone with anyone else ever again. It was hard enough trying to say good-bye when he and my mom left my cabin in Vermont. The sense of relief just hearing his voice was overwhelming, making it quite the challenge to hold back tears. All I wanted to do was just sit down on the floor and sob. Alas, it was not the time, especially when my mother was running as fast as she could from the washing machine in the basement upstairs to the nearest telephone. Note to self: *Convince Dad to install a phone jack in the basement.*

Joshua looked toward me, finished with his phone calls. "Everything okay?" he mouthed. I nodded, and soon I heard the angelic yet neurotic voice of my mom. "Rebecca! I am so glad you called! Are you all right? I was so worried about you! I kept calling and calling your house, and the court and your office and Ken and your cell phone, and *then* I saw you on the news . . . now you're with Joshua, right?"

"I always liked that guy," chimed in my dad in the background.

"Mom!" I shouted. I could hear my father attempting to reel her back in as well. "Mom! Stop! Not another word! We can't discuss anything, got it? Nothing. Not me. Not the news. Just keep watching, okay?" What was supposed to be a relaxing phone call had now prompted me to begin pacing back and forth as I stared angrily at the White House. I felt like a legislator. Joshua thought the scene quite fitting actually, as he just sat and watched the show.

"No problem, sweetie," said my mother. "Tell you what, I'll have your father book us some plane tickets on the computer, and we will meet you and Joshua in DC as early as this afternoon. We'll bring Ryan too."

As much as I would have loved to see the both of them and my brother as well, it was not the time. It was not the time, and it was not safe. "Now's not a good time, Mom," I reluctantly replied. "I'm really busy right now. I have a lot of work to do for the upcoming trial."

"But Becky, honey, I need to see you. I need to see that you are okay in person. We can go for a nice, safe walk along the reflecting pool by the Lincoln Memorial. Do you remember, when you were a little girl, how infatuated you were with Lincoln? A president and a lawyer? Remember? You did all your history reports on him. Won't that be nice? It will get your mind off things. Besides, sometimes a girl just needs her mom." My mother was outright sobbing at that point.

Ouch. Not the thing to say right now, Mom. "Mom, listen. This is not an opportunity to go sightseeing for Joshua and me. Other people are attempting to sightsee *us.* Another time, Mom, okay? I promise."

My mother's voice began to crack. "Okay, if you insist—"

"Listen, I have to go. Tell my beloved brother that I was asking for him, okay? I'll call again when I can. I love you all." I hung up the telephone without tipping off my mother to my own sadness, missing each and every one of them. Joshua appeared behind me and wiped a tear from my cheek. "It will be over soon," he said reassuringly. "I promise. Things will go back to normal."

"Thanks, Josh," I replied, leaning back into his protective chest. "I know." I was really starting to become annoyed with welling all the time.

Later that day, Attorney Rinaldi informed us that we could go home for a short time: two whole days, as a matter of fact—just enough for us to check up on our homes and retrieve some things since we would be needed in the District for a while. At that point, Mr. Taristo had arranged a condominium for us through a friend working for the United States Postal Inspection Service. Our new abode was located in Alexandria, Virginia, just outside of Washington, DC. It was nothing like the suite that we had last enjoyed (or the one before, for that matter, which we would have liked to have had a chance to enjoy . . . perhaps our doubles would let us know just how impressive the amenities in the suite actually were), but it was high on a hill and overlooked all of DC. The view was simply spectacular, especially at night when we could gaze out at all the monuments that were perfectly illuminated from the balcony outside an oversized living room with saddle-colored leather couches and arm chairs, cherrywood bookshelves, and an entertainment center that only the most creative people in Hollywood could ever dream up. Oh, and did I mention the giant gas fireplace? I will admit that I always did prefer a wood fireplace, but cleaning random fireplaces in DC was not exactly on my list of stress-relieving activities at the time, and I was not about to get picky.

Our new haunt also offered two bedrooms, an eat-in kitchen, a dining area decorated in antique lacquerware, and a large Carrara marble bathroom—with a separate standing shower and Jacuzzi tub. I was getting quite used to the idea of my living space routinely including a Jacuzzi tub. Still, I adored my porcelain tub, which by now surely sported a thick layer of dust in the cabin back home; that is, if it was still intact.

The two U.S. Marshals who were detailed to us most of the time (and the ones we grew to like the most), Sean and Matt, secretly escorted us back to Boston on a private jet and again into Vermont. I did fight an incredible amount of guilt not visiting my family, let alone alerting them to me being in the area. We were so close yet so far away. Still, Joshua and I were subject to special instructions that required us to get back to the District as soon as possible. Plus, the fact that we had details assigned to us only further solidified the fact that we weren't out of the danger zone yet. Even five minutes of passing hellos could result in a lifetime of mourning, and no one was willing to risk that.

Joshua's visit did not take long. His place had already been left a bit on the messy side, so there weren't many surprises awaiting him there. He had actually gone upstairs without me, grabbing a few things and coming right back down. I felt bad sending him alone but chose to stay in the car, unable to bear the thought of walking through the threshold where I last held Miranda.

My home was (to no one's surprise) a little more disturbing when we arrived. After the Marshals made sure that it was safe for us to go inside, I walked up the old familiar wooden front stairs ahead of everyone else through the front door. In the living room, all of my furniture had been turned upside down, cushions were torn and strewn about, and pictures were ripped out of the frames. In the kitchen, cupboards were ajar, and pieces of dishes and glassware were broken into little pieces on the floor and on the counters. The refrigerator door was open, and the icebox (along with everything in it) had melted. Everything stunk of rotting food, not to mention the moving white rice. Oh, right. That wasn't rice. Lucky me.

Upstairs my clothes were scattered everywhere. My mattress had even been taken off the bed and pushed to the side. Glancing again at my disheveled bed, I made a mental note to get rid of the entire set: it was time to rid myself of bad memories and start anew. That and the towels too. And the toilet seat. Anything Charlie's bare ass or other parts would have touched was now destined to have a permanent date with the local dump.

The boxes in the extra room were opened, but it was the only place that really remained undisturbed. As I had described earlier, most of the containers held books and the like, and the last time that they were obviously touched was when I first placed them on the floor on move-in day. I sighed, thinking that I hadn't had enough time to unpack and sort those, let alone redo the rest of my house in its now-less-than-pristine condition.

I then made my way slowly toward the bathroom. Angrily stepping over the cover to the toilet, I glanced down at the porcelain tub. It was perfect. Apparently it was the only clean, safe, apparently untouched item in my home. After a minute, Joshua walked into the room behind me. "We'll get it clean. Don't you worry. *Together*." I gulped, now sick of fighting back my tears, nodded, grabbed a few things, and we made our way to my office downtown. "You know, not for nothing, but did they *have* to empty the liquid hand soap on the hallway rug too?" I said, rhetorically of course, and sniffled. "This whole place is going to need to be sanitized."

"Sanitized?" yelled Sean, looking around in the hallway downstairs. "I was going to suggest that you consider bringing in a Catholic priest." Matt smirked in amusement.

As we pulled up to my office with Matt at the wheel, Sean handed me a key. "Obviously, they had to have the locks replaced, Rebecca." I accepted the key from Sean, and we all began the long climb upstairs.

My office was not in any better shape than my home, although fortunately, it did not take long for Joshua and me to reorganize my files: they were in the same general area in which they were left. My Rolodex was missing, which irked me, and so was my answering machine and my desktop computer. Then again, so was my answering machine, phone book, and computer back home. Knowing that I couldn't worry about anything at that point, I tidied up the rest of my files and left them neatly on the conference table for Attorney Cohen. As we turned to leave, Mr. Hatley appeared in the doorway, flushed and out of breath. "Oh, Becky! Am I glad to see you!" he exclaimed, sloppily running toward me to award me with a big sweaty hug. "I had no idea what was going on!" he continued. "People had broken into the store and into your office, and then there were all the federalies." Mr. Hatley stopped abruptly and looked at Sean and Matt. "Uh, no offense, sirs—" Our *federalies* rolled their eyes as Mr. Hatley continued. "Anyway, they were all coming in and going out, and Financial Investments was temporarily shut down, and then your name came up on the news, and I had no idea what to do. You were gone!" Mr. Hatley then threw his hands up in the air. "Nowhere to be found! I was so worried!" Joshua, Sean, and Matt were all staring at Mr. Hatley, silent and dumfounded. Mr. Hatley had barely taken a breath, although his excited voice echoed down the stairs and into the store below. Joshua looked at Matt and crinkled his nose, obviously displeased with the pungent smell that permeated from Mr. Hatley's armpits.

"I'm so sorry, Mr. Hatley," I stated, pursing my lips and almost instinctively taking only shallow breaths myself. "I'm awfully sorry." His wife really ought to think about investing in some shirts that didn't so easily display sweat spots. Ick.

"Oh, it's no bother," he replied. "It wasn't your fault. We'll fix this place up good as new in no time. The wife says the building needs renovations anyway. Speaking of—"

I wisely interrupted my old friend, to the great relief of my travel companions. "Uh, Mr. Hatley, I'd love to talk, but I do have to catch a flight back to DC right away. Can I leave this key to my office with you? Attorney Cohen from the courthouse will be picking up some of my files to cover for me. Judge Haley's in charge of the whole thing if you want to give him a call in the morning, okay? He's expecting to speak with you."

"Sure, Rebecca. I'd be happy to. Stay safe, and we'll see you soon." With that, we finally made our way back down the stairs to the open air and out to the car. "Who the heck was that?" said Joshua.

"Don't ask. He's my landlord. He's a sweetheart and a gentleman and a hard worker."

"I can smell that," Joshua replied.

"Leave him alone, Josh. He's harmless. Still, he will talk your ear off forever if he had the chance."

"Quite the character," said Matt with a smile, looking in the rearview mirror as we drove away.

A week later, Joshua and I sat at our final meeting at the Supreme Court. Attorney Rinaldi was thrilled to report that the trial would take place sooner rather than later. Defense counsel had already filed several preliminary motions to dismiss and motions to exclude evidence, but the prosecution's case was so tight that all were denied. The defendants' final tactic appeared to be to simply defend. They would allow the prosecution to present what they had, and defense would rebut without calling anyone to the stand or offering any rebuttal evidence. That being said, trial was scheduled for the following month.

"Next month? That's almost unheard of!" Joshua exclaimed, surprised but thrilled that we would be done with the matter soon. "Yes, it is rare, Josh," Attorney Rinaldi replied. "But you must remember: the defense team consists of lawyers representing

some of the best defense firms in the country. Everybody wanted a piece of this
action, and a lot of the work is being done at reduced rates. These firms have plenty
of resources and plenty of money at their disposal. If you ask me, though, they
made a few grave mistakes in the process as egomaniacs bumped heads. Still, where
this case is so highly publicized, the judge has made sure that no one has used any
delaying tactics whatsoever. That's why we're able to move this thing along. Besides,
we have everything worked out, and the defendants don't want to drag this out if
they can help it, given all the media coverage. If this was any other case, believe me,
the discovery schedule would be delayed, evidence would be questioned, *lost*, held,
manipulated . . . any number of things to the point where the case would be tried
five years from now, not to mention the bail issue, where everyone's being held. Good
news, though: you two are two of the few that will not be sequestered. That being
said, you are both welcome to watch the trial from the courtroom if you like."

"Great!" said Josh excitedly.

"We wouldn't miss it for the world," I replied, determined to see the case through
to the end.

I enjoyed meeting with the prosecutors at the Supreme Court. There was
something about sitting in one of the most prestigious buildings in which an attorney
could sit, working on a case where the goal was to save (and recover) an obscene
amount of money for an enormous number of people while giving the general public
back a sense of trust and relief, perhaps even their lives. It was symbolic really and,
after all we went through, almost completely worthwhile.

Per Justice McNaught's request, everywhere that Joshua and I went, we continued
to be escorted by two U.S. Marshals, primarily Sean and Matt. We were absolutely
forbidden to take public transportation, let alone rent our own car, so we did feel
slightly spoiled as we were ushered around in a safe, bulletproof vehicle with tinted
windows. Because Sean and Matt executed their duties so well, there were times
when we began to feel relaxed enough to venture out on our own (especially if we
weren't needed to assist with trial preparation), but we were still instructed to remain
under the watchful eyes of our bodyguards.

Despite our desire to be let loose as we were in what seemed like another lifetime,
we did not need much convincing to enjoy the company of Sean and Matt wherever
we went. We looked at it this way: if those guys were serious enough to be willing to
take a bullet for little old us, they were more than welcome to come along. Besides,
all we had to do to get a serious wake-up call was turn on the television or glance at
the front pages of the papers at the paparazzi who flooded the sidewalks for quite
some time outside the Willard Intercontinental Hotel. Joshua and I shared many a
laugh seeing the undercover agents' faces on the front pages of the newspapers and
magazines as "going off to court for the day" or whatever caption worked with the
scenario. Our undercover doubles cleverly wore signature items so that the curious
would purposely spot them: for example, my double was always spotted with her
hair up in a french twist and routinely wore oversized brown sunglasses, a skirt or

khaki pants, and the same brown flat-soled shoes. Joshua's double would normally be seen with smaller mirrored sunglasses and a Red Sox baseball cap, jeans, and running sneakers. The agents were actually detailed from the United States Postal Inspection Service, another federal agency that also played a major role in the FI investigation itself. Allan, after all, did use the mail as part of his scheme. Anywhere a letter or package went with United States postage, a federal agent from the Inspection Service would follow closely behind with a smile. Anyway, it certainly made things easier for us to move around the District as needed.

"So these guys aren't the postal police?" asked Joshua.

"No, Joshua," Matt replied. "*Big* difference. Believe me, you don't want to mess with those guys."

Joshua seemed confused, never having heard of the inspection service, which prompted Sean to chimed in. "Don't get him wrong, Josh," he said. "Matt knows what he's talking about. The Inspection Service are a serious group of guys. The agency was started by Ben Franklin more than two hundred years ago. The only reason they are the ones posing as you two is because they happened to have a couple of agents that better fit your descriptions. Believe me, there was a lot of playful bantering going back and forth between them and the FBI because everyone wanted to play dress-up on this case."

"And stay at the Willard," added Matt humorously. "Nice gig."

"You know, I can't imagine what actors and actresses go through with all that on a daily basis," I stated.

"Oh, I know," said Josh. "No acting for us if this law thing doesn't work out, right?"

"Not unless Sean and Matt decide to leave the marshals and go private," I replied. Sean and Matt laughed. "Hey, Matt," said Sean, "at least they haven't shown any interest in singing. You heard Josh singing in the shower from the hallway the other day." I laughed while Matt animatedly cringed. "Ooh, you're right about that, Sean. That was a little rough." Having no comeback, as he was caught completely off guard, Joshua sat back in his seat and blushed.

Since Attorney Rinaldi decided that we were no longer needed to assist with trial preparation, Sean and Matt suggested that Joshua and I take some much-needed time to decompress over in Georgetown. Neither of us had been there before, so we were looking forward to seeing what all the buzz was about.

Georgetown was beautiful, reminding me of Beverly Hills, California, as we passed all kinds of upscale spas, salons, boutiques, restaurants, and furniture stores. It was nice to take our time, slowly making our way in and out of stores (with the marshals not far behind us, of course) and sauntering at our own pace down the old uneven brick cobblestone sidewalks toward the Potomac River. "These sidewalks remind me of Beacon Hill," said Joshua. "Yeah, they do, don't they?" I nostalgically replied.

I was thrilled to be given the opportunity to upgrade my pathetic wardrobe in such an incredible area. I was in desperate need of new suits anyhow and definitely wanted to look my best for the trial, as did Joshua. Somehow we thought that neither the Court nor our alma mater would appreciate our appearing in the cheesy FBI or Washington DC attire so kindly purchased by Mr. Taristo from the vendors outside the hotel. Still, I will admit that we did wear our new apparel from the U.S. Supreme Court with great pride—in the apartment at least. We couldn't dare risk getting noticed by the wrong people.

Joshua, as always, was particularly patient with me and even insisted that I have the boutiques tailor my suits, which I rarely, if ever, did back at home. It was just like old times: me running into dressing rooms with an armful of clothes and Joshua, my fashion critic, eagerly anticipating a personal fashion show with each. The rule was that the armful of clothes had to include something wild and crazy, something I would never in a million years otherwise wear or buy. When it was time for Joshua to shop, he would follow the same rules. At that point, we didn't care that Sean and Matt were watching. The only thing that would have made things better would have been if we could somehow convince them to dress up too. Unfortunately, they just weren't feeling it that day.

Later that evening, we dined at Sequoia, at the suggestion of Mr. Taristo. Sequoia was a high-end restaurant in Georgetown, alongside the banks of the Potomac River. Every so often, a pair of U.S. Customs helicopters would fly by, executing a routine patrol of the area. At first I was a little alarmed but soon became accustomed to the occasional rumble. Matt explained that it was just another means of ensuring the safety of the District, particularly after 9/11. My attention then turned to the trees that were located both inside and outside the restaurant, decorated with delicate little white lights, which brought a unique air of romance and relaxation to diners as the sun began to set. Joshua and I happily enjoyed a table adjacent to the oversized windows while we sipped champagne and dined on lobster bisque and only the finest-quality filet mignons. Securing that spot did, however, come with some convincing of our apprehensive pair of federal escorts.

The situation was a little awkward for us at first, as we originally insisted that Sean and Matt dine with us. But they graciously declined, instead enjoying their own meals far enough away to give us privacy, but close enough to ensure our continued protection.

The next morning, we returned to Georgetown, this time to stroll through Dumbarton Oaks gardens. Dumbarton Oaks was a nineteenth-century mansion that rested on ten acres of gardens proudly displaying cherry trees, herbaceous borders, forsythias, magnolias, and the most amazing roses of every color and size imaginable. The mansion itself apparently offered collections of art objects, rare books, artifacts, and manuscripts for inspection, but we were more interested in taking in the fresh air while we stopped and actually smelled real roses. It was absolutely exquisite, and a wonderful place to relax. The mansion on the premises had ironically been acquired by Harvard University many years before our visit, which gave the place a homey feeling for us while we lounged on one of the many beautifully sculptured benches scattered about the serene premises—so close to the busy city, but giving us at least a temporary feeling of being so far away.

"You know, Josh," I said, cradling a warm cup of coffee. "Yes?" he replied as he watched a couple of squirrels frolic around a tree. "It's so nice to relax, but what do you say we do something a little different, perhaps a little more *exciting*?" Joshua acted surprised, yet concerned at the same time. "I'm game . . . I think," he replied with a crinkled brow. "You always make me nervous when you use that mischievous tone. Don't you think we've had enough excitement for a while? Although I must admit I am relieved to see that you haven't lost your sense of adventure."

"I'm talking about *controlled* excitement," I replied, quite proud of my idea.

"Be *frightened*," Joshua said, singing a verse from *The Phantom of the Opera*. He was pretending to be reluctant, but in reality, he was eager to do something new. "So what is it exactly that you have in mind?" he asked, animatedly rubbing his hands together.

"The International Spy Museum!" I announced, my hubris magically illuminating the gardens while the sound of a chanting choir echoed in the heavens above us.

"Ahh," said Joshua with a raised eyebrow, a half smile, and a snap of a finger. "Let's go." With Joshua's approval, the marshals happily brought our rejuvenated selves over to the International Spy Museum in the District.

The museum was better than we imagined. Matt prearranged for us to go inside so that we would have a degree of privacy and safety, while he and Sean waited outside for us. Joshua and I traveled up to another floor in an elevator, which played exciting "spy" music to get us in the mood and sported all kinds of multicolored iridescent lights. When the doors opened, we were welcomed onto a level where we were "briefed" on a role that we would take on as an international spy. We then watched a brief five-minute film about the museum and the history of spies throughout time before being ushered into another room to check in with "border security," which was basically a computer testing how well we memorized our new secret identities.

Having made it *through the border*, we were free to roam about the museum, learning by many hands-on exhibits, how spying developed throughout the years. "Wow, this place is incredible!" I said to Josh, looking all around in awe with a childlike sense of curiosity.

"This was really a great idea, Beck!" he replied, toying with a computer. "Too bad we didn't do this before all the FI stuff huh? We certainly could have used a lot of these tips!"

"Like picking a lock?" I replied in jest. "You know, you do lose your keys an awful lot, my friend."

"Wiseass!" Joshua replied with a smirk.

As we roamed around, I began to look over my shoulder and brush my hair behind my right ear. "Josh," I whispered, "do you feel like we're being followed?"

Suddenly Joshua began jerking his head around, crouching down, and sprinting around the room, his hands formed in the shape of guns. "Yes, as a matter of fact, I do. Quick! This way!"

"Josh!" I said sternly, but more quietly. "I'm serious!"

Joshua stopped the antics. "You're just being paranoid," he replied, admittedly scanning the room himself. "The guys are outside. We're fine. They are the only ones who have been following us. You should have the feeling of *not* being followed right now. Lighten up, babe."

"No seriously. I'm getting really bad vibes."

We continued on through a few more exhibits and realized that we had taken more time than we had originally expected. Soon I heard the sounds of another group who had begun to catch up with us. "Hey, look at this!" Joshua exclaimed, pointing to the ceiling, obviously no longer worried about any followers and oblivious to the ones who were destined to appear at any second. "It's an air duct! You can go inside and listen to people like they did back in the day!"

"Right, riiiight," I replied, doing my best to hide my face while scanning the new people that were preparing to enter the room. "You know, I thought we were supposed to be alone. Don't you think that Matt and Sean would have gotten us out of here before these people came in? I know we're a little bit behind schedule, but you'd think they'd call or something."

"Wanna go in?" said Josh, obviously ignorant of what I had just said as I checked my cell phone for messages. Nope. Nothing.

"I think that's for kids," I replied, not quite as eager to wedge myself into some tiny crawl space and a little upset that Joshua obviously did not share my concerns. I wanted desperately to leave the building at that point and tried my best to remain calm. Suddenly I noticed that my cell phone was showing no signal. It was then that my survivor skills ominously urged me to hide.

"Come on. I dare you!" uttered an extremely persistent Joshua, grabbing my arm and dragging me around the corner as the group of people began to arrive. "Have you ever been in an air duct, Becky?"

"No, I honestly cannot say that I have, Josh," I replied, feeling frustrated and trapped.

"Well, now you'll be able to say that you have," said Joshua, guiding me into what I hoped wouldn't become a metal coffin.

Up a small set of stairs I reluctantly climbed, which led me into the dark metal air duct. Fortunately, it did have some small windows through which one could peer into the room below (and more importantly, breathe). Once I was completely inside, I felt Joshua push me in even farther so that he could have a look as well. "Stay on your belly and keep quiet," he whispered, taking on the part of a real spy. I, however, was struggling with my cell phone, my purse, and my apparently accurate sixth sense. Suddenly the voices of a couple of men below made Joshua and I freeze.

Two men, both wearing the same black scally caps—one who stood at about five foot eight and probably weighing in at about 280 pounds, the other at approximately five feet nine inches and about 225 pounds—were walking in an unnaturally slow fashion around the room directly below us. At that point, they were the only ones in the room as the rest of the group had continued on to the next exhibit. The thinner of the two began to talk, "Someone oughtta get those two. Especially that Rebecca chick. You know, if we bumped them off, we could be the next Allan Richardses." Joshua grabbed my ankle and squeezed, protectively, but also apologetically for not having taken me seriously in the first place.

"*Richards*, Lou. Richards. Not *Richardses*, you donkey," said the heavier man, pulling up a pair of oversized gray sweatpants under a black button-down cotton shirt. He wasn't exactly a contender for the next male fashion icon.

"You know, Denny, I could have sworn they were in here. Hey, what about the air duct there? Let's check that thing out!" Denny pulled Lou around the corner and started up the stairs. Joshua curled up as far as he could, and we both held our breath.

"Are you kidding?" said Lou. "We can't fit up there. That's for kids, for Christ's sake!" As Lou was going on his tirade, the air duct buckled, and I accidentally scraped my phone on the metal wall. *Please don't let them have heard that, please*, I thought. I knew that damn thing would buckle.

"Heh?" said Denny. "Hold on. Did you hear something?" Lou pulled an extremely disappointed Denny back down the stairs by his suspenders, which held up a pair of black pants over a cheap light blue long-sleeved cotton shirt (again, another sample for the fashion icon slush pile). "That was *you*, you moron. These stairs are attached. You're going to break the thing. Now let's keep moving before they get out of the building. We'll never find them then."

As the pair left the room, my cell phone chirped, its service finally back in business. "Turn that thing down, will ya?" said Joshua. "We gotta get out of here!" *Thanks, Josh. What a novel idea.*

I wiggled out of the shaft as quickly and quietly as I could. "I'm sorry!" I said, my heart pounding. "Then again, need I say it?"

"I know, I know, Becky. *I told you so.* I'm sorry too. Let's go."

As we climbed out of the air duct, we could hear Lou and Denny still arguing in the next room. "Hey, Lou," said Denny, "so do you think they're onto us here? Looking for that Vermont chick and the boyfriend and all? I mean, really. This is a *spy* museum. Or maybe . . . this is all one big test, and when we get to the bottom, there's a recruitment station if we've passed our security exit points at the end, ya know? Wouldn't that be so cool?"

"You are such a dope!" said Denny, marching forward and slapping Lou on the back of the head. "No, this is not a recruitment center. And keep your voice down, will you? Did you take your meds this morning? You're just babbling on and on . . . thought after thought after thought. You're driving me crazy!"

Lou was entirely unfazed. "You're just mad, Denny, that I made it through border security at the beginning and you didn't," he replied, playing with the buttons on a case that displayed a pencil with a secret camera inside. "Don't worry. When the president asks me to be his personal spy, I won't rat you out. I promise."

Denny, on the other hand, had reached boiling point. "How many times do I have to tell you? This is fake! And we wouldn't have lost these people if you hadn't insisted on getting through your precious security checkpoint! We're not here to play around!" Pounding his fists together, he stormed off in a huff.

Joshua and I had no other choice but to carefully retrace our steps and get back to the Marshals as fast as we could. We had trouble getting back on the elevator as group after group began to pour out of the elevators and onto our floor. Luckily, we finally made it down without being stopped or, even worse, noticed. I, of course, made it down irked.

Once we had made it safely outside, we found Sean speaking with the local police, and two local cruisers were parked out in front of the building. Seeing us, Sean immediately ushered us into the car, climbed into the passenger seat, and we all rushed away with Matt at the wheel. "Wow, you guys are good . . . So? What happened?" said Joshua.

"Yes, they were monitoring you guys upstairs," Matt replied, looking in his rearview and side-view mirrors. "Those clowns were just a couple of drunks who frequent the ESPN Zone, Hard Rock, and Capital Brewing Company. On top of being charged for their intentions with you, the thinner guy stole the cigarette lighter off James Bond's car. Believe me, they won't bother you anymore. You have nothing to worry about with them. It's all good. That first group and the rest that arrived contained the museum's undercover security. Everyone in the area knows who Denny and Lou are. I guess these guys had hidden in the bathrooms after spotting us arrive and recognizing the names from the news. Anyhow, they slipped past the guards and started milling around, jumping into the group directly after your originally private unguided and, I guess now, *not-such-a-good-idea* tour." *Ya think, Matt?*

Matt continued, oblivious to my attempts to stifle my internal sarcastic dialogue. "Once we saw them on the cameras, we had no choice but to let the groups start through, and we were able to catch them in the act. Before their antics, they had paid for the tickets and weren't technically considered trespassers yet. We needed something solid in order to move in. You were never in real danger, guys. Don't worry."

Joshua and I were relieved, but still felt more comfortable with the idea of spending the rest of the day back at the condominium, watching our old favorite movies starting with *When Harry Met Sally*. "At least our friends today have good taste in pub grub, huh, Ms. Albright?" said Josh, as we were at last curled up on the soft leather couch under a couple of blankets, popcorn bowls in hand. I rolled my eyes, still worried about other creative criminals out there who had the potential of crossing our path, looking to impress Allan. "Yes, Harry," I replied, resting my head on Joshua's shoulder.

"No more risky extracurricular adventures for now?" asked Josh.

"No more risky extracurricular adventures for now," I answered, praying that my statement was accurate.

CHAPTER TWENTY-NINE

A S MUCH as I feared other copycats dreaming up their own grandiose ideas of somehow impressing Allan by attacking Joshua and me, I had no other choice but to refrain from questioning my trust with Matt and Sean. Besides, if I really wanted to lose sleep over things, I could focus instead on the angry South American groups (with my luck, they would be drug lords) who were suddenly cut off from their endless supply of precious payoffs, in large part because of me.

Our lives were soon engulfed by the Financial Investments case, which was soon nicknamed by many as "the trial of the century." Lord knows how many of those there would be in my lifetime. In any event, every media entity covered it, a few of which included twenty-four-hour live telecasts. In fact, the story was so widely publicized that the mayor of Washington DC ordered the streets immediately surrounding the federal courthouse to be completely blocked off, redirecting the traffic elsewhere. The media and the public, many chanting and holding homemade signs that showed their disgust for Allan: "Let Allan have a taste of his own food!" "Make Allan the Beefeater!" "Allan is no longer *Rich*-ards!" And my personal favorite: "You thought you could save money but can you save yourself?" They gathered in the street as far as security would allow—all just to catch even a brief glimpse of the players involved.

Sean and Matt escorted us to the Court in a new high-security Ford Expedition with bulletproof doors and tinted windows. Our new ride offered so many high-tech gadgets in the car, and Matt drove so fast, with blue lights flashing, that Joshua and I felt like we were part of some type of presidential motorcade. The awkward part of the whole scenario was that although we were assured our safety, the Marshals still insisted that we wear bulletproof vests into the courthouse. Talk about role reversal: we were victims, not defendants. Still, if Joshua had his way, we would all be dressed in full-blown raid gear: helmet and bulletproof personal raid shield included. I sarcastically suggested the Pope-mobile.

I must admit, however, that once we escaped the crowds, the courtroom itself was extremely impressive. It was large, immaculate to the point of sterility, and fully equipped with the capability to use nothing but the most advanced media technology to ease the understanding of the truly complex and difficult cases. The walls were all crafted out of rich mahogany wood and proudly displayed oil portraits of former judges. The vaulted ceilings, which held hundreds of small round fluorescent lights, seemed high enough to commingle with the stars themselves.

Facing Judge Jack B. Gaviston's bench, the jury members were assigned seats in a raised area to the right against the wall, not far from the court stenographer. To the left was an oversized "dock" area where defendants would enjoy the proceedings, near the chief probation officer's station. The judge's intricately carved mahogany bench was prominently raised above everyone. To its right, attached yet sitting slightly lower, was the witness stand. Centered out in front was the clerk's desk, set just below the judge. On the floor, facing the clerk, were four tables: two for the prosecution near the jury and two for the defense near the dock.

Behind those tables, a couple of rows of seats were made available, and specifically designated for attorneys and agents. This area was otherwise known as The Bar. The Bar was separated from those designated for the general public, who were located behind the bar and separated by a small mahogany wall with carvings that matched the judge's bench. Centered swinging doors granted access to the bar from the gallery where the general public sat. In the far back of the room, there was yet another separate section, which was reserved for the media and their equipment. I recalled reading somewhere that with the rapidly growing changes in modern technology, many courthouses across the country were redesigning their courtrooms in similar fashions. In fact, some offered such excellent acoustics that one could whisper in the dock and still be heard anywhere in the courtroom. That extra addition, of course, was considered to be a major flaw in the opinions of most defense counsel.

The prosecution's case began with three and one half weeks' worth of testimony from various witnesses who represented groups of victims from across the country. Some of the witnesses personally had experienced food poisoning, some witnesses had family members who had died from food poisoning, and other witnesses or family members had suffered industrial losses at such places as oil refineries: all at the hands of Allan and his cohorts. Other victims unsurprisingly represented stores who lost money when food was pulled from the shelves, and the last group represented victims, furious with having been swindled by Allan and Financial Investments. These victims could not, however, explain how Allan was responsible for everything that happened.

At the end of the victims' testimony, the case turned to Joshua and me. Between the two of us, our testimony took up almost an entire week. I served more as a summary witness, where my testimony focused on a detailed explanation of how Financial Investments customers were tricked into thinking that they were investing in real stocks and mutual funds: "Well, Attorney Rinaldi," I explained, "customers chose a rate of risk for their investments: low, moderate, or high. Statements were sent out to them monthly, each of which looked real and, for the most part, followed the actual performance of the stocks in the market. On top of that, quarterly reports were sent, again tailored, which mimicked the actual stock market with carefully constructed graphics going up and down in all kinds of various colors. Most investors signed on for the long run. They didn't know much about stocks, let alone care to follow them in the paper. And as the victims testified earlier, most consumers just scanned the pretty graphics on the statement each time they received them and then either threw them away or put them aside."

"How did clients of Financial Investments make payments, Attorney Lawson?" asked Attorney Rinaldi, wearing an obviously expensive gray-and-black tailored suit, her black hair pulled tight in a french braid secured neatly into a bun.

"After the initial deposit, clients most often allowed Financial Investments to withdraw directly and automatically from their bank accounts, paychecks, and credit cards—unless they paid in cash or by check after receiving a statement—assuming that their money would just pile up. The automatic withdrawal was the method clients were encouraged to use by FI. It was the clients' expectations that years later, when they needed to cash in, a sum of money would be waiting for them. All they had to do was just say the word. Allan seemed to rely on the notion that many people are willing to take risks to some degree. It is human nature to take risks if the reward is large and the perceived risk is small. It is human nature to want easy money."

Many people around the courtroom nodded, and others pursed their lips while I continued my explanation. "Now like gambling, anything can happen with the stock market, so nothing would be Allan's fault: Allan could point to the 'market' if there was ever a loss. The problem was, nothing was ever filed on behalf of these people. These people owned nothing." The members of the jury, all who impressively dressed up for the occasion (heeding the warning that the case would be televised), sat in their chairs, most shaking their heads.

"So how, in your opinion, Attorney Lawson, was the scheme so successful?"

I scanned the jury and took a deep breath, discreetly playing with a loose button on the jacket pocket of my new olive green suit that I purchased in Georgetown, making a mental note to take Joshua's advice and always have my suits tailored. "The reason that the scheme was so successful was for the most part, employees of the lower levels of Financial Investments were legit, so there really wasn't any acting involved: every FI representative held degrees and experience in the area. As far as these lower-level people knew, everything was on the up-and-up. The few that ever reached executive level were already a part of Allan's scheme, strategically planted in the lower levels to monitor legitimate unsuspecting employees and create a false hope of opportunities for eventual advancement. Lower-level employees were mainly hired to follow the stock market and advise and maintain clients. To anyone walking in the door, these guys were real. They even taught at Conifer Community College not far from the company in Vermont. Higher-level employees were in charge of 'securing the stock,' which, as I learned the hard way, rarely, if ever, happened. The only stock secured was stock owned by and for Allan personally, or perhaps someone who was connected with his scheme."

The media's mumbling from the back corner of the courtroom began to elevate a little too loudly, and the judge shot them a strong look of admonition. Immediately the undertones came to a sharp halt, as no one wanted to risk their precious spots in the courtroom. It took a lot of debate before the learned and rarely overturned gray-haired Judge Jack B. Gaviston allowed the media, let alone the general public, access in the first place. As ordered, the trial took place in a room with no windows as it was.

"Please continue," said Attorney Rinaldi.

"No problem," I replied, mindful to stop fidgeting with my button. "Allan and the other higher-level executives—mostly from New York, under the careful watch of his brother Jim—took care of the rest by depositing the money in several layered bank accounts. Initially, client funds were deposited into the general Financial Investments account. Approximately 6 percent would be withdrawn monthly from that account and then transferred into a second high-interest account in Tucson, Arizona."

"Okay," replied Attorney Rinaldi as the jurors began to resume taking notes, several obviously not thrilled at the idea of discussing anything to do with math.

"Now," I continued, doing my best to speak slowly and clearly, "the Tucson account was classified as an expense account. But it was tracked by Allan in his office in Deering as a 'reinvestment account.' That was one of the things that first tipped me off. A percentage of the funds from that account was then transferred to a third account in Las Vegas, Nevada, again labeled 'reinvestment.'"

"Now I know what happens in Las Vegas is supposed to stay in Vegas, but I'd like you to tell me more about Las Vegas," said Attorney Rinaldi, smiling comfortably, scribbling notes of her own on her legal pad, and pleased to regain the attention of a few jurors whose eyes had begun to glaze over in expected boredom.

Attorney Rinaldi's tactic had worked. A couple of the younger male jurors—numbers 2 and 6—leaned forward in their seats, waiting to hear some juicy details, which in their minds most certainly would involve at least half-dressed well-endowed women. At the same time, two of the younger female jurors—numbers 9 and 10—from the opposite end made eye contact, hopeful that they would hear something exciting involving at least some half-dressed meaty men.

"Sure," I replied. "The Las Vegas account was held in the name of Harold Weston, a fictional character who replaced Ron Peters on certain documents that Joshua, uh, I mean, Attorney Tameron and I had reviewed. Ron Peters was actually the deceased landlord of the building in New York housing the New York branch. No one knew that Mr. Peters had been murdered over a decade earlier in the depths of South America: his personal bills were all paid off, and taxes were filed yearly on his and his property's behalf. Sadly, no family members ever came forth until this case became public to question Mr. Peters's existence. Interestingly, each year rent was increased by Mr. Peters and marked on the books as paid in full, in cash, which Allan naturally wrote off on his taxes. He was big into that: writing things off on taxes." Finishing that statement, I was painfully aware that I had grossly disappointed the jurors, who sat back in their seats.

"Did any other dealings take place in Las Vegas?" asked Attorney Rinaldi, continuing her line of questioning.

"Yes," I continued. "Funds from the Las Vegas account were withdrawn occasionally and transferred into an account at the Grand Royale Hotel and Casino—Las Vegas's biggest hotel and casino—under the watchful eyes of Bobby Resterson, head of security. Anytime the need arose, Bobby made available from the casino any number of bank checks, left blank. The bank checks were then gifted to executives of major industries when they accepted invitations to stay at the hotel. They consisted of mostly credit card, oil, and food, nationwide, also working for Allan on the side. You know—like Aquicard, Energec Oil, and the Conifer Meatery—the ones that have been referenced in this trial. Mr. Mulcahey and the Deering sheriff even received a few of those checks themselves from time to time." Everyone turned to face Mr. Mulcahey and Sheriff Patterson, sitting in shackles next to each other with several other defendants in the dock whose cases had not been severed. Mrs. Virginia Patterson, the sheriff's wife, sat in the back of the courtroom, surprised and steaming, knowing that she had never seen a dime of the money, let alone an invitation to accompany her husband of forty-five years on a trip. She had been under the impression that her husband was out quail hunting *again*.

Attorney Rinaldi paused for a moment and then continued her questioning. "So tell me this: what would Allan and his company stand to gain in exchange for the checks?"

"Well, other than pure bribery to keep the scandal quiet, these checks were used by Allan to control the stock market. For example, should the alleged value of the FI accounts get too large, Allan would need to arrange for the market to drop, thus making it appear to the victims that they had 'lost' money so that they would expect less if they ever tried to cash in. As we talked about earlier, FI, at least on paper, invested client funds in certain companies in a few industries such as the meat industry, where Allan had highly placed executive friends who could cause a problem.

"In exchange for the checks, the meat industry—like the Conifer Meatery, for example—might be faced with, *say*, bad hamburg, and the value of their stock would drop immediately along with the decrease in sales while meats were quickly pulled from the shelves. The key thing to remember is that the 'problem' was created at Allan's request by his industry buddies, but they needed to involve the public and make it real. Simply announcing a recall or a reported accident would not be good enough. In order to escape suspicion, they needed to cause contaminated food to be sold to the general public, to cause major oil-refinery fires, to allow personal financial information to be accessed by unauthorized people, and, in the end, to allow others to report the problem. That way, the market would naturally reflect the impact of the problem. The courtroom was completely silent, and I was very aware that they were listening to my every word as I continued to explain. "Eventually consumers would come back and 'reinvest,' taking advantage of the lower price of stock, especially those living in the meat and farming communities wanting to support their neighbors. Companies in the meat industry—if they were part of

Allan's scheme—would then increase their selling prices *as necessary in an effort to keep people safe*, where in reality, procedures and machines remained the same. The situation was win-win for everybody, except for Financial Investments clientele and the average consumer, especially the occasional poor soul who ate bad food at the behest of some food industry puppet trying to impress Allan. Since Allan and his associates controlled when these catastrophes would happen, they could easily sell their personally owned stocks within a safe-enough window before the incident was to happen, then buy back in immediately once the prices dropped. So long as the timing was right and the catastrophic accidents were shuffled a bit amongst the industries, no one would have any reason to question Allan or his closest associate assistants' personal portfolios." Looking back toward the media, I was impressed that they remained silent, they too giving me their undivided attention. "In addition," I continued, "these market manipulations were used to control the exposure to the FI investors. If a client, who was owed a substantial sum of money, looked like they were going to withdraw their money, a well-timed market crash would save FI from losing a great deal of money and would protect Allan's scheme from being discovered." One elderly juror—juror number 5—sat in her seat with her mouth dropped, thinking of the meat loaf she had left for her husband for lunch. Juror number 4 took notice out of the corner of his eye and reached out to close it, keeping his incredulous attention to the prosecution's continuing big reveal.

"So are you telling me that people other than Mr. Peters died as well, Ms. Lawson?"

"Yes, I am. We heard from some of those families earlier. Some died, and some were treated for food poisoning. And it was not an accident."

"Was the meat industry the only one affected?"

"No, no, no," I continued, shaking my head. "Let me give you another example: Oil companies followed a similar plan. A 'tragic leak' would suddenly occur in a remote area or a semicontrolled explosion at an oil refinery like Energec in any one of the Southern states, and Financial Investments would pay for the cleanup from South American funds, or other real estate companies it owned, claiming, of course, charitable deductions on the taxes. Stocks would naturally plummet, people would reinvest, and prices would increase. Like the meat industry, the situation was win-win: for Allan and Financial Investments." Juror number 4 then dropped his own mouth, and juror number 5 promptly lent her assistance to close it. Having a perfect view of the scene, the clerk smiled slightly from behind a file folder.

"Attorney Lawson, do you have any information concerning South America?"

"Yes, I do, as a matter of fact," I replied. "Allan had also opened up one of his many South American bank accounts in his deceased mother's name. A portion of the South American funds from that account, along with the Las Vegas bank checks, were paid to various government officials of different levels and agencies, who promised to keep the scandal quiet. Employees of Financial Investments who were deeply involved in the scheme likewise received a commission for their services,

and many enjoyed their own bank accounts in South America as well. You can even
see some of the documents in the pictures that I took, which you had admitted as
evidence earlier in the trial."

"Yes, thank you, Attorney Lawson," said Attorney Rinaldi, pleased with the way
the trial had been going. "Is there anything else that you would like to add?"

"I don't think so. I know Agents Doug Asterly and Jordan Miller from the FBI
have much more to add. In a nutshell, funds to Financial Investments were endless.
Every four weeks, executives met in South America to party, receive funds and
instructions for the following month with their respective parts in the scheme."

"Thank you, Attorney Lawson," replied Attorney Rinaldi. She then turned to the
judge. "I have nothing further." As the defense had no questions for me, Judge Gaviston
smiled and nodded in my direction. I then resumed my seat to the right of Joshua
(sporting his fancy new navy blue pinstriped double-breasted suit, which had also been
purchased and finely tailored in Georgetown) in the front row of the bar behind the
prosecution table. Allan and Charlie, as well as the guests of the entire dock, stared at
me with looks of hatred and revenge as I carefully walked to my seat.

When they weren't shooting threatening looks at the parade of witnesses called
to testify against them, Charlie and Allan continued to angrily stare at me for the
remainder of the trial. At first I was uncomfortable, but my anxiety was short-lived
as my own anger began to fester at what they had done to me and to the thousands
of others.

Charlie and Allan were furious with each other as well. During one of the final
recesses, one of the exchanges between the two became heated, much to the delight
of the rest of the courtroom: "I always hated when you used the 'I wasn't thinking
because of the stress of my job' excuse to cover your being an asshole," barked Allan.
He then turned to Len Jacobs, his leading defense attorney: "And who, by the way, is
taking care of my home, my mail, my bills, my plants, and my cat? If she doesn't get
fed, I'll sue everybody here and the United States of America!" Charlie's head snapped
as he turned from gawking at Attorney Rinaldi's legs to face Allan intently.

"Don't worry, Allan," snickered one of the assistant prosecutors, making cryptic
notes on a fresh yellow legal pad. "We have your mail covered, and I have a strong
hunch that after this, your credit may be a tad questionable."

After Allan's tirade, Charlie gulped. "Uh, Allan? I've been meaning to tell you
something. I was caught up in the job, I swear, and, uh, about your cat."

Charlie leaned toward Allan and whispered into his ear. Allan's mouth dropped.
"You DUMBASS!" he screamed. "And what's with raping the girl anyway, you sick
fuck! I never told you to do that, and now they're wrapping me into that too!"
The prosecutors were laughing as they and the media feverishly took notes, the
media, of course, leaning as far forward as possible with dictation machines and
microphones.

"Hey! Keep your mouth shut, will you?" warned Attorney Jacobs through
clenched teeth, his voice stern and frustrated, commanding much more presence

than his general appearance. Attorney Jacobs stood just over six feet tall, with medium-length dark wavy hair pulled back in a ponytail, revealing extremely oily skin (fluorescent lighting is rarely flattering on anyone) down which the occasional beads of sweat easily ran. Joshua's personal favorite was the pinky ring: "I mean, really, can you trust anyone with a pinky ring?" he remarked.

"Quiet, Josh," I replied, remembering the ring Allan routinely wore on the pinky finger of his right hand and wondering if Attorney Jacobs smelled as bad as Mr. Hatley.

Charlie looked directly at me in a sickening, seductive way as I shifted in my seat. "Consider our little tryst a perk of the position," he sneered, sending a wink in my direction. Joshua squeezed my hand and gently turned my head, but not without first shooting a piercing, territorial look at Charlie. My stomach was filled with disgust, knowing that the entire altercation had been broadcast live for all the world to see, including my poor mother, who, I later found out, was caught by the strong arm of my father as she almost fell off the couch back at home in Massachusetts. Obviously, no one back home had yet been told the entire story about my relationship with Charlie.

"You were told to date her: *to keep an eye on her.* That was it!" continued Allan. I looked at my shoes and partially covered my eyes with my right hand as half of the television cameras focused on me for a reaction.

Attorney Jacobs was furious. "I said enough!"

"Where's Nathan anyway? He's my real attorney!" shouted Allan.

"In the dock, Mr. Richards," snickered Attorney Rinaldi. Everyone turned their attention back to the dock where Nathan Harmot, Allan's former attorney, sitting in the upper-left corner along with the other defendants, raised his cuffed hands (one which, by chance, also happened to display a pinky ring) in a meager attempt to send Allan a little wave and a smile. Watching the entertaining display, I noticed that despite the fact that the majority of the defendants wore business suits, somehow those shackles just always seemed to strip the air of confidence in any argument that might suddenly stem from their lips.

Just as things had begun to get interesting, the bailiff returned to the courtroom: "All rise!" he shouted.

People hadn't even begun to fully stand when the sainted Judge Gaviston stormed up to his bench. "Order! Order in this room!" he shouted, slamming his gavel against the bench several times. I, of course, didn't hear a thing, picturing Miranda's collar on the floor of Dave's car in Connecticut. Suddenly it hit me: Miranda was alive? Charlie killed Allan's cat? But what about her collar? Attorney Rinaldi quickly passed a note back to Joshua and nodded in my direction:

> Miranda's *fine.* She's with Joshua's neighbor.
> Forgive me for neglecting to tell you?
> —MR

Joshua and I smiled as a tear made its way down my cheek. Doug, sitting in the row behind us, leaned forward and patted my shoulder.

Attorney Rinaldi, fighting to contain her amusement at the defendants' bickering, called Doug to the stand. After he was sworn in by the clerk and answered Attorney Rinaldi's preliminary questions concerning his background, the scheme continued to unfold: "So, Agent Asterly, what would happen to the Financial Investments customers who wanted to collect their funds?" she inquired, still desperately trying to mask a grin from the earlier events.

Doug was calm, clear, and all too eager to explain. "Well," he said, sitting forward in his seat, "in those situations, a meeting with a Financial Investments representative was scheduled. The customer was instructed to bring with them all of their stock certificates and most recent FI statement. The FI representative would then compare the amount of money the customers thought they had invested with the most recent statement received from FI and with what FI had on their computer. That would determine whether or not to put the guys on the top floors on notice that a big account was in danger."

"Could you tell us a little more about the stock certificates?" asked Attorney Rinaldi.

"I'd be happy to," continued Doug, scanning the defense tables with a sarcastic smile. "Each certificate was fake. They were all printed in South America and shipped back every month with the visiting executives, who traveled mainly through Florida's Sanford International Airport."

"Why South America?"

"Allan and his brothers spoke the language fluently. Plus, Allan went on vacation there many times. He loved it. After spending so much time there, he decided to buy a bunch of property, and he bought *a ton*. Of course, on television, they always glamorize being able to hide things down in that area, and Allan was drawn to that style of life. The fact was he gave a lot of money to the right people down there, and they loved him—they protected him. What better place to print money and certificates, right? Especially when Allan assumed that the people printing them didn't know what they were." Doug then turned to face the jury. "It was Allan's theory that he could continue any operation he wanted down there no matter what the size and still hide from anyone poking around at his stuff in the United States if they ever began to question him. Truth was, it did work . . . for a while."

"Thank you," Attorney Rinaldi responded, putting on a pair of black-rimmed reading glasses and collecting another legal pad from one of the assistant prosecutors. "Now say a customer after the meeting still wanted out. What then?"

"It was rare for a customer to leave the company. Usually they changed their minds after they were offered a fake certificate for an obnoxiously larger amount, just for being a 'valued client.' Depending on the area of the country the customer was from, their certificate might be from an industry to which they could relate, like beef or spinach or oil . . . you name it."

"What do you mean by 'an industry to which they could relate'?" continued Attorney Rinaldi.

"Okay. Let's take Vermont, for example. Most of the Vermont customers had families and neighbors who worked on or owned farms. Most people ate beef, so it was like they were supporting their families and neighbors by holding stock in the trade like the Conifer Meatery. Plus, the amount of the certificate was tempting."

"Was there a catch?"

"Of course. The catch was that the customer had to agree not to withdraw from their accounts for a period of time."

"Was there a penalty?"

"Yes. The penalty would be a complete forfeiture, including the amount of the consumer's original investment."

"Ouch!" blurted juror number 4, swiveling in his leather seat.

"Order!" exclaimed Judge Gaviston as he struck the bench with his gavel. Juror number 4 was already putting his hand up apologetically while the others giggled. Attorney Rinaldi and those at the prosecution table were beaming. The media and the people in the back of the courtroom couldn't help but laugh. "Quiet please!" barked out the main court officer while the others who had strategically placed themselves around the room shot everyone respective authoritative looks demanding silence.

Attorney Rinaldi continued: "Did the customers ever question this agreement?"

"Sure. But the representatives, or 'financial advisors,' simply responded by saying that it was for 'the customer's own financial good.' Otherwise, they would never save, let alone, ever make any money."

Attorney Rinaldi nodded dramatically as she began to cross the room slowly, fiddling with her black-and-gold Cross pen. "And what if the stockholder died?"

"Oh, beneficiaries, and even their attorneys, did come in occasionally to cash in their accounts. But they too pretty much bought into the scam, and eventually left the office with their own accounts. The employees at Financial Investments were very convincing. These lower-level employees believed that the company was legit and that they were helping these investors. Heck, like Attorney Lawson said earlier, they taught at the local community college just outside of Deering, Vermont."

"Go, Bobcats!" shouted an obviously deranged young man from the back of the courtroom as though he was in attendance at a football game.

"Okay, that is it!" furiously shouted Judge Gaviston. "Remove that man!" Before the judge could finish the last sentence, the unruly spectator was surrounded by three court officers who immediately began to escort him from the room, all wondering how he ever made it through security to enjoy one of the few seats that remained available to the general public.

"I knew Brent was up to no good!" blurted out Allan, looking at me with a sick, sarcastic grin. Again the judge's gavel echoed in the courtroom. Many of us began to wonder if he had a backup gavel behind the bench since surely, the head of the present one was destined to come flying off. "Missster Richards! Another outburst, and you will be removed from my courtroom as well. Do you understand? This is my FINAL warning for everyone!"

"I apologize, Your Honor," said Attorney Jacobs.

"Good thing you didn't get *Brent* fired," whispered Joshua. I rolled my eyes. "Good thing Doug covered his bases and was a good employee," I whispered, squeezing Joshua's hand.

"Now, Mr. Asterly, please continue," said the judge. Doug nodded and continued. "During my time at FI, I saw that each time it appeared that a major investor was trying to take their money out, there would be an 'accident' in whatever industry that person was most heavily invested. Attorney Lawson talked about that a little bit earlier."

Once Doug was finished testifying, Attorney Rinaldi called Jordan to the stand, having her focus mostly on Financial Investments' major corporate accounts. "Ironically, the biggest group of customers were the same major companies nationwide and worldwide whose names were most often used on Financial Investments' fake stock certificates. Little did these companies know, however, that Allan had allies planted on the inside of each," said Jordan.

"So how were these companies affected, Agent Miller?" inquired Attorney Rinaldi.

"Basically, Allan was able to convince each company to invest and turn over management of their retirement accounts to FI. Allan's brother Jim, the accountant, was easily able to put together a convincing pitch, and where his other brother Ted worked for Aquicard, a company that originally turned over their retirement accounts without question, other companies soon followed suit. From that point, these accounts were treated just like the other FI accounts. They, of course, received statements that looked official as well."

"So are you saying that people on the inside of these major corporations, all under Allan's direction, convinced their bosses to turn over the corporate pension plans to FI?"

Allan looked down and rubbed his forehead while Jordan continued. "Yes, and it was an easy way for Allan to gain large sources of money, which he knew would be fairly constant and could lead to additional individuals giving money. In exchange for their services, Allan's associates on the inside would receive large bank checks and trips. Certain select ones also knew about the manipulation of the stock market and profited from that as well."

"And Allan used the companies' names without permission on his fake stock certificates, sometimes to convince a customer to remain invested?" asked Attorney Rinaldi.

"Yes."

Sensing the end of the prosecution's case, the jurors began to grow restless in their seats, and Judge Gaviston decided to call a quick recess. Since the trial had gone well into week 4, everyone, including the media, needed to take a break and absorb all of the information they had heard. When the jury returned, most were sarcastically rubbing their hands and cracking their knuckles in preparation to continue taking feverish notes. "So do you think that instead of giving us so much money per day and a free lunch, we can put in for a manicure too?" whispered one of the jurors under her breath as she made her way back into the courtroom. "You aren't kidding!" chimed the stenographer, shaking out her own weary hands.

At last, Attorney Rinaldi was ready to wrap up her case. Jordan resumed her seat on the witness stand once more, and the topic turned once more to "Brent Thompson" and myself. "Allan was getting the feeling that Brent was untrustworthy," continued Jordan. "Brent apparently asked one too many times how he could move up in the company, and Allan decided that he needed desperately to remove him. The question was how." Jordan then turned her attention to me and continued. "Eventually Allan decided to use an outsider—a small-town lawyer who was somewhat new to the profession with time to spare, limited clients, and a good reputation in the community—to make it work. Allan also figured that he could avoid prosecution if his scandal was exposed by hiring a lawyer—not just to defend, but more so, to 'touch.'"

"Touch?" said Attorney Rinaldi.

"Allan had read just enough law to make him dangerous. He thought that he could hide behind what's sometimes referred to as The Confidential Communications Doctrine. Basically, it's a rule about protecting clients' secrets, like a priest or a doctor. Of course, Allan needed to trust his new corporate counsel and figured that a young single female would be easily manipulated."

"And who did he choose?" asked Attorney Rinaldi.

Jordan turned to me again sympathetically as I took a deep breath. "Attorney Rebecca Lawson." Jurors began to glance my way, appearing sympathetic as well. I just stared straight ahead toward the detailed carvings on the front of the witness stand, hoping to redirect the attention back to Jordan.

"In Allan's mind, Charlie, an attractive mysterious man, was just the perfect person to get inside Attorney Lawson's personal life and test her. Plus, where she wasn't a corporate attorney but a general practice attorney in a small town, he figured that she would dwell on a few recurring themes that she had studied for the bar exams: she would first zealously protect her client and, secondly, stand behind the theories of attorney-client privilege and confidential communications." I felt my face turn red with anger as Jordan's comment echoed throughout the courtroom, praying that others wouldn't start to view me (especially my current clients) as being too naive. I had already built a strong reputation for myself in Deering, and the last thing that I needed to add to my already-busy agenda was to start from scratch again. Ugh.

Finally the focus shifted back to the witness stand. "Originally, Attorney Lawson investigated Brent and reviewed Allan's company with Allan's express permission. Allan claimed that he was audited on a regular basis to ensure no problems with the company, but as we already know now, he had his own different definition for *auditing*. Anyway, investigations, including Ms. Lawson's initial review, revealed nothing. Then suddenly, Attorney Lawson begins to receive strange threatening calls regarding Financial Investments, telling her not to represent the company. She was then told by Charlie, pretending to be a CIA agent, that he needed documents and a statement from Attorney Lawson. Wisely Ms. Lawson stalled and refused, instead choosing to investigate deeper on her own."

"Please continue," Attorney Rinaldi replied, glancing over at the jurors who appeared to be not only following Jordan but also hanging on to her every word.

"As Ms. Lawson continued her investigation, she grew more and more suspicious of the activities of FI. Eventually Ms. Lawson was able to track and compare the FI statements certain of her clients had received with actual stock market reports published in newspapers and trade journals. After some time, Ms. Lawson began to note differences in the figures provided to her clients by FI and reflected in the stock reports. This led Ms. Lawson to engage in her own covert operation, if you will."

"What do you mean by 'covert operation'?" asked Attorney Rinaldi, smirking toward the jurors.

"Ms. Lawson recruited some current and former FI employees, as well as others, to assist her in removing discarded materials from FI. She was then able to reconstruct what was going on at FI by using these materials and by reviewing the pictures she took after her 'interns' had finished their week at FI, and Allan was kind enough to throw a party to celebrate. As for the pictures taken at Allan's party, yes, they were all taken with Allan's permission and sometimes suggestion. He could have hidden documents, but his ego stood in the way of his usual facade, and he forgot to hide anything. In fact, he welcomed outsiders who were armed with camera equipment into his private office with open arms to take the pictures we saw earlier. The public, including the local newspapers, at least for that night, had unlimited access to his office."

"Okay," said Attorney Rinaldi, displaying an air of seriousness that kept everyone focused.

"Finally, reviewing everything once again with the new information, Attorney Lawson found definite illegal activity, including the murder of Mr. Peters and the so-called industrial accidents. At that point, she decided it was best not to call it to Allan's attention. The fact was she had decided to give up nothing—no pictures, no documents, no statements. In doing so, Attorney Lawson did abide by her ethical rules while she tried her best, along with the help of Mr. Tameron, to figure out how, while following these rules, to alert the proper authorities to the situation."

"And how would she do that?"

"Ethical rules vary state to state, but let me give you an example. Down here in DC, client confidences and secrets can be revealed to prevent criminal acts by some person. In this case, Attorney Lawson reasonably believed that Allan and those working for him would likely kill again or substantially harm someone, *perhaps even her*, if she did not disclose the information. Becky called Mr. Mulcahey only after she had realized that Allan's people had already killed one person—Mr. Peters, the landlord in New York—and, of course, when she was at a point where both she and Joshua were in danger themselves. Another reason to disclose is to prevent intimidation of witnesses in court proceedings or bribery. Other than that, attorneys may disclose when required by law or a court order, or when requested by a government attorney as authorized by law. Fortunately, Attorney Lawson was wise to wait for a court order. You may recall that Charlie didn't represent himself as an attorney for the CIA. Maybe that would have helped him a little if his victim wasn't so smart, but I doubt it. Nothing got past Attorney Lawson. Ms. Lawson got pulled into this scheme in an attempt by Allan to cover himself. It turns out that Ms. Lawson, faced with different ethical problems, did everything she needed to do to uphold her obligation to her client and the courts." Phew. My clients should be proud. Oh, and my mom too, who back at home had made it back onto the couch and was nodding proudly at my father. "She takes after me, you know," said my mother.

"Yeah, something like that," said my father, chuckling. "Now shush. I want to hear this."

"Quiet! The both of you!" said my brother, Ryan, placing an extra large pepperoni pizza on the coffee table and taking a seat on the floor next to it.

"Thank you for explaining that to us," said Attorney Rinaldi. "So back to Brent," she continued, grinning as she reeled everyone back in.

"Brent Thompson, as you know, is simply an undercover name for my partner, Doug Asterly. Our boss, Mr. Mulcahey, had met Allan on some golf course in Georgia and was eventually drawn into the scam himself." Mr. Mulcahey locked eyes with Jordan, obviously angered, but not overly surprised.

Jordan continued, "I had received complaints from two new executive employees in Allan's Michigan office just outside of Detroit, who had done some investigating of the company on their own. They had big dreams of partnership and wanted to know as much about Financial Investments as they could." The two employees were, as a matter of fact, still sitting in the general audience behind us, having testified a few weeks prior. Both were very excited to have the cameras face them again, and actually turned to smile for them. Not very professional, but certainly a bit of comic relief for the rest of us.

"The Michigan investigation revealed that Allan had been using funds to purchase real estate, specifically strip malls, under the fake name Harold Weston in major cities across the country. Financial Investments would then rent storefront offices in the same strip malls, again paying 'cash' at tax time."

"But when they paid cash . . ." said Attorney Rinaldi.

"They never paid a dime," Jordan clarified. "The papers just said that they did."

"So did you talk to Mr. Mulcahey about Michigan?" asked Attorney Rinaldi.

"Of course. The problem was nothing was ever done. Purposely."

"So what happened?"

"Well, eventually Doug realized that Mr. Mulcahey was linked with Allan. So he decided to venture out on his own on a mission to investigate the situation in a different way: through the FBI's division of internal affairs. He had no choice. Internal affairs instructed us to immediately leave the Boston office and come down here to the District. No one, not even Mr. Mulcahey, knew the reason why, not that Mr. Mulcahey cared all too terribly much. He was too wrapped up in his own things, especially cashing his own hefty bank checks at that point."

"Now we established earlier that both you and Doug started off working in the Boston office with Mr. Mulcahey. How did you wind up in Vermont?" asked Attorney Rinaldi, pointing toward Jordan with a now black-and-silver Waterford pen.

"After hearing about Mr. Mulcahey, and believing that the Michigan case was legit, the 'big bosses' down here in DC decided that they would reassign Doug and me to headquarters, but moved us to an office close to Deering to work undercover. There Doug landed an entry-level job at Financial Investments under the name Brent Thompson. The great thing was Doug and I were able to successfully investigate the case in Vermont, and thanks to the internal affairs division here in DC, we were virtually untraceable when we were gone—much to the dismay of Mr. Mulcahey and Allan, neither of whom realized that Doug and Brent, and for that matter Jordan and Allison, were the same people."

"One last question," said Attorney Rinaldi. "Back to basics. How did Allan Richards—how did Financial Investments get to where it is today?"

"Well, Allan did start out legit, believe it or not. He had good intentions. In the beginning, it seemed simple. He'd begin his career as a stockbroker. But then some paperwork was overlooked and didn't get filed *for a long time*. Things just slipped through the cracks. One customer threatened to report him, and Allan panicked. He ended up convincing the client to stay with the company and keep quiet by offering him straight-up cash from his very own pocket. That one payoff sparked a bigger idea: people could be bought. And everywhere Allan went, they were bought."

Attorney Rinaldi shook her head. "Please continue."

"Well, Allan, as we discussed earlier in the trial, started up his own company, Financial Investments. Eventually things reached the point where the books showed so much money that he knew that if he had several high-interest accounts going and continued to attract new investors, any losses would be meaningless. After talking to his brothers, Allan figured that the more companies he could infiltrate, the better. So executives in various companies were sought out and bribed to allow Allan control over the stock market and his scheme. But then Jim Richards, his accountant brother, either mentioned or suggested the idea of tax write-offs to Allan, and Allan's greed began to get the better of him, and he got sloppy. There were so many things Allan had going at that point that he couldn't name them all if he tried. Instead, he was just in the mind-set of 'make it happen.' With all of the money and the potential for more, Allan was focused on controlling the market."

"Controlling the stock market?" asked Attorney Rinaldi.

"Yes, control the stock market. And it turns out that he could. To a degree. Seems extreme, but the next question was, how extreme could he get? As long as Allan had people working in the inside of as many companies and industries as possible, eventually he would grab every consumer and major company around. It was a game of manipulation: manipulating the people; manipulating the system; taking advantage to the point of abusing tax breaks; buying secrets; and, unfortunately, taking a few lives in the process. So long as the only ones questioning him were the occasional clients trying to cash in their accounts, he was safe."

The courtroom was completely silent at that point as everyone listened intently to Jordan's testimony. All that could be heard other than the echo of Jordan's voice was the passionate scribbling of notes by anyone with a pen and paper, each of whom hoped that their personal investments that were unrelated to Allan were in of themselves legit. Others worried if the food they had ingested during the day's lunch break had been safe to eat.

Sensing the tension, Jordan took advantage of her undivided attention: "It became all too easy to buy off a consumer, so eventually Allan conducted his business with no intention of ever purchasing real stock or paying out on a single consumer's account. Just goes to show you: with the right person, the right reputation, and enough money, you can go far. Too bad he wasn't honest."

"Now what about the employees who weren't in on the scheme?" asked Attorney Rinaldi, reading from a small note handed to her from one of her assistants.

"They, the lower-level people, like Doug, were basically legitimate. They were gophers who were responsible for all of the grunt work. But when it came to securing stock, they were instructed to send the files up to the higher levels for 'processing.' In reality, nothing was ever done except for investing the client's money in Financial Investments accounts, which was tracked: blessings and curses for Allan."

"Blessings and curses?"

"A blessing for Allan as he was quickly able to use the so-called accounts to figure out how he could get a client to reinvest more, and he usually did. A blessing for us, as we know exactly what every client paid into the company and how much money they lost, making our investigation easier. A curse for Allan, as again, we didn't have to waste any time verifying exactly what every client paid into the company and how much money they lost to easily bring charges."

Soon Attorney Rinaldi rested her case, and the defense had nothing to present. Soon the trial was over: guilty verdicts across the board, followed immediately by the sentencing hearings, which resulted in lengthy jail terms ranging from thirty-five years to life.

The ecstatic roar of the crowd outside as the verdict was read could be heard from several blocks away. Those of us inside the courtroom were nervous to leave at first. We had been occupying a courtroom that was, in theory, designed to be soundproof from the outside. Not only could we hear the albeit-somewhat-muffled roar of the crowd, we could also feel the rumble beneath our feet. I supposed at that point, I was in a better position than any of the defendants. But I did question exactly how the U.S. Marshals would get us out of there and back to our not-as-secure condominium unnoticed and without being followed.

Allan, in particular, was in an entirely different position: he was going nowhere fast. He had dipped into so many industries securing his "contacts" that people everywhere salivated at the thought of their own personal revenge. Some thought that perhaps Allan was safer in jail, as there was nowhere in the world his safety was ensured. Then again, others thought that he may not have been so safe in jail either. Many, including those in Las Vegas, who were having quite a bit of fun placing bets on the outcome of the trial, quickly turned their attention to a new question: how long would Allan last *anywhere*?

EPILOGUE

AT THE conclusion of the sentencing hearings, Joshua and I were flooded with requests from the media. Our families and friends were as well. I stopped using my old clunky dust magnet of an answering machine, instead opting to bring myself into the modern world with the voice mail service through the telephone company. Still, the mailbox was always full, to the point where I had no other choice but to change to yet another "private" telephone number. People also got ahold of my and Joshua's cell phone numbers, forcing us to get new ones.

Ken kept me informed of the mail that arrived daily by the bagful. For a while, a delivery truck had to make a special stop at my home and at the office as the letter carrier could not carry my and everyone else's mail on foot. It was pretty surreal to receive volumes of cards, candy, flowers, and proposals, which continued to arrive on a daily basis.

Thankfully, my computers were returned to me, as they had been sitting on the floor of a closet in Charlie's secret apartment not far from Conifer Community College. I never did get my Rolodex or my phone book back and had no idea where to begin searching for it. It irked me to no end as they contained information about basically everyone I knew—everyone who had at some point entered my life, whether it was family, friends, colleagues, clients, or even a reputable local plumber. Considering though the number of people who were traveling in and out of my home and my office, I had no choice but to consider my precious bible of contact information lost for good. I supposed that if strangers from all over the country could find me, the people who really needed to get in touch with me would. As for the rest, I'd just have to send out my Christmas cards as I received them, along with a request for missing information as I began a new phone book and Rolodex.

Almost everywhere we went, we were followed by a sea of media. "You have certainly mastered the art of *no comment*, Rebecca," Joshua said, laughing at my reaction to requests, which was the same each and every time.

"All attorneys should master the art of *no comment*," I replied as we at last enjoyed a private leisurely stroll down the National Mall, past the Smithsonian museums, hand in hand, no longer in need of the Marshal Service, and, at the time, temporarily out of the limelight of the media. For the first time since the trial had ended, we were able to wear jeans and sneakers once more, as well as our U.S. Supreme Court shirts, proudly in public. "I never was a big fan of speaking with the media, especially with cases pending. Some attorneys see the press as an opportunity for free advertising," I said, kicking a pebble down the path. "Others use the press as a tactic to get into the minds of people who might become jurors, or as a way to taint an area to the point where the judge has no other choice but to order a change of venue. Some even use the media just to get people involved in their cause. The civil suits will be starting on the heels of this. No one should be talking too much right now. That's just my humble opinion."

"Duly noted, Counsel," said Joshua.

As we passed the famous rust-colored, sandstone Victorian-style Smithsonian Castle, with the majestic white U.S. Capitol Building at our back, I spotted a group of children who were enjoying a picnic with their family: the father was proudly showing them for the first time how to fly a kite. The music of the famous carousel out front of the Smithsonian Castle magically put everyone who passed by in a happy, playful mood. "You know, now that Allan's behind bars, I look differently at everyone now: even kids. All those parents squirreling away money for their children like Marie LaValle, their future investments will finally be safe too. It's nice."

Joshua stretched out his arms and began to project his voice deep, loud, and strong (actually, the word I'm looking for is *obnoxious*): "Rebecca Lawson: as always, out to save the world, especially the children!" Knowing that I was horrified at the attention he was drawing to us by everyone within fifty yards, Joshua resumed his normal voice. "You're right, though, Beck. I was thinking the same thing: a picture of innocence. Of course, I was also wondering how many of the—what, three hundred million—Americans come to the National Mall thinking that there are stores here. I know I did."

"Actually, this place is considered by many to be the cultural heart of DC with all the memorials and museums on both sides of this park."

"It is pretty impressive," said Joshua, glancing about. "I like how there is a direct line from the U.S. Capitol to the Washington Monument, to the WWII Memorial and right down to the Lincoln Memorial."

"Yes, there is no fooling around here," I said. "It's very direct. Symbolic, really. Kudos to Pierre L'Enfant for designing this big place back in the day. Too bad he didn't live to see it finished."

"Yeah, your buddy Lincoln there got it started again after the Civil War, huh?" said Joshua, teasing.

"See? He's a guy who means business," I responded, beginning to get the giggles again, more so because I was picturing Joshua projecting his deep, resonating, obnoxious voice while sporting a big black top hat and red tails, acting as the master of ceremonies at Ringling Brothers and Barnum & Bailey Circus. "So, Josh, once the civil stuff is all done, what are you planning on doing with your life?"

Joshua smiled and began to act in a more dignified fashion, changing his image to show off his best English accent, his hands now clasped behind his back and a long blade of grass clenched between his teeth. "Well, I've had *many* offers, you know. After all this media attention, I have fans." Rolling my eyes, I playfully pushed him lightly on his shoulder. "Yeah, you're a real hottie," I teased as he pretended to lose his balance.

"Ouch!" Joshua replied dramatically, nursing his shoulder. "Seriously, though, I think I'll do something different with my law degree, but I'm not exactly sure what I'll do yet. I guess I have a few ideas up my sleeve. One thing is for sure: it's definitely time for me to get out of the library. I'm ready."

"Well, you know," I replied, "you have my number if you need a lawyer."

"Hey, Becky? I have a question—well, more of a request, actually."

"Oh yeah? What's that?"

"Well, I think I know what I would like you to get me for Christmas."

I turned to face Joshua with a very sarcastic, analytical face. "Oh?" I replied. Admittedly, I was beginning to become slightly concerned.

"I was thinking that you could make me one of those emergency preparedness kits."

"Like for a terrorist attack or a hurricane?" I asked.

"Naw . . . for hanging out with you!" he replied as I smacked him playfully again. "You know," he continued, "disposable, flexible plastic double cuffs in case I need to restrain a bad guy; some Mace, of course; a police baton; a LED flashlight; . . . maybe some cut-resistant gloves; a seat belt cutter . . . you know . . . things like that. Oh, and one of those spike systems for tires to put a damper on those pesky Suburban attacks. They can really sneak up on you, you know."

I was howling uncontrollably at that point, curious to see just how far Joshua would go. "You're forgetting one thing, Josh," I stated, egging him on.

"Oh yeah? What's that?"

"Duct tape!"

"Sure! Bring it on!" he cheered, thoroughly enjoying the addition.

"And while we're at it, how about the number of a local locksmith?"

"Yeah, that too," he replied, motioning with his arm.

"Anything else?" I asked.

Joshua paused dramatically. After a few moments of pretending to think, he responded. "No, I think that should do it."

"I'll see what I can do," I replied. What a nut.

Joshua put his arm around my shoulders, and we continued our stroll down to the white stone Washington Monument, the fifty flags surrounding it waving patriotically in the breeze. We then turned right toward the White House. Looking up, I noticed that the sun had begun to set in the distance behind the Lincoln Memorial. "What do you say we grab some dinner at the rooftop restaurant at the Hotel Washington?" Joshua suggested. "After all, it is our last night here to really relax in the District for a bit before the civil matters go forward. Why don't we watch the sunset from up there?"

"Sounds good to me," I replied, turning my focus to the sudden rumbling of my stomach. "I'm starving!" As I looked back toward the great orange Southern sun making its way behind Lincoln, I knew that I would miss sharing the Alexandria condominium with Joshua. We did make good roommates, and although our entire saga was frightening and more often than not *dangerous*, we did have fun and certainly shared the ultimate war story. Plus, who knew that he was such a great kisser?

Trenstaw University Law School already had possessed a fine reputation, and it probably goes without saying that the trustees were thrilled with all of the national media attention. The undergraduate school enjoyed the attention as well: they had not only educated both Joshua and me, but unbeknownst to them, they had also kept safe some of the most precious documents relating to the Financial Investments case in its lockers. The boys in the security office, of course, acquired an interesting habit of crediting themselves by telling people that our evidence had been kept secure as a result of "Trenstaw's Finest."

Trenstaw University continued to really thrive after that, and applications for admissions increased for both the law school and the undergraduate school by a record-breaking 58 percent, beating out most of the Ivy League schools for the next two years. Eventually both schools were able to acquire more property in Boston, which they impressively turned into dormitories for the students to accommodate both the undergraduate and graduate school's growing community.

Deering, a community many people otherwise had not heard of, was essentially placed on the map, much to the delight of my neighbors. I found it especially hilarious to watch interviews with Ken, Mr. Becker, and Mr. Hatley on the news and entertainment programs—all quite proud to be one of my closest friends and, of course, eager to boast their own businesses as curious tourists began to frequent the area.

Ken's interview with *Access Hollywood* was especially entertaining. Mrs. Whitfield, sporting her famous purple hair, walked directly into an interview with Ken, who was sitting on the front steps of his store with Nancy O'Dell and Billy Bush, two of the show's star reporters. "Oh, thank goodness I caught you, Ken!" Mrs. Whitfield exclaimed, taking a seat beside him while looking directly into the camera. "I was so worried for you and for the store when things kept being pulled from the shelves!" Ken's overfriendly intruder then turned to face Billy, sitting next to Nancy diagonally below them, wide-eyed and openmouthed, while Mrs. Whitfield continued to ramble with her animated hands. Ken, at the same time, could do nothing but continue to duck and weave while adjusting the microphone on the collar of his navy blue blazer. "I actually played a major role in the Financial Investments case for Ms. Lawson," said Mrs. Whitfield, oblivious to her unwelcome arrival. Leaning forward, she grabbed and began to squeeze Billy's knee. "It was *my bank* that issued scholarship money to the students who won the contest, you know!" Billy was unsure what to do as Mrs. Whitfield wasn't exactly sitting in the most ladylike position when she leaned forward, revealing the bottom of her white lacy bloomers from under her purple-flowered bishop-style dress.

"That's nice," replied Nancy, redirecting the attention back to Ken while sending one of her assistants "the look" to escort Mrs. Whitfield from the area. "So, Ken, you were saying?" said Billy, stifling his signature giggles while Nancy rolled her eyes and mouthed the word *Wow!* to the rest of the group. Mrs. Whitfield was whisked away, still talking up a storm and adjusting her famous purple hair.

Besides the thrill of being interviewed on camera for national television programs, some of the more excitable events for the residents of Deering were the flurries of visits from Hollywood producers who were eager to make movies that depicted the Financial Investments scandal. For the next year, people pitched ideas and scoped the area for plays, televisions, books, and blockbuster films surrounding Deering and its part in the scandal. Of course, Deering was such a quaint and almost completely undisturbed little town that many producers also kept it in mind for other projects that were completely unrelated to Financial Investments.

Joshua and I were treated as though we were real celebrities for quite some time. Still, we probably could have done without the high school pictures, movie clips of high school plays, and whatever else the reporters could dig up. Lucky us. I just wished that the world would remember that my hair was in style at the time they were taken. Joshua thought I was cute. Yeah, so was Rudolph.

Soon the civil actions began (mostly wrapped into class action suits). Since I was not needed to serve as a witness for either side, I was invited to serve as cocounsel. After several weeks of negotiations in Washington DC (and the invaluable assistance of a major accounting firm), a settlement was reached so that all injured consumers received their due sums. The Associated Press reported that the national economy was saved from a major market collapse, bigger than any economist had ever anticipated. In fact, for quite some time later, economists on the news routinely mentioned the market's "near miss" when presenting their stories or holding roundtable discussions. Conspiracy theorists from then on were all over every incident, which involved pulling food from the shelves or a major accident at an energy plant. They and many others were convinced that someone new was somehow attempting to "pull an Allan" and manipulate the market as well.

As a result of the Financial Investments scandal, companies (particularly the bigger ones like Aquicard) began to institute detailed security programs to make sure that history did not repeat itself with the next brazen criminal mastermind by either improperly investing or staging incidents. Treaties between the United States and several South American countries were also developed in an attempt to thwart similar illegalities in the future.

Some people called me a national hero, although I didn't feel like one. I was just glad to be alive, and relieved that everything was finally over. As frustrated as I occasionally became with my colleagues before I met Allan, working on the Financial

Investments cases in the judicial heart of our country made it all seem worthwhile. I believed in the concept of justice again, and I believed in the judicial system as a whole again as well. It was comforting, and a great privilege, to be in the company of those who shared the belief as strongly as I did. What I learned was invaluable, and I found that the things that I used to silently consider to be either intimidating or annoying in and out of court finally began to vanish. I had become part of a bigger picture and acquired so much more experience in such a short time that things were put into a new perspective for me.

It was never my intention to go to law school to make a difference or change the world. I went to law school to learn the profession of law. But somewhere along the way, I guess I did make a difference. I changed the world for thousands of people. Maybe even millions. Go figure.

Once I was nestled back home, Ken and Marie were married, and the whole town was invited to the celebration, followed by a beautiful reception on a perfectly sunny and warm day on the lawn of Deering's little white church. Marie's daughter served as matron of honor, and Jacqueline and I served as bridesmaids. Marie's son, who had become very close to Ken, was Ken's best man.

Five years later, I was proudly sworn in as a federal district court judge in Vermont, after strong recommendations by the president, the attorney general, Justice McNaught, and Judge Haley. The media once again flooded the streets of Deering to cover the—in my opinion—unnecessary festivities held this time in my honor. Of course, all the reporters by then were smart enough to steer away from Mrs. Whitfield and her famous purple hair, although each camera shot inevitably included a splash of purple to some degree.

My eyes, admired so genuinely by Joshua in the Hay-Adams Hotel, have seen a lot in their day. They started out as blue and are now hazel with specks of blues, golds, and greens—symbolic, really—reflecting the many perspectives I now have for situations in life. My vision, although healthy, now includes a "blind spot," which is monitored yearly after a series of stubborn migraines: my only souvenir reminding me that I too was once a victim of domestic abuse, thanks to an ex-boyfriend named Charlie.

Wrinkles have developed around my eyes from smiling and squinting at the sunshine. Joshua calls them happy lines. I am glad to have seen this much so far, and I am looking forward to many years more. If I am ever unfortunate enough to lose my sight, I will still be grateful from having seen so much: both the good and the bad. Sometimes we have to see ourselves through difficult times. Still, with patience and, in my case, prayer, friends, and relatives—both living and deceased—we do find that life does find a way of correcting itself.

This tale may seem as though it is being told by someone late in life. Instead, this tale is being told by and about someone who has lived a full life in a short time. As Abraham Lincoln once said, "And in the end, it's not the years in your life that count. It's the life in your years." Although it was certainly a challenging situation, I have made my peace with it, and have grown from it, thanks to my continued attempts to master the art of the open mind. An open mind makes us better people—whether we are lawyers, doctors, preschool teachers, or simply friends. An open mind helps us to get through the challenging times when we feel a little less prepared. An open mind allows us to see the beauty in the ugly and the good in the bad. And most of all, an open mind allows us to heal; that way, we can help others when fate sends them spiraling in a similar direction.

I have happily accepted the fact that I am a magnet for bizarre situations. Having said that, my tale is not complete by any stretch of the imagination. It is, in fact, a beginning—a beginning that includes a new life based upon friendship, trust, love, and happiness, as expressed in a poem, which I lovingly dedicated to my husband, written five years after the Financial Investments cases were closed and three weeks after our wedding:

You Are My Everything—You Share My Soul

You hold me: I swear my heart touches yours;
I taste your soul through your gentle lips;
at last, the fantasy of many who yearn:
the feeling of love and to be loved in return!
I prayed for so long—for the concept of love,
then I opened my eyes, it was you who I saw:
a miracle sent from above.
Our first kiss was electrical,
though I'd watched your lips for years;
I still melt in your arms, and melt with your smile;
you dissolved every one of my fears.
I long inhaling the air you breathe, your scent upon my clothes;
Each second with you I savor, and I cherish;
You are my everything—you share my soul.
When I gaze into your eyes, if a mere glance,
I see love for eternity; you make me wise,
strong, beautiful, healthy, and somehow altered my priorities.
I pray we live a million years; souls entwined for millions more.
Thank you for having me share in your life;
and more for the honor of being your wife.

—The Honorable Judge Rebecca Tameron

Breinigsville, PA USA
24 January 2010
231276BV00005B/77/P